THE
HAPPIER
DEAD

IVO STOURTON

SOLARIS

'Man comes and tills the field and lies beneath,
And after many a summer dies the swan.
Me only cruel immortality
Consumes; I wither slowly in thine arms,
Here at the quiet limit of the world,

Why wilt thou ever scare me with thy tears,
And make me tremble lest a saying learnt,
In days far-off, on that dark earth, be true?
"The Gods themselves cannot recall their gifts."'

'Tithonus', Alfred, Lord Tennyson, 1860

OATES SLEPT WITH his earpiece in so that if an emergency call came over the wires, it wouldn't wake Loretta. She was grouchy because he'd had to cancel Christmas with her parents. Work wouldn't let him leave London. He'd been getting up the courage to tell her for a few days, and had finally broached the subject that evening over dinner. Even after all these years she still got scared when he went out late at night, and her fear made her angry at him, so when the bleep tickled his eardrum he rose as quietly as he could.

The earpiece was programmed to caller ID, and Oates heard a recording of his own voice whispering, "*That bloody girl, that bloody girl*". Lori stirred at the shift in the mattress, but said nothing. He padded out onto the landing, and stood there in his boxer shorts. He waited with his hands on his hips, deciding whether or not to pick up. For a few seconds sleep kept duty at bay, then yielded.

"Answer," he said.

"Hey there daddy-oh. How are you doing?"

Her voice had a scratchy, narcotic edge. He could hear someone laughing in the background, and the steady repetitive beat of club music.

"I'm sleeping."

"How's the little lady?"

"Asleep."

"How are those two lovely kids?"

"What do you want?"

The voice on the other end giggled, amused with itself.

"You know what I want. I want the inside line."

"I don't know what you're talking about."

She tittered again.

"I'm hanging up."

"Wait! Just tell me what you know about the Avalon call. Murder, right?"

"What?"

"Avalon, the Great Spa. Come on granddaddy-oh, wake up!"

"I don't know what you're talking about, Grape."

"Don't tell me I scooped central! I'm everywhere, I see everything," she whooped. "I'll bet you hang to the left."

Despite himself, Oates put his hand over his groin on the dark landing.

"There's been a murder at the Great Spa. I reckon it will be pretty juicy, with all that money about. I reckon it will need a delicate touch."

She broke off to shout at someone in the background to fetch her a beer.

"Well they haven't asked me, so you're wasting your time."

"Okay. Sure. All the same, I wouldn't bother going back to bed. Cross your heart you'll download to me if they choose you?"

"Go to bed, Grape."

"And don't let them make you sign any confidentiality stuff! I want to know what goes on in there, I want–"

"End call."

Oates looked back over his shoulder into his darkened bedroom. He wanted nothing more than to crawl back in beside his wife, but there was a job coming. Whatever else Grape might be, she was seldom wrong.

He opened the door to his sons' room, and listened to their breathing in the darkness. The shapes of trains on the wallpaper were discernible in the moonlight, and on the ceiling there was an arrangement of luminous stars that he had stuck up at Harry's insistence. He worried about that boy. Harry was so keen on staring at the stars that one day he might fall straight down a man-hole. Mike would be alright, he could already take apart the engine of Oates's old motorbike, and sooner or later he would be able to put it back together.

The atmosphere was warm with the sweet scent of children's bodies. He inhaled the smell. If he had to go he wanted to take it with him into the night outside, the way a soldier carries a love letter into battle. The house was silent but for their breathing; outside the city rustled faintly in the cold night. As his eyes got used to the darkness, he noticed that Harry had tied a skipping rope around the door handles of the wardrobe. Oates had checked it for monsters at bedtime, but his dad's word was obviously not quite good enough.

What he would do to anyone who hurt his boys. If he let his mind wander, sometimes it found its way to that thought. It was the only thing to alleviate the unbearable tenderness he felt listening to them sleep. It was part of what kept sending him out into the streets. In the shadows of the bedroom he could feel his nascent retribution, like a dog keeping watch over his children. He knew that revenge for their injury was a particular temptation for him, offering as it did the chance to earth once and for all the fury that was in him in an act of vengeance beyond reproach.

He went across the hall to the TV room where he kept a spare uniform ready for late night calls. He stood for a moment, bare-chested, and looked at the photograph sitting on sideboard. His daughter and his two sons all a-grin, wrapped in towels on Brighton beach. He shook his head and returned to dressing.

As he strapped the Velcro across his sides, as the heavy body armour settled on his broad chest, as his fingers splayed in the rough gloves, he changed his being, and there was nothing domestic about the eyes that met his in the hall mirror. He picked up the pad and pen from the radiator cover and leant the paper up against the wall. He tried to think of what to write for Lori. Once the call came through he might not have much time, but without any idea where he was going it was hard to know what to say. He didn't want to upset her, or make a promise he couldn't keep.

He was still holding the pen over the blank page when the call from central came, and it was the Chief Superintendent himself. A body of a guest, a financier named Mr Prudence Egwu, had been found in his room at Nottingham Bioscience's Great Spa, Avalon in Essex.

"It's not the best time to be leaving the family, John."

"Oh, don't you worry about all that. Besides, with good luck and a stiff tailwind you should be back by the end of the day. They reckon they've already laid hands on the man."

"They reckon?"

"Well, he's confessed. But I've had a look at his file. It doesn't look like he knew the victim, and he's a gentleman of restricted means."

"Who is he?"

"He works as some sort of groundskeeper in the spa. Most of the staff sleep outside the dome, but apparently they do have access through the night."

"So you think he's an Eddy?"

"I was rather hoping you might do the thinking on this one."

There had always been Eddies, men who confessed to the crimes of others out of loyalty, desperation or greed, but such cases had been few. The real evolution of the phenomenon had come with the Treatment. You couldn't compensate a healthy man for thirty years of his youth with money, but if you could promise him a thousand more, what was three decades inside? Now Eddies were the scourge of the court system.

There was a grim humour to watching an interview play out, when an officer had to reject a confession, and the solicitor spent the whole interrogation trying to convince everyone that his client was guilty. Oates knew he had a reputation for winkling out the Eddies, for spotting the glint of inconsistency in a well-briefed confession. It worried him, being known for a nose, because it gave his opinion on a tricky case a weight that was hard to carry.

Oates tried to recall when he first heard the word 'Eddy', but he couldn't pinpoint it. Eight years ago? Ten? Bhupinder had a theory that it came from a children's character called Ever-Ready Eddy, a particularly reliable collie dog with a smiling, compliant face that showed up on t-shirts and lunchboxes. The Superintendent insisted it came from Edward the Confessor.

"Okay. Anything else I should know?" Oates asked.

"You've not been to the Great Spa before, I take it?"

"No. Why would I?"

"Well, quite. There's something a little uncanny about the whole project to my mind. I'm rather jealous of you, parting the curtains of all those myths and rumours. I've had a chat on the phone with their management, and it seems you and your team may find the place a touch disorientating. Apparently they maintain their effect by absolute fidelity to period detail. We've had a request from their marketing department…"

"Come on, John."

"A very polite request to respect that period detail. Once you're inside the crime scene I don't care what you do, but I've given standing instructions that everyone on the team is to dress in the clothing provided."

"You must be joking."

"If I was joking, I would say a rabbi, a priest and an imam walk into a bar. I intend for this to be a proper investigation, but in order to do that I need to make sure we've been as accommodating as possible along the way."

"Right."

"What?"

"I said alright."

"There are some very .distinguished noses under that dome, and I want them left in joint. It's going to be a delicate balance. I've chosen someone with a light touch. Bhupinder and most of the team should already be there when you arrive."

Oates said nothing. It was odd to hear his boss echoing Grape's words so exactly. She must have hacked into a conversation or an email between the Superintendent and whatever higher powers he consulted when he allotted the case. He could feel the responsibility curling up in his stomach, getting comfortable for a long stay.

"Give my regards to your lady wife."

"She's asleep."

"Sensible woman," John said, and rang off.

Oates took his trenchcoat from the hook in the hall. He left his note, groped his way down the stairs, opened the front door of his house, and stepped out into the London night. The streetlight refracted in the drizzle. The downstairs neighbours had left the weights off the lids of the bins again. He didn't want Lori to wake up to a garden full of rubbish as well as an empty bed, and the foxes had lately taken to knocking over the cans. He picked up the bricks and set them as quietly as he could on the metal covers.

He could smell smoke on the crisp night air. Something burning down by the river. Along with the dead leaves on the windscreen of his car there was a leaflet stuck under the wiper advertising cleaning services. The first line was misspelt. Oates could sense the wake of hope stretching out behind the flyer, maybe all the way to China or Somalia, smoothing into the void. The street was silent, his neighbours' windows dark, chintz hanging down to hide the goods in ground floor rooms, and keep the modesty of first floor bedrooms. In the wee hours of the suburbs, he felt like the last man on earth.

Tacked to the inside of his front door, the note he had left for Lori read: *Case in Essex. Should know more by morning. John says it's a quick one. Love to the boys. PS Keep safe.*

AS HE DROVE down Putney hill and on into central London he thought for the hundredth time about applying for a move. He felt guilty at the idea, he would be leaving the others with even more work, but he wasn't sure how many more notes Lori was willing to read. They were understaffed on the murder squad. All the jobs that involved death were short on recruits. A friend of Oates whose father had died had had such difficulty finding an undertaker that in the end he hired a taxidermist to help him with the corpse and built the coffin himself. He remembered it even in Syria, between his first and his second tour, the strange adjustment to the way the men regarded risking their lives.

It was just as he set out for his second six months that Nottingham Biosciences had confirmed the rumours surrounding the successful development of the Treatment. After that, being a soldier just felt incredibly shitty. There had always been the risk of dying, but at least you knew that everyone, even the fattest banker sitting in the softest seat in the City, was going to keel over sooner or later. "Do you want to live forever?" the Captain would ask them before they left the gates of the compound on patrol, invoking the war movies they had watched as boys. It made them laugh, it made them feel better, not because they were happy to die, but because they knew that everyone did in the end. It helped to put things in perspective.

Knowing that you were risking your life to try to keep a stable Middle East, so that a rich stranger wouldn't lose his pension in oil shares, and that a hundred years after your funeral parade he might still be drinking champagne and chatting up your daughter's granddaughter – that changed everything.

It hadn't happened overnight, but he could remember someone from his regiment being awarded a posthumous George Cross for conspicuous gallantry, and when the news came through one of the lads had called him a fucking idiot for getting blown up in the first place. Not in a friendly or consolatory way, but dismissively. The Sergeant had knocked his teeth down his throat for it, but before the Treatment no one would even have dreamed of thinking like that, let alone said it out loud. They might have thought it a waste of a friend's life, but not in a way that made a mug of him. This was before people really understood how the Treatment worked, certainly before people understood how much it would cost, but every man suddenly had the thought that if he could only make it home alive, he actually might be able to live forever. That made the Captain's rallying cry a lot trickier.

Nothing changed the rationale for killing, just for risking your own life. If anything they had been quicker with the trigger that last tour, and friendly fire incidents had increased so steadily that by the time Oates had come home his mates were attacking their own shadows.

Back home, back in peacetime, the distaste for death had spread. It wasn't just yours anymore, it was anyone's that seemed uncanny. Suddenly no one wanted to be a soldier, or an undertaker, or a fireman, or a paramedic. No one wanted to look after the elderly, or work the murder squad. A death in the family was something subtly shameful, the way Oates imagined a pregnant and unmarried daughter must have been in the 1950s.

THE ONLY THING that hadn't changed was the journalists. People might not want to be directly involved with death, but they still found it fascinating. Especially the violent, and the kind that the papers liked to call 'senseless'. He had transferred from the army to the newly formed Domestic Order Unit in his early twenties, straight off the Hercules from his last tour in Syria. He and forty men, five from his squad and the others strangers, had walked down the ramp onto the tarmac at RAF Lyneham, the damp and the gentle grey light so alien after the desert. After they got their papers a couple of the single men went for a drink in a pub in Chippenham, and his Sergeant had told him about this new outfit that was starting up to deal with the trouble in London.

That was how he met Lori. She came up to him after a night of rioting, and said: "Thank you. You guys are doing a great job, trying to keep us safe." That had been nearly twenty years before, and ever since then he had been hounded by journalists.

Grape was the least objectionable one he had come across, partly because she was unaffiliated, partly because she was good at getting him information in return, and could be trusted to sit on a secret until it hatched. She was a news puppy, running an independent blog that covered crime, home affairs and, when real stories were thin on the ground, the odd tidbit of celebrity gossip. He had visited her site once. It was as lurid as most. She was pushy, but he knew it was a precarious existence; she depended on a steady stream of scoops to keep her hits up, so the advertisers would keep buying space on her page.

The only strange thing about her was her forgetfulness. You couldn't establish a running joke with her, you had to remind her of the details of previous conversations. She existed in a constant present.

Thinking of Grape and the heads-up she had given him, he spoke into his earpiece: "Text that bloody girl – victim's name is Mr Prudence Egwu. Don't publish until we've spoken to his next of kin. End text."

OATES DROVE DOWN through Chelsea and along the Embankment. The good citizens of the day had relinquished their claim on London, and each of the people he saw posed a policeman's question simply by virtue of being out in the rain and the small hours of the morning. There was a lone jogger puffing her way along the pavement by the swollen grey river, her face set in grim determination to be fit and thin for someone, and a group of young men from the St George estate hanging around the edge of Pimlico. Their cigarettes glowed in the darkness.

There were a lot of police on the streets, walking in twos with their thumbs hitched in their stab-proof vests. A young black man had been run over by a police van in Peckham, and two days of mounting disorder in the suburbs had left the city restless.

On Parliament Square the black bomb barriers glistened in the wet, and the protestors huddled in their tents beneath the statues of Churchill and Roosevelt. The rain soaked their cardboard placards, dissolving the demands. There were ranks of rough sleepers under the bridges. Still and silent in their bedrolls, they reminded Oates of rows of body bags, and of how heavy they were when you had to drag them into long lines under a hot sun.

Past Blackfriars, robotaxis bore the tired lawyers back from the honeycombs of midnight offices to their sleeping wives. Oates had a feeling Grape was out there somewhere in the east; he had never asked her where she lived, and she wouldn't have told him if he had, but you could hear the lairy pride of Bethnal Green in her voice.

It took him almost an hour to make it out to the eastern edge of the city. The first thing he saw was the light atop the great dome, glimpsed through a screen of trees as he came out of the City through Canary Wharf and crested the hills on the edge of Essex. It was a shining red beacon designed to warn away the planes landing at City airport, but with the rise and fall of the earth, the darkness and the distance, it was impossible to get a sense of scale. He carried on along the Λ13, but the buildings hemmed in the view as he came through Rainham, flats stacked on top of fast food outlets and boarded shops, and it wasn't until he passed the London Road that the staunch ranks of the Victorian High Street fell back, giving a view of the Great Spa nestling in the girdle of the M25. When he saw it for the first time, his instinct was to pull over on the hard shoulder of the motorway, to get out of his car and stare at the structure whilst the traffic swept eastwards beside him.

In the five years since construction of the dome of the Great Spa had begun in earnest, Oates had resisted exhortations to visit the building with a certain grumbly pride at his own refusal to be excited. He had secretly been hoping for some job or personal errand that would take him out east so that he could see it without having to go to see it, but no such occasion had presented itself, and as the building moved from construction to completion, and the commentary moved from protest and excitement to simple awe, his stubbornness had compelled him to perpetuate his initial whim. He had seen photographs, he had even succumbed one evening alone in the living room to watching footage of a flypast by a BBC helicopter, but no photograph or recording of the thing could prepare you for the impact. The pace of the cars around him slowed perceptibly along with his own, as if the vast building exerted a gravitational pull at its periphery, and Oates craned forward over the wheel to get a full view.

The building was composed of two distinct parts – the central structure was a dome stretching a kilometre and a half into the black, rain-strewn sky. It was the shape of an upright egg half-buried in the earth, so that the walls rose quite steeply from the ground and tapered into a rounded point. At its uppermost limit, the great red beacon on the top was so close to the rainclouds that the light illuminated them from beneath with a cherry-red glow, giving the sky above the spa the look of a vast special effect, a stage show for the passing motorists. Down the sides of the dome there trooped long lines of maintenance ladders studded with blue lights. Around the circumference where the dome met the earth was a chain link fence which must have been thirty feet high, though, beneath the rise of the dome, it looked like a toy; a spot of detailing on a model prison.

The chain link fence was supplemented with guard towers at hundred metre intervals, their eyes turned outwards on the world. Beyond this, green fields stretched away to the M25 on one side and the edges of the east London suburbs on the other. They were illuminated in the glare of stadium lights erected around the building's edge, so that the residents on the London side spent their nights in a perpetual false dawn.

The second part of the structure consisted of two giant tubes snaking away from the dome, extending half a mile in either direction. Along the sides of these were a series of buildings accessible from the outside of the structure, and Oates guessed that these were maintenance buildings and accommodation for staff. The whole edifice was so grossly out of proportion with the world around it that rather than being part of the landscape, it seemed to alter the dimensions of the sky and the earth to accommodate its own needs. Oates had the queasy impression that the whole scene existed not on the land, but deep beneath the ocean, and the Great Spa was not an artificial thing, but organic, a vast anemone spotted with bioluminescence, drawing in men and women like curious amoebae across the fields and motorways.

The purpose of the giant construction was not so much mysterious as vague. They didn't administer the Treatment in there, that much everyone agreed. The Treatment was handled in a single Nottingham Biosciences clinic in Harley Street. They had been performing it for years before the Great Spa was even talked about. But you had to have had the Treatment to stay there. Nottingham had originally called it a health spa, a place its clients could de-stress, and it was that description which had given birth to the nickname that was now so universal that most people would have been hard pushed to remember the official one – Avalon.

Oates thought being eternally young and rich would have been enough on their own to massage the stress out of most men, but apparently not, as the Great Spa had been hoovering up footballers, potentates and billionaires since the day it opened its doors if the press were to be believed. He knew as much from Lori's gossip magazines. He never read them, but she left them on the bedside table and beside the bath, and somehow just having the damned things in the house stimulated a kind of gossip osmosis.

He saw the signs for the exit from the A13 onto the road that led to the spa, and he found that as the distance closed with the dome the effect of its size receded, as the height and width of it wasted their energies beyond the edges of his windscreen. At the exit itself there was a huge billboard bearing the name of the spa, and the slogan of Nottingham Biosciences picked out in bright cursive lettering: *Don't fear the reaper.* Above the tagline, a woman's smiling face, youthful and bright, was illuminated in a spotlight. Someone had drawn a penis on her forehead, and in the lower right corner, the letters 'M.R.' were scrawled in red spraypaint. It was a tag he had seen going up all over London in the past few months.

Apart from himself, the road was bare of traffic. He switched off the radio and drove with the hum of the heater, and the tapping of the rain on the roof. The metronome of the windscreen wipers kept a quick time.

An avenue of high wattage streetlights set on either side of the carriageway guided Oates's rusty old car towards the gatehouse. As he approached a checkpoint, a guard emerged in the rain. His face and shoulders were concealed by a waterproof poncho, and an automatic weapon hung at his side. Oates slowed the car and wound down the window. A second guard came out with a dog on a leash, and walked around the car. Flecks of cold rain spattered his cheeks. The first guard leant down, a dripping bill above eyes and an unexpected smile. Oates showed him his police pass, and he took it and pressed it against a machine he held under his coat. He returned the card to Oates and waved his arm at someone in the guardhouse, causing the metal barrier to rise.

"What's with the dog?" Oates asked.

"Mortal Reformers. In case they put a bomb in the boot," the guard said, and laughed. There was nothing particularly funny in that as far as Oates could see.

He passed underneath the raised arm and through the steel membrane of the perimeter fence. As he approached the smooth mountain of Avalon he slowed his car, and then stopped completely. The surface of the road simply vanished into the blank wall. He stared at it, and to his astonishment the whole structure seemed for a moment to lift up from the earth on a cloud of orange light. A blink and a toss of the wipers revealed a shutter coming up in the wall, and Oates drove through into the garage beyond. The air smelt of diesel, and the concrete floor was piebald with oil stains. The shutter closed behind him, and he expected someone to emerge from the little office up a small flight of stairs to the side of the room, but no one came. For a few moments he waited, then opened the door of his car and shouted, "Hello?"

He listened, and could hear the sound of music playing on a stereo in the office. He sat back down on the driver's seat, and was just wondering whether to leave his car and head into the office when a movement caught his eye near the striplights hanging from the garage ceiling. A Painted Lady butterfly.

It was so cold in the garage that Oates could see his breath as he watched. The butterfly descended from the ceiling. It paused for a few moments on the bonnet of his car, the surface beaded with rain. It flexed its wings once, twice, and then, seemingly refreshed, it rose to rejoin its gentle battle with the light.

Oates was still watching it when a door in the opposite wall began to open. He climbed back into his car and shut the door, and so he did not at first feel the warm breath of scented air that came from inside the dome. When the door was still only half way open, the sunlight streaming through made Oates blink, and by the time his eyes adjusted to the brightness the gate had slid up into the ceiling, disclosing the entire scene beyond.

As Oates gazed out through the opening in the wall, he was reminded of *The Lion, The Witch and The Wardrobe,* a book his father had read to him as a child, and which he had read to his own kids. He thought of the moment the children push through the fur coats in the back of the magic wardrobe, and find themselves in the snow-covered forest of Narnia.

Outside the garage with its gulp of winter night, there was a summer evening. Gone were the motorways and floodlights, and in their place was a long avenue of trees, the shimmer of a breeze turning the silver undersides of their leaves to the setting sun. Fields stretched away on either side of the avenue. A bicycle with books in the basket stood propped against a tree. Dotted across the fields were groups of young men and women in whites, playing cricket whilst their fellows lay in the shadows under the trees. A man rode on a bicycle along the towpath beside the river, calling instructions to an eight as their blades dipped in unison into the sparkling water.

Beyond the river rose the red brick walls of a courtyard, and a bell tower with the purple sky framed by the arch. Around and behind this central structure was a further collection of buildings which had the unmistakable aspect of a school. The brick quadrangle and the river and the fields basked in quiet splendour. Yet as Oates watched, he detected something uncanny in the movements of the figures playing cricket. At such a distance he could not distinguish anything of their features, but the way they moved and stood prompted an instinctive disquiet.

Only the warning rattle from the roof as the gate began to descend startled Oates from his reverie, and he accelerated quickly through the closing door. He rolled on down the long drive, approaching the main buildings across the fields. As he drew closer, he saw further buildings beyond the court, undistinguished blocks of new-builds alongside the Victorian brickwork. The drive led up to a gap flanked by wrought iron gates on the other side of which was a carpark. Beside the gate was a groundsman in blue overalls. The man waved to him and gestured for the car to head through. Just as Oates passed he leaned down to peer in through the windows, and a look of horror appeared on his face.

Beyond the wall the carpark was flanked on three sides by what looked like science classrooms. Oates caught a glimpse through the long windows of benches with sinks and gas taps at regular intervals. Seeing the still interior of the room in the evening light, he had the odd conviction that he knew exactly how it would smell – the air slightly acrid with chemicals, the old dust warmed by the sun, and the happy boredom of adolescent bodies. He parked in the shadow of the beech tree in the centre of the carpark. He got out, and was wondering how to find Bhupinder when he heard a cry from behind him.

"Stop! You can't be here!"

He turned to see a portly middle-aged man with the sausage-pink skin of the colonial Englishman running towards him across the grass. He was dressed in a suit that flared slightly at the trouser cuffs, and his hair sat shoulder length. A mutton chop moustache completed the ridiculous ensemble. He looked as if he had wandered off from the set of a seventies sitcom. The groundskeeper Oates had passed by the gate was coming from the other direction, talking discretley into a microphone hidden in the wrist of his jacket. The portly man reached him first, and grabbed Oates by the arm. Oates caught his hand, and turned him neatly onto the bonnet.

"Ah, ah, ah! DCI Oates, I take it?" he said, looking back over his shoulder, with his pink cheeks pillowed on the rusting bodywork.

Oates released him, feeling compliance in the soft bicep.

"That's right."

"Well, will you please come with me immediately? It's extremely important."

The man ushered Oates in through one of the doors that connected the block of classrooms with the court, and bundled him into a bare stone toilet, pushing in behind him. The room was no bigger than an old fashioned phone box, and when Oates turned around his companion's tummy brushed up against his armour.

"I'm sorry about that, but I understood your commanding officer had been quite clear with you. You can't wear those clothes inside the school. We have a suit for you. I believe it's right that a man of your rank would not normally have been in uniform in the seventies? Perhaps you don't know, anyway, our period specialists have confirmed it. Your colleagues are all in period appropriate uniform."

"Who are you?"

"How rude of me, I'm Charles Golden. I'm in charge of public relations here at St Margaret's."

"Avalon?"

"Within the school we refer to it as St Margaret's. Listen, I will give you and your men a full briefing as soon as we can gather everyone together, and you've had the chance to change. And I'll introduce you to our director, Miranda."

"I need to see the crime scene."

"Absolutely! Of course. All the more reason to dispatch the necessaries as quickly as possible." Charles said, and clapped him on his shoulder pad, "Besides, what will people think, if they see two burly chaps like us coming out of the bogs together!" He reversed out of the room with some difficulty, pressing himself against Oates in order to swing the door inwards.

Oates was left alone in the old fashioned cubicle, with the chain flush on the cistern, and a bin for sanitary towels down by his boots. It was a dangerous position, for each moment he waited stripped him of a little of his dignity and authority in dealing with the management, and yet to leave in his present state was to defy a direct order from John. *This is where you got yourself, with a reputation for a nose and a delicate touch – locked in a toilet.*

He put the lid down, sat on it, and splashed some cold water from the taps over his face. He wondered if the PR had manipulated him into this deliberately. If he had, it was a blinding move. Be suspicious of any man who appears to be stupid, and who occupies a position which requires high intelligence. Charles seemed to Oates like the kind of boy who had always been picked last for sports at school, and had taken that shame inside himself, into the workshop of his soul, and fashioned it into something sharp.

IT WAS ANOTHER of the handymen who brought him the suit, and a leather hold-all for his uniform. He waited outside whilst Oates changed, and then accompanied him through the college to a set of rooms in the headmaster's lodge where the remainder of his team was waiting. The suit itself was a good wool, though heavy for the weather, and it had the same ridiculous flaring and wide lapels as the one Charles wore.

As they walked through the external passageways, Oates could not help but feel a certain amazement. The purple sky above them, complete with a complement of clouds to make a poet proud, was as natural as any summer he had ever seen, and the breeze seemed to move with a perfectly judged freshness through the stone passages. The sandstone walls were still warm from the touch of the sun.

It was difficult to tell with the sudden and jarring transition between the seasons, but it seemed to Oates that he had not only moved from winter to summer, but had also come backward by about eight hours when he passed through the walls of the Great Spa. Darkness was drawing in, and an early moon shared the sky. It was odd that it had risen in the time since Oates's arrival.

They passed the school dining hall, where supper was taking place, and Oates looked out over the ranks of students eating their spaghetti bolognese. They wore white shirts and grey blazers, the girls in skirts and the boys in long trousers. Though they were too old for schoolchildren, he could not detect any embarrassment at the uniforms they wore. Indeed they did not even seem to think it strange. He had never seen so many of the new-young together, even on television.

The entrance to the headmaster's rooms was a small portal in an ivy-covered wall, and Oates had both to stoop and to turn his broad shoulders as he made his way through into the cool interior of the lodge. A wide staircase, the banister posts decorated with oak carvings of previous headmasters, wound up to the first floor, and it was here that Oates found six junior officers and Sergeant Bhupinder sitting at a series of old fashioned desks before a lectern, at which stood the man who had accosted him in the carpark. They were dressed in police uniforms older than he was. Looking at them all in costume, he had an uncanny sense that they were nothing more than actors playing the role of policemen, and at any moment a director hidden somewhere in the scene would shout "Cut", and the room would come alive with a bevvy of make-up artists and assistants adjusting their lapels.

At the back of the room was a young woman, no more than a girl really, in a floral print dress. At first he wondered who she was, before he noticed the way the groundskeeper was looking at her as he lingered by the door. He was unsure of whether or not to leave, and he watched her instinctively for a clue. The groundskeeper was a tough-looking man in his forties, and from this doggish vigil at the doorway Oates surmised that his young mistress must in fact be new-young, and that this was most likely Miranda, the director of the Great Spa.

Charles was already well into his induction spiel, and Oates settled himself at a desk near the front, nodding to Bhupinder. Although Oates resented the imposition of the introductory address, he was interested in the workings of this hermetic world, and he was not disappointed by Charles's strange little list of prohibitions, all delivered with the same knowing cheek to which Oates himself had been treated in the toilets.

They were not to wear any clothes, or to use any technology that postdated the freeze date of the Great Spa, currently 18 July 1976. They were not to reference any event or circumstance occurring after the freeze date. Charles told them this was trickier than they might think, and ran through the examples most likely to trip the unwary. It was pretty easy to avoid discussing contemporary events, but harder to stop oneself from humming anachronous tunes, or using popular modern catch phrases.

To demonstrate this, Charles sang a couple of songs, and invited the men to guess the year. He did a Tom Jones number, shaking his bottom clumsily behind the lectern, and then a new R&B track, effecting a crooning vocal and swaying with his eyes closed in mock ecstasy. It broke the men's reserve, and they started calling out dates, a young man Oates recognised but whose name he could not remember joining in with the chorus of the R&B track. Oates disliked the ease with which Charles got the men onside by appearing to defer to them.

With the tension in the room dissipated, the remainder of the talk flowed quickly. Days within the spa passed on the double – a single day to night cycle was twelve hours. Oates glanced out the window at the moon, which had risen appreciably. They were not to talk to any of the students. They were, as far as possible, to avoid looking at any of the students in a way inconsistent with their roles as police officers at the freeze date. This was particularly important for any student they might recognise as a celebrity or politician who had come to prominence after the freeze date.

If there was a need to interview any student, they would first consult with Charles or 'el grande generale' Miranda (whose identity Charles confirmed by favouring her with an elaborate bow), and a member of the college staff would be present. They could not use earpieces or any other radio device to communicate with anyone outside St Margaret's, as the dome insulated the interior from all external signals. They were to make no reference to the surrounding external geography of the Great Spa, or the winter season.

"Of course, all these rules only apply to any conversation you have in an open space within St Margaret's, or a conversation you have in front of a student. If you're chatting amongst yourselves then there's no issue."

*   *   *

WHEN OATES HAD first seen Miranda, he felt the vague uncanniness which was his primary reaction to the new-young. He had not come across them very often, since the kind of people able to afford the Treatment were not the sort with whom he and Lori regularly mixed, or indeed the sort who had much to do with the police. His main experience of them had been a brief secondment with the Royal Protection Squad as a young detective, when he would see them come and go – Arab princes and foreign diplomats flanked by bodyguards.

Most chose to be returned to a state somewhere between twenty and twenty-five, but Miranda had taken this to the extreme; the girl before Oates was biologically no more than eighteen or nineteen years old. She had a thin waist, shiny hair, brow untouched by lines of grief, concern or concentration. She looked like a work experience student, somebody's niece shadowing for the day in the office. Her attractive presence filled him with the need to make conversation, to defuse any lingering sexual tension by asking her how her exams were going, or what she was doing for the summer, something to fix them both in the formal attitude of receptive youth and disinterested age. Yet in her manner there was all the assurance of earned authority.

She had sat at the back of the room during Charles's little piece, and several times, whilst the portly man sweated and worked the bellows of his charm, Oates had noticed him glance nervously over the heads of his audience, looking for the silent approbation behind them.

When the talk was done Miranda walked to the front of the room and waited for the men to fall silent. It was impossible to deny the certainty of her expectation. Six rowdy constables who had been singing and joking moments before went quiet, and when she spoke she did so in a voice so low that the men strained forwards in their chairs to hear it. She thanked them for their attention and for the cooperation she was certain would be forthcoming, and reiterated that all the facilities of St Margaret's were at their disposal. Oates half expected her to finish with a clipped 'dismissed', but when she was done speaking she simply sat back down in the chair behind the desk, and it was Charles who came forward to guide them to the room where the murder had taken place.

"Not you, Detective Chief Inspector Oates," this slip of a girl said, raising her voice over the rustle of rising bodies, "I would be grateful if you could remain behind."

The command was so peremptory that had it been made by a man, Oates would have walked right past him. Issuing forth from that girlish physique however, he simply obeyed. As they filed out, he saw some of his more junior colleagues smile and nudge one another. Bhupinder lingered by the door and looked back at him, though whether he was being supportive, or simply hoping to be included in what he imagined to be the grown-ups' conversation, Oates could not have said. He guided Bhupinder towards the door with a nod, and Charles held it open. Oates and Miranda were left alone in the schoolroom. From outside could be heard shouting, and the explosion of youthful laughter, as one person chased breathlessly after another through the shadowy stone cloisters.

"I WANTED TO apologise for the manner of your greeting."

"No harm done."

"We will get to the bottom of the confusion, but you came in by the service entrance rather than the front, and it appears the guards in the gatehouse saw your car and understood you were already period appropriate."

Oates thought of his rusted Ford; it had been almost fifteen years since he had bought it, second hand. The thought made him smile. Clearly for all the historical accuracy and scientific sophistication of the spa, they were unprepared for the intrusion of the genuinely broken-down and old-fashioned. The Met had given Oates a robocar, but it was forever in the shop, and he didn't much mind. As far as he was concerned, a car should have a steering wheel, and he hated sitting in the front seat with his hands in his lap whilst a computer did the driving.

"Do you have any questions for me in private?" she said.

"About the case? There are some things I need to see to before we begin speaking to witnesses."

"About St Margaret's."

During Charles's talk, Oates had been examining the desk at which he sat. It had the look of good old oak, impregnated with youth and boredom, scented with dust. Someone had scratched their name with the tip of a compass into the wood. Had it been a student, or one of the designers of the Great Spa straining for authenticity? It occurred to him that the figures he had seen carved into the banister posts of the stairs were not old headmasters at all. There were no old headmasters of St Margaret's. On an impulse, he asked her: "You could build anything in here, right?"

"How do you mean, anything?"

"I mean you could build, I don't know, somewhere far away. The Cayman Islands. Or ancient Greece if you wanted. Why this?"

"When we began our market research, we asked people to remember the place where they had been happiest. And we quickly discovered that their references were more specific in time than in place. Generally they remembered the point in their school days where they enjoyed the maximum freedom with the least responsibility as their best, often coinciding with their first romantic and sexual experiences. There was also a more general nostalgia for the period immediately prior to the swift technological advances of the late twentieth and early twenty-first century. We sought to evoke a generic space that would appeal to the majority of our market. Over seventy per cent of the 5,000 people to whom the government granted Treatment licences in the last year were of American or western European origin, between the ages of seventy-five and eighty, with an education completed to secondary school level or above. There were too many variations in educational background to produce a completely tailored experience. We can't take everyone back to their own schooldays. So we sought to create an archetype of the English schooling system as it existed between 1970 and 1980."

"My school wasn't anything like this."

"Yes it was."

"I haven't seen anyone pregnant. Nothing's on fire."

Miranda smiled politely. He had the feeling she was attending him with a fraction of her intelligence, whilst the remainder devoted itself to some purpose beyond his understanding. It was a feeling which put his back up.

"Your school may not have been exactly like this one, but your experience of that school would correspond with the experience you would have here, and over the duration of your stay you would begin to align your personal history more closely with your current experience. People share a cultural memory, and a bias towards the idea of a pre-technological 'golden age'. St Margaret's is a composite, an archetype, designed to invoke that cultural memory to supplant and replace the personal."

"I should be getting on."

"I thought if you could understand a little of what we are doing here, it might facilitate your investigations."

"It would facilitate my investigations if I could see the crime scene."

Miranda smiled crookedly. "You think this is a leisure facility for the idle rich?"

This was pretty much exactly what Oates understood of the Great Spa, though he might have expressed it in less polite terms. The implied subjectivity put him on his guard; he had no intention of being rude to this woman, or giving her or her paymasters (or for that matter his own) any cause for complaint. He stayed silent.

"Are you familiar with the myth of Tithonus?" she said.

"Yes."

He enjoyed the effect of this remark. In addition to the natural pleasure which anyone might feel at confounding a low expectation, he could see that Miranda was irritated with herself at having been seen to underestimate him.

"And what do you remember of it?" she said, in a schoolmasterly tone.

"Eos was the greek goddess of the dawn. She wanted Tithonus, a mortal man, for her lover. She asked the gods to grant him eternal life, and they did. But she forgot to ask for eternal youth, and he grew older and older with her forever, until he went weak and senile and she locked him away in a room to wait for the end of time."

"Very good. I asked your Superintendent for an intelligent policeman. Some people would say that's an oxymoron, but I see he has been as good as his word."

She smiled at him again, apparently thinking he would be flattered by the assertion that he was less of an idiot than the calling to which he had given his adult life implied. He understood then the extraordinary usefulness of Charles to this institution. How would his men be likely to behave if it had been Miranda who had given them their welcome?

Despite his satisfaction, Oates felt a fraud. Miranda had chosen the one academic area of which he had a passing knowledge. When he was a kid he had loved classical myths the way some kids loved space or dinosaurs, and the stories and names had stayed with him long after the rest of his limited education had emigrated from his memory. He wanted to make this clear to Miranda, in case she later discovered he had left school at seventeen and thought he had intentionally concealed it, but she continued before he could think of some way of disclosing it without sounding chippy.

"The whole of human culture has been driven by the desire to deny the fact of death. At this very moment, the world is polarised between two great forces. One the one hand, we have consumerism, and on the other religion. Consumerism allows us to deny death by purchasing a series of products endlessly associated with youth and health. Religion might appear to be the antidote, but serves the exact same purpose, telling us that death is not really death but a doorway to more life. All this death denial has fostered the most cruel abuses in human history, because when you deny the fact of death, you can avoid a proper consideration of the taking of life. We at Nottingham Biosciences have now cured death, or at least ageing. But we've found there's a certain... Tithonus Effect. Only the ageing takes place on the inside." She tapped her skull for emphasis, with a perfectly manicured finger.

The discussion had somehow turned into a lecture. Consciously or not, Miranda had come to stand behind the lectern, and her diction had taken on the pleased, emphatic quality of the academic gambolling in her own field. He was the sole pupil, held back in class on a sunny afternoon. He had never been particularly well-behaved at school, and it was amazing how the positioning recalled in him, for all his conciliatory intentions, a childish desire to rebel.

"I always knew it must be very stressful to be immortal and rich, but I never knew it was boring too. I suppose I should count myself lucky."

"What we are trying to do here is no mere exercise in leisure. This is a treatment centre for the last untreatable illness. This is a hospital for those for whom the world holds nothing new. If we can succeed here, we will truly have conquered death, and fulfilled the dearest dream of man."

"And who's the winner if you manage it?"

"Who benefited from the development of vaccines, or antibiotics, or radiotherapy? Humanity is the beneficiary of scientific advancement. Think of the effect on the environment, if people no longer felt the compulsion to reproduce to ensure the continuance of their genes. Think of the peace we might achieve, with no more need for God."

It was an answer forged in the press conference, grand words purged of all controversy. Pare down the truth of something to a sentiment so lofty, it was impossible to disagree with it. He was on the point of arguing with her, when his interrupted sleep and irritation drove him back into the arms of sarcasm.

"Are you a fan of The Beatles?"

"Why?"

"It sounds a lot like one of John Lennon's songs. Imagine."

She smiled tightly. "Imagine indeed. What we have here is a unique opportunity. An amazingly high percentage of people occupying the top positions in engineering, finance, politics and the creative industries come to us, the finest minds not only of our own generation, but of the one before.

If we're going to understand what it is to be youthful in the soul, it will be through this place. The physical environment, the psychic atmosphere of the school is important because of the state of mind it engenders in the guests. In order to make them feel young, we remove from them their responsibilities. All these managing directors and MPs and movie stars, no one can ask them to make a single decision for a blissful four weeks. And our clients study for the duration of their stay here, both for the accuracy of experience, and for the rejuvenating effects of new knowledge. And we study them. Do you see how important it is to preserve the atmosphere?"

"One of those clients has been murdered. I'm sorry if that interferes with the atmosphere, but my job is to find out who did it."

"We are all deeply saddened by Mr Egwu's death. It was a tragedy," she said impatiently.

Oates looked into the old eyes in that flawless young face. "He had a good innings. And it comes to us all in the end."

Miranda met his gaze for a few moments, and then looked away with a sigh. It was as if a favourite pupil had disappointed her with some act of minor stupidity, and she was cast back into the loneliness of her own superior understanding.

Oates was struck by the renewed power of platitudes. It was one of the most enduring effects of the Treatment, the way it had re-vivified certain old expressions. Language had grown up around the human condition like a rose around a wall, and now part of the wall had fallen the blooms of cliché swayed wildly, unsupported in the air. Miranda nodded to herself and he sensed she was steeling herself for a final attempt to enlist him.

"Have you ever looked into someone's eyes as they died?" she said.

"Yes."

"And what did you see there?"

"Pain and fear."

"How about surprise?"

"Shrapnel in the stomach is a surprise, whether you die or not."

"Aren't you afraid of death?"

"No."

"How about the deaths of those you love then?" she said, as surprised by her exasperation as he was.

They stared at one another, and for a fraction of a second Oates felt the violence in him stir in its sleep. It was a terrifying feeling. Most of the time, he could almost forget it was there, and the comforting sound of his better angels chatting to one another about traffic jams and money worries drowned out the sound of it snoring. Then someone like this said something like that to him, and the terrifying specter of his own potential rose before him once again. There was a knock on the door, and Charles inserted his head into the tension. The atmosphere made him grin.

"Not intruding am I? Only the Sergeant was asking if the Inspector might be free to visit the crime scene."

"No, we were just concluding our discussion," Miranda said, "Unless there's any last questions you have for me?"

"The Superintendent told me you have a man in custody."

"Mr Ali..." She looked to Charles.

"Farooz."

"Mr Ali Farooz. He's being held in one of the maintenance rooms outside of the main school."

"How did you come to suspect him?"

"Joe, our head groundsman, was doing his rounds in the small hours this morning, and saw Mr Farooz running across the road from the students' quarters. He called out to him –

the domestic staff aren't supposed to be inside St Margaret's at that time, but they sometimes come inside to enjoy the warmth and the atmosphere at night. I'm told it has been quite a cold winter outside our little enclave. Joe didn't think anything of it until Mr Egwu was found this afternoon. When we spoke to Mr Farooz he simply admitted it."

"I want to speak to him as soon as I've seen the body."

She nodded. "Of course. One would hope that given his confession, you and your men could wrap up your investigations overnight. Charles will be able to get hold of me if there's anything further you need. In the meantime I trust you will encourage your team to respect the parameters laid out in this evening's meeting. Your Superintendent has requested a full report from me on your departure."

She put out her hand to him, and he shook it. Her skin was very pale in the gloaming. Oates turned as he left the room, and watched her collecting her notes from the desk at the back. She paused, her features still with thought. In that moment she appeared to him like a white marble statue of a pagan god, dredged from the earth, cleaned, restored and put on gleaming display in a modernist museum.

She was layered with time – on the surface, a freshness borne of recent attention. Beneath that, an aged thing who had absorbed more than a natural lifetime of human experience, who had watched a century of history accrue from behind her impassive beauty. Underneath it all, as with the ancient gods, there was a bedrock layer that predated her creation, a force of nature to which she had given a human face. As Oates turned to walk down the stairs after Charles, he realised he did not have the requisite learning to reference the symbols in her neat dress and well-groomed hands, and he wondered what it was she embodied for those who worshipped her: wisdom, hunting, lust or war.

*   *   *

CHARLES WALKED AHEAD of him down the stairs, and he managed to restrain himself from talking to Oates until the two of them had passed through the narrow doorway into the great court. Supper was over, and the students were dispersing in twos and threes from the dining hall. The long evening was drawing in, and lights glowed in the high Victorian Gothic windows of the chapel, the bulbs of chandeliers showing warmly through stained glass.

In the fresh air with Charles's giggly curiosity beside him, Oates felt again like a schoolboy who had emerged unscathed from the headmaster's office after an interview about some crime the two of them had committed together. He knew he would have to work hard to retain his suspicion of the ebullient public relations officer, and so when Charles asked him how fierce the old woman had been he remained non-committal. Charles however had correctly judged the atmosphere when he put his head around the door, and with his prior knowledge of Miranda he seemed to intuit exactly the nature of their exchange.

"She can be quite evangelical about what we do here. Bloody hard work for a PR man like myself, to keep the wheels on when the boss goes all starry-eyed. Still, never a dull day. And she's got more of a personal interest."

"What's that?"

"Well, in perfecting the Treatment, obviously." Charles pulled his plump cheeks back in a parody of Miranda's youthful skin.

"She suffers from this... Tithonus Effect?"

"She's never talked about it. You've met her, she never talks about anything outside of her work. But I would have thought so, wouldn't you?"

"How old is she?"

"Oh, DCI Oates! You should know better than to ask that of a lady! But I should say it's a safe bet she was bent over her textbooks in these very halls when you and I were mere glimmers in our fathers' eyes, and peering into the human soul whilst we were trying to figure out what the big and the little hand do."

As they passed under the old gatehouse that housed the school reception, Oates found himself marvelling once again at the sheer size of the spa. A further street opened out beyond, with a couple of students milling around in the light of the streetlamps. Another groundsman was positioned just outside the gate. He had one of the long mechanical arms which council cleaners use to retrieve rubbish from hedgerows, and he was using it to pick up a dead swallow from the gutter. Oates had seen three of the groundskeepers now, and they all had the same bearing, the indelible imprint of a life spent in the military.

They crossed the road, and just before they entered a doorway on the other side, Charles put a hand up in front of Oates's chest, bringing him to a halt. He cocked his head and grimaced.

"Do you hear that?"

Oates listened. From a window somewhere he could hear music. It had the unmistakable sound quality of a record-player, speakers turned outwards on the summer night. He didn't recognise the song, a seventies lounge-ballad. A man's warbling voice mounted a scale whilst a female chorus ladelled sugar into the backing vocals.

"What is it?"

"It's the soundtrack to my working life. What you can hear is Demis Roussos, with The Demis Roussos Phenomenon, the only EP to climb to the top of the UK hit parade in

1976. Demis spent just one week at number one, but after that we'll have Kiki Dee and Elton John demanding we don't do anything untoward to their hearts, then ABBA will be resurrected to inform us of the age and temperament of the Dancing Queen. When we were still at the planning stage for life inside St Margaret's I begged Miranda to bring forward the freeze date by just a couple of months so we could have The Clash and The Ramones, but she thought them redolent of a social upheaval that might disrupt the therapeutic atmosphere. Demis may only have lasted from the 17th to the 24th July in the real world, but here he plays on a loop for a week every new term. You wouldn't believe the royalties we pay his estate. It's like working behind the counter of a shop at Christmas for all eternity, with Let it Snow playing on repeat. If it turns out this Ali chap went on a rampage, and you're short a motive, my money's on Demis."

"I'll bear it in mind," Oates said.

They entered a second court, a small functional space compared to the grand open vistas of the main body of the school, where the students had their accommodation in a mix of Victorian brickwork and sixties concrete and glass. Charles explained that each guest had their own room. Outside one of the staircases was a rope of old-fashioned blue police tape, and a young officer was chatting to a couple of the students who had gathered there.

All the time, Charles kept up his friendly patter, and Oates continued to resist the insinuation of his camaraderie. Charles rebounded from each rebuff with the clumsy enthusiasm of a teenage suitor. As Oates walked past the stout dormitory walls, the spa felt like a fairytale palace – the cold queen, her oafish jester, and her personal army of ex-special forces in blue overalls.

*   *   *

OATES LEFT CHARLES to supervise the conversation between the young policeman on guard outside the stairwell and the small crowd of students. The first flight of stairs was wide, but the second flight was half a ladder, a skinny little passage between the walls. He could smell death about half way up, the heavy metallic odour of spilt blood. By the time he arrived in the room, the SOCOs had already set up the Oracle and taken their readings.

The tripod, with its various sensors and lenses hanging like mechanical fruit from its limbs, stood a few feet from the body. Tiny sound waves probed the wounds, and the cameras fed the pattern of the blood spatter back into the program. The thermometers registered the ambient temperature of the room and of the corpse. Further instruments probed the stiffening of the joints, and the degree to which the blood had settled in the lower veins and arteries. When all the data had been stored and processed Oates and his fellow officers gathered around the screen to watch the preliminary analysis. In the simulation the bright orange figure of the assailant entered the picture from the left of the screen, and brought the knife down on Prudence Egwu.

The murder weapon, which lay now on the floor beside the dresser, was a distinctive African knife with a bone handle. As the scene played out, the computer registered the vital statistics of the attacker – height, six foot. Weight, 90 kilos. Probability male, eighty-six per cent. Probability age range eighteen–thirty-five, sixty per cent. Oates frowned in irritation at the data lines. He had specifically told the SOCOs to switch off the probability metrics, because it was bloody obvious that most violent crime was committed by young men, but there was a homicidal old lady or two in the world, and seeing the odds in black and white made it harder to spot her.

On the screen Prudence raised his forearm, and the first blow sheered to the bones in his wrist, partially severing the hand. Oates had only to look up to see the fan of blood pumped from the wrist across the neat cream walls of the room. The Oracle emitted the victim's facsimile scream, together with the distance at which it would likely have been audible, through the walls and on the ground below. The attacker advanced, stabbing over and over again, raising the knife almost above his head each time and bringing it down into Prudence's chest. It was those long arching blows and retractions that had thrown spatters across the ceiling. He kept striking after the victim had fallen to the floor, the assault continuing long after death. The timer running in the corner of the screen showed three am the previous night.

"Is that thing calibrated to the time in here, or the time outside?"

"In here. There's no other way to fix it, otherwise it gets upset about the temperature." The technician patted fondly at the steel legs of the Oracle.

"So that's, what... about seven pm outside of Wonderland?"

"Yeah. Maybe."

"Figure it out. Any fingerprints, DNA?"

Bhupinder shook his head. "We've run one sweep. We'll do another just to be sure, but I'd guess what little we've found will turn out to be the victim's. It's weird, after an attack like that, not to leave anything behind. Someone must have done some cleaning up. I just knew this would be a long one." He gazed morosely at the floor, toeing the edge of a pool of blood with his plastic slipper.

"Chin up. It'll all be over by Christmas," Oates said, and his subordinate grinned ruefully. "Can someone please find me a pack of cigarettes I can smoke in this place?"

He walked over to the bed, where a large photo album lay on the bloody covers. He lifted it up in his gloved hands, and turned through the pages. The first few shots of the family Egwu were truly ancient, pictures of a large unsmiling African holding a spear and wearing a crown of bones and feathers with several woman clustered around him on his ornamented chair. The brown sepia tones of the early portraits gave way to the bleached colours of nineteen seventies snaps, as the crown, frown and feathers gave way to sharp suits, afros and smiles in the later generations of Egwu men. By the time the camera had travelled all the way to the early twenty-first century, the pictures had the flat quality of print-outs from digital, and the formal portraits had disappeared entirely in favour of graduation and wedding snaps. There was even one of Prudence Egwu as a young man on safari with a smiling African guide.

Oates flicked through the last of the snaps, and was about to toss the book back down on the bed when he noticed one blank page. A picture had been removed. It had a place and date written underneath it in a neat hand: *Prudence and Capability, my two boys! London, Chelsea, September 2005.* Oates looked at the space, the white shadow cast by a little mystery.

"Ah! Another oversight."

Oates was annoyed to find the PR man leaning over his shoulder. He was wearing plastic slippers, latex gloves and a hairnet like the other men in the room.

"Who the hell let you in here?"

"One of your chaps said you had done your reconstruction thingy – amazing machine! – and I might come in. He's a City fan apparently but I won't damn a man for that." Charles grinned broadly, and scooped the album from Oates's hands. "This should really have been checked and removed at induction."

"Someone got one photo," Oates said, and indicated the missing picture. "Do you know where this is?"

"Well, not personally, no. But someone in our welcome team undoubtedly will. We confiscate any little anachronisms the guests might try to bring in and keep them safe for the duration of their stay. This picture is dated after the freeze date, so they will have taken it. They should have taken the whole album. Prudence and Capability... dear me, I would have sued my parents."

"I want to know if your people have that photo."

"Of course, Inspector! Your wish is my command and all that."

"That knife, you let the guests bring weapons into the spa with them?"

"Only period appropriate ones."

Oates took a last look around the room, trying not to be rattled by his companion's impermeable good humour. He asked him to wait outside whilst he completed his inspection of the crime scene, and Charles left with a salute. Prudence Egwu had had time to unpack. His clothes hung in the wardrobe, sweatshirts and jeans in the style of over fifty years before.

His packing case, an unusual item bound in the skin of some kind of reptile with his initials stamped on it in gold, was stashed neatly at the end of his bed. He had been looking at the photograph album before the arrival of his assailant – the light blood misting on the cover indicated it had been lying on the bed when the first blow was struck, and there was a corresponding blood-free patch on the coverlet.

He had also been drinking whisky, though not a lot. A seventy year old Islay was stoppered on the sideboard. It would have been a recent vintage, by the strange logic of St Margaret's. A single glass, still half way full, stood undisturbed on the lid of the trunk. Oates looked at it, and wondered if the stuff tasted worse for being stripped of its years. It was the kind of booze a man shared, if only to impress. Had Prudence Egwu expected visitors? He came back onto the tiny landing to find Bhupinder flicking the underside of his throat.

"We're never going to get him down these stairs," Bhupinder said.

"He's a big bugger. Still you know what they say. Take your time, he's not going anywhere."

Some of the men chuckled in recognition of the familiar joke. A constable brought Oates a pack of cigarettes in a brand he had never seen from the tobacconist on the high street which ran away from the gates of the school. Bhupinder went ahead to find Charles. Oates waited until he was outside to light up, which was a good thing, because the first puff had him clutching his knees in a coughing fit. Through watering eyes he stared at the packet: 'Pall Mall, Famous Cigarettes'. No wonder they were famous, they blew the back of your throat off. The filter was about a quarter the length of any cigarette he had ever seen. He took another drag, ready for it this time, and enjoyed the unaccustomed rush. Some things really were better in the old days.

The little crowd around the police tape had disappeared, and the court at the bottom of the stairs was empty. Night proper had settled on St Margaret's, and the students were in bed. Voices carried from the open window above. With their superior out of the room, the men spoke more freely as they began to move the body.

"Maybe this isn't the time to tell you, but this is my first."

"You've never done a body before?"

"On traffic I have, loads. Just never like this."

"Hey lads, we've got a virgin!"

"Bloody hell, he's heavy."

"What did you reckon of that Miranda?"

"Lovely lady."

"Are you joking? She gave me the willies. The tide wouldn't take her out."

The sound of laughter came behind him down the stairs. Oates was torn between storming back up the stairs and telling them to shut up, and a nostalgic wish to be able to go and join them. There was no one about to hear, and the good feel of the cigarette tipped his mood to indulgence. Charles and Bhupinder were waiting outside in the street, and he followed them to the maintenance rooms where they were holding Ali Farooz.

THE ROOM IN question was just behind the carpark. Oates knew he would only have one chance to decide whether or not Ali Farooz was an Eddy, and he stood in the shadow of the arch to smoke a cigarette and collect his thoughts. He had memorised the facts spat out by the Oracle, and he had spoken to Charles and the head porter about Ali. Bhupinder had already searched Ali's quarters, and the only item of any interest was a diary in several volumes. These had been brought to the schoolroom in the headmaster's lodge, turned into an ops room for the night. Bhupinder's dismay as each fresh item of physical evidence was brought in and set out on the desks was so comical that by comparison Oates felt himself positively cheery about their prospects.

A constable was thumbing the first volume of the diary,

others were interviewing guests and checking registers and CCTV (almost non-existent inside the Great Spa, for reasons of period fidelity), but so far there was nothing either to implicate or exonerate the cleaner beyond the testimony of the head groundsman and Ali's own confession. He was an immigrant from Kenya who had come to the country stuck between two fridges in the back of a truck. The amnesty had brought him back into the white market, and he had been working at Avalon for about three years. He kept himself to himself and had no family or friends, so far as anyone knew. The SOCOs had found no traces of Prudence Egwu's blood on his clothes or his skin, but he claimed to have washed before he was caught.

In theory, of course, there would be many opportunities to interview the suspect, right up to the point at which the decision was made whether or not to charge him. In practice, you only got one shot.

In part, it was the fault of the press. Once the name of a suspect started to appear on the net, events began to gravitate towards the named individual. In part, it was the fault of the Met's reaction to the press. Once that name was out there, the pressure was on for a conviction, and any subsequent attempt to move the investigation in another direction would invoke the intense skepticism of senior colleagues. Oates had even heard of investigations involving alleged Eddies where evidence contradicting the initial line had been concealed to avoid embarrassment, the logic being that it was less of a crime to fit up an innocent man if he connived at his own incarceration.

More dangerous to Oates than this conscious corruption was the unconscious drive to confirm a cherished hypothesis, and it was amazing how, after the initial interview and the first solid decision on the credibility of a confession, the facts that militated against the suspect's guilt moved meekly to the edge of the mind, whilst those which supported it clamoured for attention. In part it was the simple fact that if a confession was thought to be genuine, effort and attention drained away from the case through a thousand little channels, official and unofficial, as man hours were scaled back and corners cut, and as the next unsolved crime obtruded.

But none of these factors alone could explain the overwhelming significance of the initial decision. It was the pull of the explicable that sealed the deal. The commission of a crime created a gap in the narrative logic of the world, which could only be filled by the apprehension of the criminal. Computer games, TV shows, films and comics had trudged over and over along the same path, wearing the psychic groove so deep that real events were now expected to flow down those channels as naturally as rain water finding its way from the rooftops into the sewers. A believable confession fulfilled that need. If you got the first interview wrong, it was a big thing to derail the train of a moving narrative.

Oates had one superstition, brought back with him from the desert. He didn't like to think of himself as a credulous man, and he told himself that he believed in it only as a fate placebo. Still, he had never gone into battle without performing it first.

When Mike was born, and the doctor with his controlled urgency demanded a c-section, he had to sneak off to the toilets to perform the ritual, because the sight of it drove Lori mad. She was jealous of it because it predated her knowledge of him. She was jealous of the man he had been before she met him, as if the younger version of himself had been her love rival. In a sense, Oates knew, she was right. He cherished that earlier incarnation of himself, the young man with a flat stomach and a good left hook who had felt the rush of battle in the desert. The taste of the old cigarette, so different from its modern incarnation, brought it back. Sometimes, he even thought about stealing away, doing a bunk with his former self, the two of them running off to some foreign warzone.

Lori was the same with his army buddies. She was always hospitable, bringing them beers from the fridge when they had their poker nights, but some time after they had gone home he would find himself quarrelling with her about something apparently unconnected, about his leaving the scum of his stubble in the sink, or the cash he spent on booze, or the hours he worked.

The cumulative effect of this over the years had been the slow separation of Oates from his old comrades, as Lori levied these scenes of domestic disharmony as the cost of every reunion. The strange thing was that Lori was not a nag, there was nothing further from her nature, and he could see that she loathed herself during these arguments, and cast about in vain for the cause of her frustration. If you'd asked her whether she wanted Oates to keep up with his army mates, she would say yes, of course, and she would mean it too. But every time the occasion arose, she would make it more difficult, and hate herself all the while.

He couldn't help her because he felt no equivalent. She was ten years younger than him, and he didn't get the sense with her that she had ever been a different person from the one she was today. Perhaps he had taken her too young; the thought had nipped his heels right up to the day of his wedding, but he had resolved when he made his vows to compensate by never making her regret her choice. And he didn't think she ever had, with the possible exception of that single night when they got the call about Anna. He recoiled from the thought, and set about his ritual.

There had been nothing in the pockets of the suit they gave him, and he had borrowed an old-fashioned fifty pence piece from one of the groundskeepers. He flipped it until he got three heads in a row. It took him thirty tries. It was a good thing he didn't believe in luck, because the last time it had taken that many the Mastiff he was travelling in had been ambushed in a narrow alley with adobe walls outside Damascus, and one of his friends had gone home flag-wrapped in the Hercules's hold.

ALI FAROOZ WAS staring at the floor. He stood up and retreated from the table when Oates entered the room, and Oates judged he was the right height and weight for the murderer. He was heavy set, with the same big build as the victim. He was wearing a white t-shirt and a pair of blue trousers in a pared down version of the groundsmen's uniform, and there were dark patches under his arms. He had been in the room long enough for the air to carry the smell of his unwashed body. Oates did not look at him, but instead set out his papers and a Dictaphone on the desk.

They had offered Ali a lawyer, but he had refused. The clichéd pattern for an Eddy was the nervous black teenager and the ageing white lawyer with a hand on his shoulder, some experienced criminal brief employed by the same man as the Eddy to keep an eye on him, cautioning him not to speak when he risked revealing his ignorance of the details of the crime.

"Smoke?" Oates asked him.

Ali was now standing by the barred window. "I don't smoke."

Oates shrugged, and went to put the packet back in his pocket, leaving an unlit cigarette pursed between his lips.

"And I would prefer it also if you did not smoke, Inspector," Farooz blurted out.

When he heard this Oates was ready to show him who was in charge, but looking at Ali changed his mind. His expression was proud, but hopeless. The man was not trying to cheek him. He was simply trying to keep his dignity in this barred place, where he had been waiting for hours. Oates shrugged, and put the cigarette back in the packet. He gestured for Ali to sit down.

Oates had over the years built a shrewd estimation of his own effect on people, and he knew that his silent presence was a powerful lever on closed lips. He sat in front of Ali Farooz waiting for him to speak, to ask what would happen next or whether they were going to charge him. They sat like that without exchanging a word for almost a minute until the policeman himself became uncomfortable with the silence. It wasn't that Ali was playing the hard man, or staring him out. He simply had the look of a man who doubted that speaking could do him any good.

His failure to ask anything about the case seemed to Oates to betoken a simple lack of interest. It was something he had seen on the faces of black mercenaries in Arab Africa. You would never see it on the face of a man raised in the UK, black or white – the British had too much faith in their rights to be truly terrified of the police, and too much of a conviction of their own significance to accept that their feelings and actions might have no effect. The Nigerians and Somalis Oates had captured in the desert had, through the sheer hardship of their lives, gained an indifference to their fate that made them fierce fighters and docile captives.

It was this realisation which made him say, not unkindly, "You're a long way from home, eh?"

"I live in the staff accommodation just outside River Tunnel 1."

"But you were born in Kenya?"

"I was born there, yes."

"No family out there?"

He shook his head.

"For the tape, please."

"No I have no family in Kenya or here or anywhere else."

"You've been in the UK for five years, two years as an illegal, three under the amnesty."

"That is correct."

"You have no record. No previous arrests. Do you have any kind of police record in Kenya?"

"No. This was confirmed most vigorously at the time of the amnesty."

"What did you do in Kenya?"

"I was training to be a doctor."

"And you were involved with a dissident political organisation?"

Oates avoided using the name which had been given on the file, which he could not work out how to pronounce.

"Yes. It was for this I had to leave."

"What were your lot then? Islamists?"

"I am Christian."

"Socialists?"

Ali at first shook his head, then shrugged and nodded. Oates guessed he had been about to describe in detail how his personal political credo differed from socialism, and had decided at the last minute either that he couldn't be bothered, or that such theoretical niceties would go over the head of his interrogator. Either way, Oates, who had been called more things in interview rooms than a referee at a football match, felt oddly slighted.

"For the tape, suspect is nodding. That's pretty brave. Would you say you were a man of principle?"

Ali glanced up, sensing both an edge of sarcasm and an impending trap.

"What do you mean by this?"

"Well, you've never been in trouble with the police before."

"Never."

"And you believe in something so much you get chased into exile. You don't seem like a very likely killer."

"I hate them. I hate them all so much."

"Who do you hate?"

"All these, the new-young."

"Why do you hate them?"

"You tell me why they should live forever, when I have to die."

Ali's voice, which up to this time was inflected with the careful civility of a man trying to pass through foreign customs into a country he does not respect, was suddenly filled with such venom that Oates sat back in his seat.

"You tell me, mister. You tell me that and I will say I am sorry for what I did."

"So why did you come to work here, if you hate the new-young so much?"

He shrugged. "Everybody hates his job."

"Okay. So, you hate the new-young, but you come here looking for work, because everybody hates their jobs. Then one night you see Mr..." Oates pretended to flip through the pages of his notebook.

"Mr Egwu," Ali said, not too quickly.

"Mr Egwu, thank you. You see Mr Egwu and you stab him to death. Had you seen him before you decided to murder him?"

Ali nodded.

"When?"

"I see him yesterday afternoon."

"Just that one time?"

He nodded again.

"Where did you meet him?"

"In the carpark."

"Did you fight with him? Argue?"

He shook his head.

"But you decided to kill him. Do you think that was a surprising decision?"

"It was not a decision. It was just something I did."

"Mr Egwu suffered an extremely violent attack. He has over thirty stab wounds to his arms and chest. I would imagine it's quite difficult to do something like that."

Ali shrugged again, but he did not look away. "I told you, I hate all of them."

"Why Mr Egwu, and not someone else?"

Ali sat silently, and for a moment Oates thought he might have shut up shop. Then he said: "He had this snake skin case. I help him carry it in. We don't have people to carry stuff here you know, you bring your own stuff, because they don't have people to carry things at real school. Most expensive place to stay in the whole country, the whole world maybe, and you carry your own damn things! But he calls over to me as I am crossing the carpark, and he says, 'Would you mind giving me a hand?', only it's not a question, you see? So I say I am not allowed, but he says I should do it now. I say I will get in trouble if I do this, and he say I will get in trouble if I do not, and he will pay me. So I help him take it up, it is very heavy. I hurt my hand on the railing on the stairs. All the time I catch him staring at me. We come to his room at last, and I am looking at the case, and he asks me if I like it. And I ask him what is it, and he says it is real snakeskin. And he runs his hand over it, like this, but I don't say anything.

Then I think he was angry and he gives me five pounds. But it is an old five pound note, they only use them in the school. I cannot buy food and things with this. So I ask him for real money, and he tells me they take all his real money at the gate. I know this so I say he can give me the key to his locker and I will take some, just as much as he says I can take, and he tells me to get out now."

"What time was this?"

"About six thirty, because I am heading for my shift in the kitchen."

"Okay. And what did you do after that?"

"I go and I serve the students supper in hall. I think I will calm down but I do not. I think that there cannot be many snakes like this one left in the world, and this man, he paid someone to kill one of them for him. The snake needs his skin, but this man wants it, so he takes it, and he gives me a five pound note which I cannot use, because only the guests are allowed in the shops in the school."

"What time did you finish work?"

"The hall closed at nine o'clock, and we have clean-up after. I thought I would get calm. I say to me it is not so much to cry about, but I just get more and more angry, thinking about it. Miss Swatch, my boss, she says to me that if I break any of the dishes then the costs comes out of my wages, because I slammed the washer shut."

Ali stared at him. Oates could sense that he expected him to make a note of this, and to follow up later with Ali's supervisor to check if it was true. He put his pen down on the desk.

"Prudence Egwu was attacked in the early hours of this morning. What did you do between the end of your shift and the assault?"

"I sat in my room."

"And what did you do after you killed him?"

"I put my overalls in the incinerator in the basement of the science block. And I take a long shower," Ali spread out his clean hands for Oates to see, splaying the pale palms.

OATES RAN HIM through the details of the evening several times, asking him the same things in slightly different ways. His story never changed, but it had the suppleness of memory, adjusting to accommodate his interrogator's variations. After two and a half hours, Oates went to take a break. The eastern edge of the night sky was tinged with the dawn. He stood outside and played bits of the interview back on the old-fashioned Dictaphone they had given him. If he was an Eddy, he was a bloody good one. A bad Eddy tended to give himself away by not knowing the crime in sufficient detail, and a better one by presenting a story that fit together too neatly, without the roughness of a thing hewn from nature.

Often they were too keen to explain their motives; Oates had found that with real crimes, the guilty party only had a slightly better idea of their rationale than the interviewing officer. *He looked at me funny; she shouldn't have called me that; I was bored.* Those were the reasons underpinning the most violent crimes he had ever encountered. Ali's story had practical consistency, with just the right touch of the inexplicable. Maybe for once it was as simple as it looked, and they had the guilty man. Oates and the idea stood side by side in silence, smoking together in the still of the night, and by the time the cigarette was down to the filter they were starting to trust one another.

Oates brought Ali the statement to read and sign. He didn't ask him if he needed someone to help him read it, as he didn't want to insult him. When Ali was finished reading, Oates gave him a biro. Ali took the pen from him, and for a second he held it like a poor man holding a strange piece of cutlery in a fancy restaurant, unsure of what to do with it and unwilling to ask. He leant down, put his left hand on the paper to hold it steady, and signed his name. Oates picked up the paper and blew on the signature. As he did so, he felt his nose twitch. Ali seemed to him an educated man, and had been a university student. The signature looked like the work of an illiterate.

Oates took the signed confession with him to the ops room where he found Bhupinder arranging interviews with Prudence Egwu's neighbors. Having promised that each student could give his statement in the presence of a member of staff, and most of those students having reflexively insisted on independent representation, the coordination of so many people was proving a nightmare. Even when an interview had been organised, the guests made curiously unhelpful witnesses. Something in the atmosphere of the spa induced in them the sullenness, shyness or unhelpful enthusiasm that the teenagers they were playing might have felt. He waited until his second in command had finished placating an irate company lawyer who had been woken in the early hours of the morning to attend an interview with his CEO.

"You said you'd found his diary. Can I have a look?"

"Course. There's hundreds of the bloody things. He's recorded every single thing he's done since he came to this country. I swear, I've just read about him having a shit."

Oates looked at the stack of diaries, and for once it seemed that Bhupinder was not exaggerating. There were piles upon piles of spiral bound notebooks, at least a hundred in total. If it was confined to real incidents, the biography of the most exciting man alive would not have covered so many, and as Ali was unlikely to have carried any with him from Kenya, the books must deal with a period of no more than five years. Oates plucked one from the top of the stack, and read a sentence at random... *my jeans with the second button missing on the fly, and my shirt. The stain is still quite visible on the sleeve, but the button which I re-attached to the cuff is quite firmly in place, which is a good thing...*

Although the substance was a little bizarre in its mundanity, it was the form that interested him. Word upon word of dutiful detail marched in neat little ranks from one margin to the next. Oates got the impression in reading it that there was still some ghostly schoolteacher looking over Ali's shoulder as he wrote, thinking nothing of the content but ready to rap his knuckles with a ruler at the first sign of an inksplodge. It was impossible to connect the neat hand of that journal with the shaky signature hanging around looking shifty at the bottom of the typed confession.

Oates took a scrap of paper, and held a pen in his own left hand. He tried to sign his name, holding the paper steady with his dominant right. The resulting scrawl looked close to Ali's john hancock.

Bhupinder had his lunch in a Tupperware dish open in front of him on the desk. The crustless halves of a coronation chicken sandwich were arranged on a bed of kitchen roll with a housewife's loving precision. Oates knew Bhupinder lived alone, whilst his mother bugged him for grandchildren. There was something slightly melancholy about lavishing that much care on your own sandwiches. Oates reached over, and took the apple which stood for pudding in that little tableau. Bhupinder looked up, hurt but unsurprised by this fresh outrage, and he made no protestation as Oates left the room, slipping the apple into his pocket.

When he walked back in through the door of the interview room, Ali was in the same position as he had left him. Oates asked, "Have you eaten?"

For the first time in their whole interview, Ali looked unsettled. He was unbalanced by a moment of kindness.

"The men here gave me some tea. But I didn't drink it."

"Catch," Oates said, and threw him the apple. Ali caught it in his left hand. He raised it to Oates and smiled. His teeth were very white. The crunch of the bite sent juice frothing down his chin.

Oates pictured in his mind's eye the video of Mr Egwu's death he had watched on the Oracle. The blow that had killed him had come down hard on the nape of his neck, just above the right shoulder. To swing a blow like that, you'd have the knife in your right hand. Ali Farooz had signed the confession with his right hand, but when he wasn't thinking he caught apples with his left.

Oates allowed himself a little moment of pride at having detected the pretence. He had something definite to pass on to the Superintendent. He was glad for Ali, too. He quite liked the man who had faced him across the table for the last couple of hours. Eddies always thought they'd make it through thirty years inside, but somehow they never did. It was cheaper to have them killed in prison than to buy them the Treatment when they got out.

There was another, even greater reason to smile. An Eddy was the best lead you could have. He must have been hired by somebody, briefed by somebody, and whoever that person was knew the real killer and had enough cash to make his offer to Ali credible. Ali must have been an ambitious young man to accept the offer in the first place, and although Oates could not offer him the Treatment, he was confident he could guide him through the narrow pass between threats and bribes to the truth.

ONE OF THE handymen showed Oates through to a room outside the shell of the dome where his earpiece could once again pick up a signal. He had intended to call the Superintendent then Lori, but instead he found himself calling Grape.

"Hey."

"Oh, hello," she said.

"You sound pretty chirpy, considering."

"I try to stay professional."

Her impersonal tone both irritated and impressed him, as she'd been high not more than five hours before. It was as if it was poor etiquette for Oates to have mentioned it, like trying to take someone up on an excessive offer of hospitality made when they were drunk.

"What's your problem?"

"I thought we had a good working relationship, Inspector. I don't know what you're trying to pull but, for your information, I check my facts and I don't like being used."

"Two things. First, we don't have any relationship working or otherwise and if I drop you the odd tip you should be grateful, not lecture me on professional standards. Second, I haven't told you anything but the truth."

"I've been through the guest log for last night, and there's no trace of any Prudence Egwu. If you need me to put a false name out or help you out like that it's fine, but I expect a little professional courtesy, because if I start to feed my readers that kind of contaminated crap then before long they're someone else's readers."

"I don't know what to tell you Grape. That's his name. Maybe the register's wrong."

"How can it be wrong? I'm looking at the booking records now."

"I don't want to know about your hacking. And I've seen the written register and he's in there. Maybe they haven't updated it."

There was a pause on the other end of the line, and then Grape said, "You swear?", and she was young again, not the hardened professional but the girl out there somewhere in the city who Oates was helping, and he felt a strange gratitude sweep through him.

"Cross my heart."

"Okay. I'll check again. So what about this suspect then? I'm hearing all kinds of rumours."

"Oh yeah?"

"Juicy ones."

"Like what?"

"Assassin for the Mortal Reformers. Industrial spy. Government provocateur."

"His name's Ali Farooz."

"F-A-R-O-O-Z?"

"Yeah."

"Can I use it?"

"You can say we have a suspect in custody, he's helping us with our enquiries and he's an Avalon employee. That's it."

"Did he do it?"

"Come on."

"You come on."

"No."

"No you won't come on or no he didn't do it?"

"Both."

"So who is this poor Eddy?"

"He's a young guy from Kenya, washed up with the amnesty. Serves food in the canteen, porters, stuff like that."

She started to laugh.

"What's so funny?"

"You don't get it? Oh come on, it's a scream!"

"No."

"Someone tried to pretend like the butler did it."

Oates hung up. He started to walk back into the dome, and to his surprise, he found himself grinning.

"CAN I HAVE a look at the register?" he said as he entered the ops room.

"Sure."

Bhupinder nodded his head towards the desk where various articles lay in neat lines, some bagged in plastic, others loose, all bearing numbered labels. The register was leather bound and glistening with gilt at the page ends. Oates flicked through until he came to the date of Mr Egwu's arrival at the spa. It was the very last signature in the book, but there it was.

"Do we know why Mr Egwu came late?" He spun the book for Bhupinder, who eyed this new source of labour suspiciously. "Ali reckons he helped him with his bags just yesterday."

"No. I'll ask Charles."

"How are the interviews going?"

"Alright. Nothing much so far. They have a curfew so pretty much everyone was in their rooms. I can't be dealing with this speeded-up time, now it's light out I feel bloody exhausted. Doesn't seem like much of a holiday to me. Maybe it's like opera, you know: it's boring unless you're rich."

"Lori likes opera."

"Yeah? Well, she's a special case, your missus. Too good for you," Bhupinder looked up shyly to check how his joke had gone down, and at the sight of Oates' smile he gave a little nod of relief. "One thing though, the list of people staying in the school buildings looks about half as long as the list we got from the fire safety team."

"Is it the staff they missed?"

"No, we got the staff list. I spoke to that PR bloke and he says that that's right, there's only half of the guests in here, the other half we don't need to worry about."

"But he wouldn't say where they were?"

"Just that they were in another site somewhere under the dome. Completely separate from St Margaret's."

"I'll talk to him about it. Have you found the victim's next of kin?"

"As far as we can tell, there isn't one. No family, no wife, no girlfriend. We sent someone round to see his boss."

"So we can release his name," Oates said, thinking of Grape.

"Well there's one thing you should see, guv. It's a bit weird, see he used to have a brother but he's dead. Well, he was declared dead last year. He went missing about six years ago."

"Okay. So we don't need to inform him."

"Yeah, only this is the weird thing, when we started checking up on our systems, a whole load of red flags appeared. Apparently Prudence Egwu made all these complaints about our handling of the original case, even tried to sue us. We have to inform internal investigations that we've become involved with him again."

"Well he's not likely to try and sue us again now is he?"

"No, I suppose not," Bhupinder said, as if seriously weighing the risk that the murdered man would take legal action, "but still…"

"He wasn't still looking for his brother if he's had him declared dead."

Bhupinder shook his head, "That was his old job had him declared. Nottingham Biosciences."

Oates felt suddenly wary.

"Prudence Egwu's brother used to work for Nottingham?"

"Yeah. And some of the complaints the victim made were against them."

"What kind of complaints?"

"I don't know. I've only got one pair of hands you know."

"What else did you find?"

Bhupinder clicked his tongue.

"Who was the investigating officer on the original case?"

"Felix Minor."

"Oh, brilliant. Perfect."

The problem with Bhupinder was that he looked depressed and terrified even when everything was going smoothly. As a result, when a genuine problem arose, Oates found himself less prepared with Bhupinder than with any of his other men, as his attitude created in Oates a perverse sense of confidence; however bad things were, they could not be as bad as the Sergeant's collapsed expression implied.

This time however, Oates had to concede the situation looked suspicious. The victim's brother being a missing person, his employment by Avalon's parent company, the complaints and the involvement of Minor, any one of those facts alone would not have been enough to divert the course of the investigation away from his interrogation of Ali. Together however, they had an ominous look.

Oates filled Bhupinder in on the status of their suspect. No one was to be allowed to speak to Ali, and Bhupinder was to continue the investigations in St Margaret's until Oates's return. Before he left, he promised to have a word with the management, to get to the bottom of the missing guests.

Oates just wanted the case solved as fast as possible so he could get back to his family. Still, if there had to be delays, he couldn't think of two people more deserving of inconvenience than Charles and Miranda. He was quietly pleased at the idea of telling them that his men would be muddying their carpets for a few days yet. It suited his mood, to poke his stick in their spokes.

THE SCHOOL'S WORKING day had already begun, and he found Miranda among a group of spectators watching tennis practice on the sunny grass courts on the other side of the river. She was surrounded by various staff members, and the comic, slightly sinister effect of their old fashioned clothes was greatly multiplied by seeing them gathered together. The dew still lay on the grass, and students' trainers squeaked as they ran. The morning had imparted some of its freshness to the spectators. One young teacher in a nylon shirt was running up and down beside the net, shouting encouragement. Only Miranda was unaffected, and watched the game with cool attention. When she saw Oates coming, she waved a greeting, and came away from the group to speak with him.

"Have you come to say goodbye, Detective Chief Inspector?"

"I have, but only for a little while I'm afraid. I've got some business in London, but then I'll be back."

"Ah. You mustn't think me rude, it's just that as you know we run on double time here. By the time you get back from London it may well be the middle of the night again. We've already had one night of interviews and other excitements.

I do wish to avoid any further disruption to the students, routine is incredibly important here."

Oates was conscious of the effect the accelerated days were having on him. The morning sun was rising with unnatural speed. He felt jet-lagged, his body unsure of whether it wanted food, sleep or activity. In identifying this influence, he was able to diagnose a malaise that had affected him ever since his arrival. The creeping sense of loss of control, of having only one opportunity to do everything, must in part be due to the accelerated pace of the day. It was one more thing to beware, in the spa's wide spectrum of disorientating effects.

"I'm sure my Sergeant can get everyone else interviewed during the day while I'm gone, but there's some guests he's been told he can't see."

"You may continue to interview all students in the main school."

"Where are the rest?"

One of the players performed a perfect serve, sending the ball skimming low over the grass, sliding past the leading edge of his opponent's racket. The cry went up, "Ace!" Miranda clapped, holding her hands above her head. Calls of acclamation came from the group of teachers.

"The rest of the guests could not possibly have had anything to do with the murder," she said, "nor would they be in any position to give you information, helpful or otherwise."

"Why not?"

"Guests are physically segregated from St Margaret's for the first fortnight of their stay."

"Mr Egwu wasn't."

. "Mr Egwu arrived late for term. He was to have been transferred to our induction centre today."

"This induction centre inside the dome?"

"It is."

"Where?"

"You have the suspect, Inspector. One of my own men apprehended him for you. I understand he has confessed. Surely it's not too much to ask that the police should remove both the criminal and themselves from this private institution with the minimum disruption to our lawful business. I really fail to see what further help either my staff or my guests could possibly provide. Or should we prepare to try him here as well?"

"He didn't do it."

"Excuse me?"

"Whoever killed Prudence Egwu was right handed. Ali is left handed. There's been an obvious clear up at the crime scene. No DNA, no fingerprints, nothing. Now I want every single person in this whole dome brought to the gym and sat down, and I want statements. If you've got a problem with that, I will arrest you and charge you with obstructing a police officer."

Miranda still wouldn't look at him. A desire came over him to grab her perfect little chin in his hand and turn it forcibly to face his own. It was some time before she spoke again.

"I had hoped not to involve you in the detailed workings of St Margaret's. But if you are going to insist on interviewing all the guests, I suppose I must show you why that is quite impossible."

Oates followed Miranda back down to the towpath. They turned away from the school, and walked for some time in the deep green shadow of the vegetation growing along the bank. In the distance, Oates heard the ringing of the great bell in the courtyard tower. Under the shade of the trees, they met another groundsman. He was carrying a plastic bag held loosely at the top, and when they walked past Oates saw it was filled with dead birds.

Further down the river, they came upon a bend where a tree sank its branches into the clear depths of the water. Moored by a rope to a branch was a punt, and inside on tartan blankets there lay a new-young man and woman in school uniform. They were not touching, but the girl scrambled into a sitting position when she saw Miranda appear on the bank.

"The bell has gone, Stella. Aren't you supposed to be in Mr Weaver's class?"

"No ma'am. I've got a free period."

"I'll be checking when I get back. Now *have you* got a free period?"

"No ma'am."

"No you haven't?"

"Yes ma'am. I mean I haven't."

"I want both of you to come to my office before assembly tomorrow morning. Do I make myself clear?"

"Yes ma'am."

"And take that punt back to the boathouse, please."

The boy, with an ostentatious slowness, got up, stretched, and went to undo the rope from the branch. And yet he obeyed. There was something about his limited defiance which was incredibly... immature. An adult would either have told her to piss off, or would have done as he was asked without theatricality. The boy was implying that he could defy her if he wanted to, he just didn't want to right now, thank you. It was so teenage, Oates had a moment of self-doubt. Perhaps this was a real-young boy, mixed up with the new-young. But physically, he must be at least twenty. His attitude was immature even for a twenty-year-old. He was behaving like a boy of fifteen. It was clear that this was in fact one of Avalon's guests, a man in his seventies or eighties, no doubt with some business or political empire beyond the walls paralysed by his absence.

And here he was pretending to be a naughty schoolboy. The encounter left Oates with an overwhelming sense of embarrassment.

They carried on down the path for ten minutes, at the end of which they emerged into a clearing surrounded by trees. In the middle of the clearing stood a group of low buildings. They were new-build and lacked the artful dilapidation of the rest of St Margaret's. Seeing these sleek glass and stainless steel cubes, Oates could appreciate the cleverness that had gone into the architecture of the school proper. The designers had built and then distressed the school to give the impression of a continuous flow of youth, eroding the fabric of the walls and pavements like water flowing through rock. By contrast, the structures in this clearing put Oates in mind of a hi-tech industrial park, a laboratory for the construction of precision instruments.

Oates and Miranda entered one of the buildings through an unobtrusive reception. By this time he expected the blue-suited groundsmen just inside the doors. He was asked to don a body suit, hairnet and slippers similar to the ones he had worn in the crime scene. They passed through an airlock into a long chamber which reminded him of a distillery. Arranged at regular intervals throughout the warm interior were a series of great glass cylinders filled with a translucent liquid the rich colour of honey, tinged a coppery pink where the lights on the ceiling shone through. The liquid was sufficiently viscous to hold in its interior a galaxy of tiny bubbles and suspended particles which caught the glare of the bulbs from the ceiling like dust motes in a beam of sunshine.

The air was slightly humid, and Oates could make out, through the distortions of the curved glass surfaces, workers in white overalls moving silently between the

casks. He became aware as he moved further into the room
of a deep throbbing, as of an engine buried somewhere in
the floor. It was as if he had entered the bowels of some
huge ocean liner far beneath the level of the sea, where the
pistons turned the great propellers.

The vats themselves were fifteen feet in height with a
flat top sealed in metal, tapered to a rubbery teat beneath.
Within the liquid, suspended with no part of them touching
the glass, were the bodies of the new-young. Oates stood
in front of one of the curved surfaces, and looked into the
face of a famous actress.

She had stalked the silver screen since Oates was a kid,
although her name was a stubborn blank. He had snuck
into an 18 at the local cinema to marvel at her tits when
he was fourteen years old. By the time he made Detective
Sergeant, she was playing the hot mother of teenage kids
in big-budget dramas. When Mike was born, she was
clocking up awards as a mad matriarch in a big TV show.
Shortly after that she'd had the Treatment, and was back
to playing sex kittens. The papers had been awash with the
return of a big screen idol, and Oates had been pulled up
by an erotic déjà-vu quick enough to give him whiplash.

She was quite naked in the amniotic sac, her knees drawn
slightly up to her chest, her arms positioned defensively
with the loosely clenched fists almost touching her cheeks.
Her nudity made her look more perfect and less human.
He was so used to seeing her on screens, in the flesh she
looked not quite to scale. Down the length of her forearm
there ran a tattoo in gothic script, *omnia causa fiunt*, the
colour of the ink enriched by the surrounding jelly. He
moved closer to the glass, fascinated by this opportunity
to observe such a famous face at close proximity, without
the fear of her looking back.

He could make out the tiny declivities of the piercings in the lobes of her ears. As he gazed at her smooth face, he realised the reason for the unnatural sense of stillness. She wasn't breathing. He could see the tiny pulse of blood in her carotid artery, but her chest was motionless, and between her lightly parted lips he could see the golden jelly filling her mouth. A metal tube coiled its way through the fluid, and passed up one of her nostrils, taped in place with a piece of white surgical tape. All at once one of her tawny arms twitched, and he started from the surface of the vat, almost spilling backwards.

"This is one of our missing guests. Do you still propose to interview her?" Miranda asked.

"Is she awake?"

"We have repressed her higher brain functions. She is in the state that exists before consciousness, a kind of deep sleep." Miranda put her hand on the glass, and gazed fondly at her guest.

"She looks like she's having bad dreams."

"She is not having dreams of any kind. What you see is reflex motion, similar to a baby kicking in the womb, establishing muscle tone."

"How long do they stay in here?"

"Ten days, immediately after their arrival. Would you like to see a birth taking place?"

"No thanks. I was there for my eldest and that was enough. You have any kids?"

"No."

"I didn't have you figured for a mum."

"I've always thought it a neat trick, the way nature infuses the reproductive process with morality. We think we are being selfless when we take care of our children. We hold the loving mother as a symbol of moral rectitude. And yet all we are doing is protecting the passage of our genetic material. The Treatment relieves one of that particular hypocrisy."

"There can't be more than forty in here," Oates said, assessing the ranks of vats. "My Sergeant reckons he's yet to see almost a hundred. Where are the rest?"

As they left, from somewhere in the depths of that humid room, he heard the coughing and screaming that accompany a first breath of air.

THEY EMERGED INTO an internal corridor, windowless but with many doors leading off at intervals of about ten feet. There were no portals in these doors, and Oates followed Miranda as she opened the first one on their left, and led him into a small cubicle. Inside was a politician Oates recognised. He had been a senior figure in the cabinet of the previous government. Politicians never had the Treatment whilst they were still contesting elections. Nothing makes a man seem more out of touch than becoming immortal. But straight after they'd been chucked out of office, they'd disappear from view for a while, a few years a least. You'd lose sight of them, until one day they popped up on some speaking tour or charity fundraiser, all the wrinkles and grey hair smoothed away by the gentle hand of Nottingham Biosciences. Because the Home Office were in charge of granting Treatment licences, immortality had become like the honours system, a perk of long public service.

The man was curled on his side. Beneath his body was a long foam bench, the cushioned surface cupping his hips and shoulders. His head lay awkwardly in the arms of a large middle-aged woman. His face was turned in towards her chest, and her arms were wrapped around his muscular torso. She was rocking him gently, and whispering to him.

One of her great breasts swung free from the nurse's smock she wore, and sat squashed between her ribcage and his cheek. Oates watched as the man's cheek, slightly blue from a recent shave, undulated with a rhythmic sucking. The woman looked up at them and smiled pleasantly.

"How is Clarence?" Miranda asked.

"He's been ever so good. And such a hungry boy!"

The man shifted slightly at the disturbance, and his nurse returned to shushing her charge.

"We teach them to suckle," Miranda said to Oates. "We teach them to soil themselves again, to cry out for assistance rather than helping themselves. We teach them to dispense with any conception of personal dignity, with any conception of self-reliance."

The politician turned to look at Oates, and his eyes were glassy. The long wet teat slipped from his lips. His dimpled chin and his nose glistened with thin milk. The smell of that milk was everywhere in the room, and, with the warmth in the air, Oates could feel the drowsy pull of it. He felt comfort settle on him like a hand on his shoulder, and the very next second a wave of nausea made more intense by the contrast. Minister for Education. That's what the man had been. He'd been a fat, bald statesman with bushy eyebrows when Oates had last seen him on the news. Returned to his twenties he was quite handsome. He raised a hand to Oates, and smiled a gurgling smile. When his lips parted, Oates could see he wore rubber caps on his teeth, presumably to spare the nipples of his wet-nurse from adult incisors.

"If I spoke to him, could he understand me?"

"Have you ever felt very drunk, and then something terrible happens, and you suddenly find yourself stone cold sober? That would be the effect on one of our guests if you were to interrupt any given stage of their upbringing. We do not interfere directly with the mental process, beyond the soporifics administered in the womb stage. We rely on the primal memories to re-emerge of their own accord. These first two weeks lay the foundation for the rejuvenating effects of their fortnight at St Margaret's. It cleanses the soul of experience. Do you remember the children's story about the wind and the sun? Each of them wants to make the man take off his coat. The wind blows and blows to force it off, and the man just pulls it tighter and tighter. Then the sun comes out and warms him, gently, gently. And in that blissful warmth, he gladly shrugs it off." She reached down to touch the man's face, with a genuine tenderness that surprised Oates.

"The adult personality is like the coat we wear against the world. The men and women here tend to be the strongest, the most powerful, the ones who have had to clasp their coats very tightly against the gale. Then they come here, into the warmth, and we help them to take it off."

"Why? Why would anyone want this?"

"To be young again."

They walked out through the door and back into the sunshine. Oates took a deep breath. Despite the warmth of the artificial sun, he shivered. He felt as if he had just walked through a spider's web, and even after he had brushed it away there was still the feeling of the residue on his skin, and the suppressed fear that maybe the spider itself had come with him somewhere just out of sight, on the back of his coat or in his hair. He took out one of the old-fashioned cigarettes, and lit it. They stood silent for a few minutes, Oates trying to regain his composure, and Miranda waiting patiently for him to do so.

"I had a case once," he said at last. "Rich bloke used to pay this woman in the West End to walk up and down his back with great big stilletoes on."

"That hardly seems the kind of peccadillo requiring the attention of the police."

"She used these railings either side to hold her weight. One day she slipped. She was a big girl. The spike went right through his ribs. It took four lads just to unpin him from the floor. That's what that reminded me of. Those businessmen who like to be spanked."

"It may look disgusting to you. A medical intervention is seldom attractive. I dare say you might find bowel surgery or an open-heart transplant equally repellent. But believe me, we give these people relief from their suffering. They can have a second first kiss. For a time, they can take pleasure in life again."

"How many more rooms are there like that one?"

"Another fifty. We are expanding, of course."

"And how long do they stay here?"

"A fortnight in this induction block, and then straight into school. The first day or two they are a little shaky, but the mind gravitates very quickly to that perceived ideal of happiness in late adolescence. The only problem is time and expense. It costs a tremendous amount to take a guest through a full upbringing. We use the double-day cycle within the dome to alter the guests' perception of the passage of time, but it never seems long enough. They are always so reluctant to leave. And the effect is temporary."

Oates recalled the sight of the new-young men and women he had seen playing cricket on his arrival, and knew what it was that had been so uncanny. The way they moved wasn't right. If you looked closely at one of the new-young, you could see in the way they held themselves something distinct from the real-young. Although they might be no more than twenty or twenty-five biologically, they carried in their flesh a memory of the little injuries which begin to accumulate in age, and from which recovery is incomplete.

Oates had felt them himself, these little intimations of death. His right ear sometimes clicked from having a rifle fired against it for so many years, and the cochlea shrank from the siren. Another decade, two maybe, and he'd be starting to go deaf. A young man knows he will live forever the way a fanatic knows there's a god, whatever the evidence to the contrary. Oates had been an immortal in his own mind when he first went to war. But as he had aged, his body had told him different.

The new-young, most of them at least in their seventies, had heard those intimations of doom. Sometimes on a news programme or a TV show you'd see them from behind, and they would look old for a fraction of a second, despite their agile figures. Deep in their fresh new bones was buried the memory of what it meant to get arthritis in the fingers, to lose your sight, to feel your knees when you climbed the stairs. It made them cagey of their perfect bodies where a healthy young man or woman was generous with their strength and beauty. They believed in death, these rich immortals, in a way the real-young never could, though the real-young would be in the ground soon enough when compared to the new-young's eternity.

Yet it was not this instinctive care which Oates had seen out on the playing fields, and on the tennis courts that morning – rather its opposite. The twenty-somethings on the playing fields ran and called and tumbled over in a bundle of flailing limbs. The way they moved had not only the sureness of young adulthood, but even the coltishness of late childhood. Their running was undisciplined, experimental, as each new step provoked fresh amazement. They were testing their powers like pubescent girls with their new beauty, pubescent boys with their first muscles.

"I'll need to speak with everyone who might have had any contact with Mr Egwu since he came into the spa."

"None of these people could possibly have met Mr Egwu."

"I want them all out of their tubes."

"You would be destroying millions of pounds worth of therapy, as well as upsetting some of the most powerful people in the world. And, as I told you, as you have seen for yourself, it would be pointless. Our phase 1 guests are quite unconscious, and our phase 2 guests will have very limited recall."

"I couldn't care less about their fucking holiday."

"Detective Chief Inspector, as I have tried to explain to you, this is not just some leisure exercise. These people are really suffering. You have no idea what the Tithonus Effect can do to the mind. It must be stopped in its early stages. It is horrible. It is horrible!"

Miranda's voice had risen in volume as she spoke, and her final words rang out in the empty clearing. Oates felt a surge of satisfaction. For the first time, he felt her entire attention alight on him. Had he been pushing her, unconsciously, for just this engagement?

"I'm sorry."

"You're not sorry. You are pleased. Is there something here that has angered you? Do you wish to punish these people? Are you jealous even? Or do you think they deserve it?"

"I've got a job to do and I'm going to do it."

Miranda nodded, and the flash of passion was gone in an instant. Her air of distraction returned, and whatever luminous element of her consciousness had briefly turned on Oates, its light passed again into the interior of her thoughts.

"We'll see. You are an admirer of classical mythology, Inspector. Did you ever wonder why the ancient gods were so cruel? Why they were so violent?"

"No."

"No?"

"It just made sense to me. More than a loving god anyway."

"I have. I have given it a great deal of thought."

"And?"

"The classical gods weren't really deities in the modern theological sense. They were neither omniscient nor omnipotent. They were really just people. People who had been doomed to live forever. I think they acted as they did because they were bored."

THE GUEST ENTRANCE to the dome was accessed through one of the shop fronts on the High Street, and Oates was shown to a storage locker where his clothes and personal effects were neatly arranged. Putting on his body armour, he felt time and identity return to him. The multiple layers of fantasy within Avalon had unsettled him. It had amplified in some way the conflict between his desire to see justice done, and his need to get back to his family. A trailing thread of his personality had snagged on the chain link fence of the spa on the way in, unravelling behind him as he walked the corridors of this wind-up toy of a world.

The setting that Nottingham had chosen for their fantasy retreat had not helped. Miranda was right to say that St Margaret's was generic, but it had more of the flavour of a posh grammar or even a private school than a normal comp. It reminded Oates of reading *Brideshead Revisited* (there had been a limited number of books in his camp in Syria, and most of them belonged to the officers), and being disgusted by the author's attempt to corner the market in halcyon youth, staking out the idealised territory of late adolescence like a private garden in a London square, giving the keys to the upper classes.

At least with a book you could banish the characters by throwing the thing across the room. The Great Spa was real. There was something obscene about this generation of the rich, clawing their way back into the womb, insulating themselves from the decade they had shaped with all its riots and decay. Eternally young, they could afford to wait for a better day.

He thought of Ali Farooz, and the hatred which had almost convinced Oates of his guilt. Looking back, he understood that the hatred had seemed authentic because it was. Oates could feel it himself – didn't every mortal man, woman and child have a blood feud with the new-young, who would never die?

The Great Spa had overmastered him. He had wanted to be like a sheriff in an old Western, riding into town in his rusty Ford bearing justice for those who thought themselves beyond its reach. But Miranda had seen him coming a mile off, and in accommodating her requests and playing dress-up, Oates and his team had confirmed to her and to her clientele that the normal rules did not apply even as they sought to enforce them.

Outside the spa, with the cold caress of the armour on his trunk and the cigarette smell of his raincoat, he stood once again on solid ground. He knew that whatever unease St Margaret's had raised in him, he must confront it before he returned. The resolution to the case lay within the walls of that artificial summer from sixty years ago. Yet inside it, he was vulnerable. Inside it, he was a stranger in someone else's past.

Oates decided to take the seventies suit with him. He didn't want the management to have any excuse for delaying entry on his return, and they could hardly say the clothes they had given him were not period appropriate. Plus it was a nice suit, and the only other one he had no longer buttoned at the waist. When they finally ushered him out the door and back into winter, the cold wind turned his head. Oates's car had been driven around to the carpark outside the guest reception, and it stood among a gleaming host of Bentleys, Mercedes and customised Jeeps. Some of them were robocars, particularly the sports cars, but not all. A robocar would only look pricey to someone poor. If you were really rich, Treatment rich, you kept your steering wheel, and hired a man to turn it for you.

Seized once again by the odd adolescent defiance, he reversed into the car behind him, cracking the headlight. He pulled away as the car alarm lit up, delivering its shrill summons to the security guards through the double doors. As he headed down the motorway the great dome of the spa appeared once more in his rearview mirror, a souvenir snow globe with a thousand youthful memories shaken up inside, glittering with reflected light as they drifted down through the past, with a murder suspended at their heart.

THE RADIO SAID that there had been more disturbances in the small hours in London. There were bins and cars set alight in Tottenham, and groups of rioters had emptied some of the stores. A shop selling high-end trainers had been looted and fired on Camden High Street. The flames were still going in the morning. "I can't leave you alone for five minutes," Oates said to the city. He called Lori.

"Did the kids get off for school alright?"

"Fine. Mike's a little rattled."

"Yeah."

"How's the job? Will you be able to pick them up this evening?"

"We'll see."

"They'd like it if you picked them up."

"I'd like to be able to do it."

"What do you want for supper?"

"Oh, don't worry about me."

"It's no bother, I'm going to the shops now."

"I'll probably just get something out."

"It's not good for you, you know. Eating all that junk."

"I know."

"Well, what time will you be back?"

It was amazing how they could both feel these confrontations coming. They neither of them wanted the conflict, but every step they tried to take to avoid it seemed to hasten the clash. He felt as if they were not two people in a conversation, but two drivers late at night who swerved to avoid one another in the same direction. He fought to hold on to kindness.

"I'll be back when I'm back my love. As soon as I can."

"Okay."

"Okay then. I love you."

"Bye."

"Bye."

"End call," he said, but she was already gone from the line.

As he drove in the grey morning, Oates thought of a time just after he and Lori had moved in together. One of the things he loved about his wife; despite the fact she was neat as hospital corners to look at, she liked to eat her dinner in bed, and didn't care if you got crumbs on the mattress or ketchup on the spread. He'd never been with a girl who would let you eat in bed.

Oates had bought a pallet of microwave lasagna from the cash and carry, and they lived off it for about a month. It was an Indian summer and they slept with the windows open and the street noise.

When October came they had to close the windows and the curtains for warmth. The first night with the sash up and the drapes closed she said she couldn't sleep with the smell of lasagna hanging in the room. She had got up to take the two empty microwave dishes back to the kitchen, and Oates had leapt naked from the bed and blocked her way. He told her that he couldn't let her take out the dishes, because if she got to cleaning up their bedroom she would eventually leave him. "I'm a slob and I can't change! You have to stay a slob too," he howled, and she was laughing so much she could barely hold the trays, and he chased her around the bed.

She leapt on the mattress and flanked him with a springy quickstep, landing lithe at the door. Before she made her escape she turned and grinned at him, and kicked up a naked heel. "If you change you'll leave me," he shouted breathless from the floor, and the neighbours banged on the adjoining wall and told them to shut up.

Coming back into London he noticed a curious thing. The traffic should have been flowing into the city, but the red taillights ahead of him were few and free moving. It was the other side of the road that was busy. People were leaving London. He passed one spot where the traffic had slowed to a halt on the other side of the crash barrier, and saw a kid with his duvet drawing finger faces in the condensation on the back passenger window. More than anything, Oates wanted to get back to his family. But the body of Prudence Egwu lay between them like a fallen tree across the road. There was no way round but to clear it.

FELIX MINOR WAS bent. His conviction had left dirty fingerprints over every case he had ever handled. Minor had been caught out in a big purge of the Met following one of their periodic institutional scandals. This one concerned the distribution of goods at police auctions. Under pressure from the government to crack down on the assets of convicted criminals, the Met had increased the seizure and subsequent resale to the public of paintings, cars, boats, clothes, furniture and houses belonging to gang lords laid low. The officers in charge of such auctions could not bid for the items themselves, but they did administer the timing and advertisement of the sales.

It had become a perk of the job after resolving a big case to arrange an auction at very short notice and at an inaccessible venue, tipping off a few favoured dealers in advance. These stooges would scoop the loot for a song, and split the profits with the team of officers who had recovered it.

The arrangement had all the makings of a mass corruption, being a grey practice underpinned by a corresponding sense of entitlement. Such systems unravelled when the balance between greed and prudence shifted decisively to the former, and so it was when a journalist's land registry search revealed that the multi-million pound house of a drug boss had been sold for the inexplicable sum of £100,000 to a property magnate with links to New Scotland Yard. The Met had appraised the officers involved with the dispassion of a surgeon observing a soldier's poisoned limb, and Minor had found himself just below the amputation line.

The experience had embittered him, trapped as he was between the knowledge of his own guilt on the one hand, and the knowledge of everyone else's on the other. He had deserved his punishment, but there were those above him who had deserved more, and who had been spared. Because of this, he was unable either to sustain himself with the knowledge of his innocence, or to embrace repentance, and the shrapnel from his crimes stayed buried in his bones, slowly poisoning the blood.

Oates felt the reflection of this paradox in himself – Minor had been his governor once or twice in his early days on the service, and he was no better or worse than most. He had liked the older man. Nevertheless, Oates felt a strong condemnatory reflex towards him now, precisely because his sin was one which Oates himself might have committed.

The things that happened to policemen in prison had happened to Minor, and now he haunted the pubs in Soho.

He occupied a space between the forces of crime and the forces of the law, and belonging to neither he talked to both.

Oates left his many-miled Ford in police parking at St James's and walked up towards Piccadilly Circus. Night and day haggled over central London long into the morning, and the city was still dimly lit beneath the pavement sky. As he came up Lower Regent Street he saw the statue of Anteros framed against the giant electronic billboards on the other side of the square.

It was his favourite statue in London. It had originally been built to commemorate the great philanthropist Lord Shaftsbury, and so the sculptor had chosen Anteros, the god of selfless love. But poor Anteros just didn't have the brand recognition of his elder brother Eros, god of mad desire. They were twins and they looked identical, so people started calling the figure Eros. When the burghers of London found out that their stiff-collared Victorian hero was being commemorated by the naked boy-god of lust, they re-christened the statue again, calling it 'The Angel of Christian Charity'. But you didn't go to Soho for Christian charity, and Eros stuck. Wasn't that London all over, mixing up love and lust, then getting embarrassed about the whole thing and trying to conceal it with some posh sounding name?

Even Eros was having a tough time of it these days; the god of desire was reduced to a tiny black silouette against the famous billboards on the other side of the circus. The face of the Nottingham Biosciences model, twenty foot wide from ear to ear, bulged in projected 3D from the surface of the largest hoarding. The flawless young girl mouthed their slogan, "*Don't fear the reaper*". Oates spat on the pavement and trudged on through the curtain of rain, the tourists and the cars and the buildings staying out of his way.

There were a couple of pubs Minor was known to frequent, and Oates had decided to begin by looking in at the Moor's Head. It was open twenty-four hours, and was a good bet this early in the day. Away from the main tourist drag, the streets narrowed and cobbled up. The shops began to specialise, and to conceal rather than display their wares. In the cafés there were a few stragglers from the nightclubs, drinking coffee and resenting the day. The second hand book barrows on D'Arblay Street smelt sweetly of damp paper.

The vices of the whores and the dealer on the corner of St Peter's Street seemed quaint beside the chain restaurants and clothes shops looming on Oxford Street, and the monstrous dome of the Great Spa out on the ringroad. Their sins were like the disobedience of children playing in a warzone. They had enough respect to stop hawking as Oates walked past in his uniform, and he nodded to them. The people in the Great Spa paid for their own security, but these people were under his protection or none. This was old London, hoarding itself against the future in the dank little alleys.

The Moor's Head was dingier inside than the grey morning. Oates clocked three large men at the bar, their backs a wall of black leather. A tramp sat beside the door, nursing the half of bitter that stood between him and the cold outside. The pub had a wooden partition to separate the saloon bar from the back of the house. He knew better than to ask after Minor, and went round to look for himself. The door in the partition was set low, and Oates had to stoop. Minor sat at a wooden table beside a lead-latticed window in the snug. The diamond-shaped panes of glass were old enough to be thick at the bottom, and steamed by the radiator beneath the windowsill. On the sill itself there was a sheaf of flyers for West End shows, strip clubs and warehouse parties, all of them long passed. From somewhere round the corner came the sound of a quizz machine gobbling change.

"Can I get you a drink, Felix?"

"Get you a drink, he says."

"What's that you're drinking?" Oates said, motioning to the tumbler of brown liquid on the table in front of him.

"Fruit squash. I've given up the booze for Lent." He grinned up at Oates.

"How about a whisky?"

For a few moments Minor was silent, and Oates thought he might tell him to piss off. Then he shrugged, and shouted, "Horace!" The barman came to the side of the saloon bar, turning a clean pint glass against a dirty cloth. Minor stuck his finger in the air above the table and waved it around three times. "And for my esteemed guest, Horace."

The smell of whisky made Oates feel nauseous. He hadn't eaten since he left home. On the stack of flyers there was a laminated menu, and he picked it up. When he moved the menu it left a darker outline of itself against the coloured leaflets, where the sun had bleached them.

"If it's breakfast you're wanting I'd go somewhere else. For a copper the spit's the best thing in the food."

"Thanks for the tip."

"To what do I owe the pleasure of your company? Or maybe you just want to chat over old times, eh?"

Minor gazed up at him. Drink had dug the intelligence from his brown eyes and a wet cunning had welled up to replace it. Perhaps it had been a mistake to visit the old man. The whiff of disgrace still clung to him, and a handshake made you want to wipe your hand on your trousers. It was so unusual for a senior officer to seek Minor out that he must guess Oates was badly in need of his help. He should have sent Bhupinder, or even rung the pub's old phone, but the moments of powerlessness in St Margaret's had goaded him into taking action himself. It was another little defeat at the hands of the spa, and of its mistress.

"Can I sit?"

"You're drinking aren't you?"

It was too late to dissimulate. His only chance was to be straight with Minor and to try to pay whatever price he wanted for his help. Even if he had something to trade, Oates knew the pleasure of having him in his thrall might be so extreme that Minor would simply refuse to tell him anything.

"I was hoping you might be able to help me with something."

"Oh yes?"

"An old case you worked."

"See now, this is embarrassing. I'd love to help, but they've asked me to leave the service."

"Come on Felix. I'm asking you as a favour."

If Oates had hoped the direct approach would shame him into helping, he was mistaken. Minor was inoculated against shame, or rather he felt it so consistently that a little variation in the dose made no difference. He was not however insensible to his own pleasure, and he was grinning now.

"I know how you're asking me."

"So what do you say?"

"Must be a real emergency."

"It won't take a minute."

"If it's an emergency maybe you could deputise me."

"I could get it out of the files. But it'd be quicker coming from you."

"I'd not be sure of that."

He was about to offer Minor a smoke when he remembered he still had the old-fashioned pack of Pall Mall. The former policeman was sure to notice, and the last thing he wanted was for Minor to catch the whiff of big money. He thought about trying to bum one off him, but decided against it. The frustrated need for a cigarette made him aware of his big hands, and he laid them on the table.

"So this is your favourite haunt now is it?"

"It's the same as anywhere else."

"A little dingy if you ask me."

"You're the one doing the asking."

At that moment Horace loomed above their table, and set down their drinks. Minor was given a single dram of whisky, and Oates was given a pink concoction in a cocktail glass, with a maraschino cherry fastened to the rim, and a faded paper umbrella part submerged in the surface. He heard laughter behind him, and when he turned around the three big men at the bar were grinning at him over their shoulders like a set of dingy gargoyles built to guard the pumps. Minor cackled and slapped his thighs.

Oates popped the truncheon from the panel on his leg. He brought it out beneath the table, and pressed the button on the side to extend the sleek, heavy length of it. As it slid into position, it gave an oiled click like a dislocated finger popping back into place. He set the truncheon down on the table beside the glass.

"Drink it," he said to the barman.

One of the men sitting at the bar went to rise from his seat.

"You sit down," Oates said mildly. The man at the bar hesitated for a few seconds, his buttocks quivering in mid-air, before settling back with a creak onto the stool. He obeyed not because Oates willed him to, but because he could sense Oates willing him to defy the order, to furnish the spark to ignite the moment into the conflagration of battle. Horace tried to laugh, and went to turn away from the table.

"Is that not what you wanted then? I'll get you another."

"I said drink it."

Horace licked his lips. He looked to the man who had almost risen, but his hopes of salvation were dashed by the sound of the man's arse settling back into its foundations. He stared at Oates for a few seconds, and gritted his teeth. With a look of hatred he grabbed the stem of the glass. He made to chuck it back.

"Sip it."

"What?"

"Don't down it. Sip it."

The barman raised the glass to his lip, and sipped. The slurp sounded loud in the silence of the bar. Oates risked a glance at Minor, and saw his eyes shining with the reflected light of another's humiliation. They waited in silence as Horace drained the glass. Oates stood up.

"Now eat the cherry."

Quickly now, his eyes on the ground, the barman obeyed and dabbled for the bright little fruit with his dirty fingers. He popped it in his mouth and munched once before swallowing.

"Now stay still."

Oates took the little cocktail umbrella from the glass, and lifted it towards Horace's eye. The barman flinched away at first, but Oates put out a hand to his shoulder and patted him, like a groom reassuring a skittish horse. He popped the umbrella up with thumb and forefinger, and brought the pointed tip closer to the watery swell of the barman's eyeball. Horace had astigmatism, and the bloodshot belly of the eye protruded, pregnant with jelly.

"Don't blink and you'll be alright," Oates said.

Tightening his grip on Horace's shoulder, he brought the tiny wooden point of the cocktail stick just up to the downward brush of the blinking lash, and then thrust forward to lodge it behind the barman's filthy ear. He heard one of the men at the bar exhale.

"You're going to wear that umbrella for the rest of the day. I might swing by here before closing. I've got some errands to run. If I come in here and you don't have that umbrella behind your ear, I'm going to break your wanking arm here and here." He tapped Horace's right elbow and forearm with the point of his baton,. "And not a man in this room will see a thing. Will you, my new friends? Now, I'll have a whisky same as my old colleague here. And you can treat yourself too."

"That's real police, that's real police now," Minor said, wiping the tears from the corner of his eye.

"I'll have you out of here old man," the barman said.

"Have another cherry, Horace! It's on the Inspector. You're alright Oates, I always said you were alright."

As Oates sat back down, Minor clapped him awkwardly on his armoured shoulder. All his former antagonism was gone, he was expansive. He asked what Oates wanted to know, and Oates told him, omitting any mention of the murder, the Great Spa or anything else likely to pique Minor's interest. Minor was so elated by the confrontation that he didn't even ask.

"I remember that Prudence Egwu. He asked us and asked us to find his bloody brother. In the end he lodged a complaint, not a general one mind, a personal one against me and the officer in charge. He was mad, but they have to investigate the complaints, even the mad ones. And he had the money to keep it going."

"What happened?"

"What happened? Nothing happened. He was mad, same as I said. We looked and we looked and we found nothing.

You know he actually said to me if it had been a white fellow had gone missing, we would have found him. I said only if he was hiding in the coal shed, son. He didn't like that!" He smiled at the memory of how little the dead man had liked it.

"Did you get anywhere with tracing the brother?"

Minor shook his head emphatically. "He just vanished. Well, people do, don't they?"

"Any leads? Anything odd about the case?"

"Plenty of odd stuff, but all talk. There was talk at the time of all sorts, because of what he did. Some people were saying a competitor of Nottingham had kidnapped him, like they had some underground lab somewhere to keep him chained up, or else they'd done for him to stop him perfecting the Treatment for Nottingham. Some people said Nottingham had nabbed him to stop him going over to the competition. We even had a call saying he'd been kidnapped by the Chinese secret service."

"What did you think? Personally I mean."

Minor shrugged. "He was an odd-bod. Didn't have much of a life outside his work, except some charity bits and bobs, and church. Nothing tying him to the world but his ideas, and that's a thin enough tether for anyone. Could be suicide, could be he just left."

"Did you ever find out what he was working on?"

"No. But the brother told us all his research was gone. Don't ask me how he knew. Tried to tell us it was proof of his kidnap theory."

"Did you ever hear mention of something called the Tithonus Effect?"

"No. What's that?"

"Just something someone said to me. Did he ever give you a picture of his brother?"

"You'll find something on file."

"This complaint..."

"You want to know if there's trouble there for you?" Minor grinned. "There's no nasty surprises on that one, saving what was there before we came on it. He was a very rich man, that Mr Egwu, and I think he hired his own men to keep looking after we'd dropped the case. But you can speak to the senior officer if you really want to check."

"Who was that?"

"Don't you know? Superintendent John Yates of the Met."

Oates prided himself on his poker face, but something must have shown, as Minor smiled at him.

"Ask for you special did he? I bet he did, I bet he did. He used to ask for me special."

Oates changed the subject, and the two of them chatted about people they had both known. Minor claimed he wanted news of them, but whenever Oates told him anything that looked like a divergence from the historical position, he just snorted and cited some incident from his own time on the force. He produced these anecdotes as if to refute the present, like a paleontologist brandishing the fossil record at a Catholic bishop. "Dick Owen will never go higher than Chief Inspector. I remember..." Bhupinder called, but Oates ignored it. They ordered another round, Oates asked for that cigarette after all, and for a while what with the smell of the pub and the old stories the two of them were friends again. They had settled into a brief silence when Minor said, "I was sorry to hear about your girl."

Oates looked round quickly to see if any of the men had heard. They gave no sign, but still Oates felt the reference get loose on the floor of the pub. Once it was out he would never get it back, it would be away in the walls, chewing at the wiring of his authority.

"Yeah," he said, as he got up to leave, "take care of yourself, Felix."

"I'm alright, Detective Chief Inspector. It's you as should be watching your back," he said, and with that the moment of warmth between the men was dispelled, and Oates went back out into the rain. From the street he took one last look through the grimy window of the pub, and Horace was still wearing the umbrella perched at a jaunty angle behind his ear.

He shook his head for Felix Minor. Drink had made him paranoid, with all the self-aggrandisement of a full-blown 'they' out to get him. The psychic injury done him by his conviction had left him stranded in his glory days. Minor and Miranda were like two pilgrims walking the same trail, the old man in his dingy little pub where no one had changed the carpet in thirty years, the new-young woman in her state of the art pleasure dome, each of them searching for the shrine of their own youth. Minor was, if anything, more successful – his grievance provided a watertight seal against the present. Perhaps every man and woman walked their life on a see-saw, and one day a single footfall tipped the balance between the significance of past and future.

Oates remembered his own mother looking through photographs in her retirement home in Southend-on-Sea, and the signed picture she had been sent by a favourite pop-star, himself long dead. The past had become reality for her, and she spoke to her son quite cheerfully of their father, dead for ten years, as if he had just popped next door. Oates could accept that fate for himself, even the quiet horror of the doilies and the soft seaside rain, but it seemed as if the fulcrum of significance was retreating inexorably backwards, so that fifty and then forty and then thirty years old were somehow unbearable.

He thought about what Miranda had told him of St Margaret's, that the real secret of promoting the feeling of youth was to remove from people their sense of responsibility. He could understand that, because the thought of his kids and the murder and his men back at the spa made him feel old. He could see the temptations of the retreat into the womb, where even the burden of conscious thought could be dispensed with, without needing the courage to let go the gift of life.

THE MORE HE considered what Minor had told him, the less he liked it. Why would a man with a grudge against Nottingham book himself in for a holiday at St Margaret's? Why for that matter had they taken the booking, and why had Charles not seen fit to mention the history to Oates and the investigating officers? As a public relations officer he could hardly be unaware of a man publicly making accusations of foul play against his employer, even if it had been five years ago. Why had John not warned him?

Oates couldn't share Minor's enthusiasm for the idea of deliberate deception. Being part of one of the institutions routinely fitted up for conspiracy had taught Oates to dismiss conspiracy theories out of hand. The kind of people who believed in such things were either half-mad like Minor, or else deeply innocent of the world, toys still in the packaging of their teenage bedrooms. Apart from anything else, the Met lacked the funding and organisation required for a decent conspiracy. Perhaps his boss simply hadn't spotted the connection. Only the files with their archival memory had picked up the link.

Still, it was too much of a coincidence to have the company implicated, however loosely, in one brother's disappearance, and for the other to turn up murdered on their property half a decade later. If Prudence Egwu really had kept paid men on his brother's case, perhaps they could give him more information. They must have written reports, submitted expenses. Oates knew there wasn't a front garden in the suburbs more meticulously kept than a private detective's expense forms. He remembered the victim's address from the file. He decided to drop round there to see if he could find any record of the investigations before the tech team arrived.

He took the Underground. When he sat down on the padded bench, he saw someone had scratched the letters 'M.R.' with a coin onto the carriage window. By Notting Hill Gate tube station the shops were still open, but the shopkeepers had taken their goods from the window displays. One store selling cephoscopes on the corner had nothing in the window but a handwritten sign saying *No stock or cash kept on premises*. The street where Prudence Egwu had lived swept down from Camden Hill, wide and tree-lined. The houses themselves stood back from the road, with gleaming black front doors beneath porticos at the tops of stairs. Despite the cold Oates grew warm as he toiled up. The house was near the brow of the hill, overlooked by nothing but sky. The door had a keycard lock, and he used his police pass to open it.

The entrance hall was flagged with black and white marble tiles. Oates opened the set of double doors on the left hand side and whistled. The dining room was thirty feet long. He flicked the lights. Down the length ran a long mahogany table, polished to the point where a ring of dim stars floated underneath the chandelier. The chairs were green leather buttoned in shining bronze, with wooden eagle claws for feet. On the walls there hung a picture composed of a couple of childish squares in oil. It was altogether the kind of room that seemed too expensive to be the property of any one man, but existed in Oates's mind as a place which could be hired out by the rich for weddings and funerals.

The thing that affected him most deeply was not the opulence of the furnishings, but the space. Space was the rarest thing in London, and as the space for the body was curtailed, so the mind was similarly circumscribed. The physical barrier presented by the walls of his cubicle at the office and the be-suited bodies of tired men on the tube prevented his mind from wandering as effectively as if his thoughts had been creatures of flesh and blood. And what was that sound? Silence! No chatter of phones, no hard drive whirring, no traffic, no television, no neighbours moving in the walls, shattering the illusion of solitude. With this much quiet, a man could be dignified. The room made him uncomfortable in a way no blood spattered back street could ever have done.

He pulled one of the seats out from the table, but it looked so clean he hesitated to sit down. He set it back in its place, being careful to align the balls clutched in the carved talons with their corresponding dents in the thick carpet. He pictured the financier with no next of kin to hear of his death, sitting alone at the end of that long table, flanked by twenty empty chairs. Oates thought fondly of the clutter of his own home, and the toys on the carpet.

He went over to look at the modernist painting. He couldn't see the point of it, and the very fact that someone like him thought it pointless would be part of its attraction. He knew instinctively that there were people in the world, rich people, who would think that this painting was worth more than him and a thousand like him. And in financial terms, they would no doubt be right. The working life of a DCI would not produce enough money to move the painting from a wall in this house to a wall in someone else's. It was offensive for a thing like this to hoard millions between the four wooden planks of the frame, when the Met had not the manpower to protect the weak of the city.

He went over to the silver drinks tray standing fully crewed with cut crystal decanters on the sideboard beneath the painting. He wouldn't normally of course, but his encounter with Minor had forced him to break the seal, and he needed to take the edge off his irritation. He liberated the whisky bottle from its silver collar, and poured himself a measure.

Oates left the room and wandered back down the hall to the study, and knew he had found what he was looking for. Above the desk there was a portrait of Prudence Egwu as he had been before the Treatment, an elderly black statesman in a suit and tie, standing with his hand resting on a globe. Oates raised the glass to him.

One side of the office had been converted into a strong wall. A safe-like box about a foot in depth was fitted with a panel over the surface, and a shutter of bonded steel a couple of inches thick that could descend over the entire recess. The shutter, which locked with another keypad at the wall, was raised. Out of curiosity Oates passed his police card over the keypad, and it bleeped red. Someone had gone to the trouble of disabling the factory settings; only the proper code or a warrant frequency would release the lock. Inside the alcove were hundreds of paper files in slings. Oates knew that men like Prudence Egwu trusted the physical security of their homes over the computer. When you kept important files on your computer, you never knew whose skinny fingers were reaching up the wires to rifle them.

A couple of the folders had been pulled from their moorings, and lay strewn on the carpet. Oates squatted to leaf through the pages, but without context they were meaningless. He found graphs, columns of numbers in a spreadsheet, photocopies, some with notes written in a tidy hand in the margin. The labels of the files still hanging in their slings were marked with letters and numbers, and gave no clue as to their contents. He looked up, and noticed the cameras hanging in the corners of the room.

The security panel was mounted on the wall of the study. Oates set down the glass on the desk blotter, and scrolled in fast rewind backwards through the hours since he had been woken by Grape's call. The grainy screen showed 1:45am as a masked man approached the front door and entered the keycode. As the door opened the intruder looked back over his shoulder at the empty street, craning out from the portico with an almost comic furtiveness. Oates tracked him through the hall, where he switched the light on, stood for a few seconds, then thought better of it and switched it back off.

In the few seconds of illumination, Oates was surprised to see that the mask he was wearing was an ornate Venetian titillation, with tiny bells hanging from the colourful papier-mache crest. He used a lighter to see his way through the hall to the study. He entered another code into the panel of the strong wall, which lifted into the air. He did not need to pause to read the files, by the light of the flame he carried he removed two neatly from their slings and slipped them into a leather satchel. Then he pulled others from the shelf and spread them over the floor in a simulation of disorder. He went back out through the hall, and closed the door behind him. On the doorstep, blithely unaware of the external camera, he removed his mask to reveal the face of a handsome young man.

With the mask off, the expression made Oates want to protect him from whatever it was he had gotten himself involved with. He looked so proud standing there, and so relieved, already congratulating himself as a master criminal as he prepared to slip away into the night with his illicit bundle. Oates waved to him on the little screen. *I'll be seeing you later*. He looked forward to finding out what was in those missing files.

The awareness that he was not alone in the house dawned slowly on Oates. It was an atmospheric phenomenon, brought to a sudden focus by the sound of a muffled shout from upstairs. Oates removed his gun from the mooring in his belt. He walked softly into the hall, risking a look up the stairs. He returned to the security panel and worked the keypad. *Number of occupants in house?* **Three.** *Location?* **Study, one. Master bedroom, two. Would you like to signal the police? All our alarms are silent and confidential!** Oates lingered over the question for a few seconds, and pressed 'Decline'.

He mounted the stairs, grateful for the deep pile of the carpet. The sounds were coming from a closed door on the second landing; as Oates drew nearer, they took on the unmistakable quality of a man or woman being beaten. There was the sharp sound of a slap, and then a muffled cry, the rumble of a low voice and the shrill quaver of a desperate response. He pressed his ear to the door to try to gauge their position in the room. He stood back, and kicked the door in.

In the first instant of apprehension, the thing on the bed in front of him was a monster. It seemed to be tearing itself apart, one half begging for release, the other half urging on the coupling. Like some horrible manifestation of his own conflicted instincts, the thing incited violence and begged for peace from two different mouths. After a few seconds the image of the demon dispersed, and Oates realised that it was a man raping a young woman whose arms were handcuffed to the posts of the wide headboard. The man was so intent on his work that he did not even hear the crash of the door behind him, but the woman, whose wild eyes stared over his shoulder, saw Oates and her screams intensified.

Oates holstered his gun. He grabbed the man's shoulder and flung him backwards. He stumbled off the bed but managed to keep his footing, his erection bobbing in the air in front of him in an obsequious greeting. He was a young guy, late twenties and well built, a fact from which Oates took a momentary savour; no need to hold back with a guy built like that.

The man had the presence of mind to cast about him for a weapon, and his eyes alighted on an open backpack on the floor, from which protruded an effusion of metal and leather objects. He dipped for it and came up clutching some kind of sex toy, two vibrating balls attached to a length of silk. Just for a moment the two men paused, breathing heavily, and looked at the absurd device with which he had armed himself.

He swung one of the love eggs at Oates. It bounced with a harmless clatter against his shoulder pads, and Oates punched him in the face. As the blood began to flow from his nose he cried out, "No, no, no," in the high-pitched, querulous tones of an old lady remonstrating with her Pekinese. He turned to run, but Oates grabbed him by the hair and hurled him through the door of the bathroom. He hit the marble wall of the tub. He scrabbled to right himself on the bathmat and had found his feet before Oates could get through the door. He went to slam it shut, but the floor of the bathroom was wet and his feet went from under him. He collapsed backwards into the tub, and Oates was on him. He grabbed him again by the hair, and all the time he kept saying, "No, no," only now there was no more sense in it than a dog's barking.

Oates noticed that the soap in the tray beside the bath still had its wrapper on, as if this was not someone's house but a fancy hotel. He held the man's head under the tap and turned it with his free hand. The flared spout erupted with a pressurised stream of freezing water, and Oates left it on. When he finally shut the water off the "nos" had stopped, as had the struggling, and the naked man turned on his side to glub and spit mouthfuls of water into the gold plughole. Oates took off his coat and hung it over the towel warmer. He dried his hands, took out his handcuffs, and yanked the man's wrist over the edge of the tub to fix it to the pipe running underneath. Finally he picked up the pair of trousers that lay crumpled in the corner of the room, and husked the wallet.

"What do you want? I'll give you anything you want, just please, don't hurt me."

This raised a giggle from the room next door.

"You fucking bitch!" the man shouted. "You set me up, you little fucking whore! When this is over I'm going to find you and I'm going to..."

Oates shut the door to the bathroom and walked back over to the taps. He pulled the porcelain handled lever that switched the flow from the taps to the shower, and then turned the hot tap instead of the cold. He allowed the scalding rain to fall on the writhing flanks of the man for a second, and a cloud of steam filled the air. Being clothed before the pink and naked figure in the tub made Oates think quite suddenly of Mike, who had finally stopped his dad from coming in the bathroom to hoik him out of the bath at the age of six. Oates liked to hold the towel for him, to wrap his warm body in white folds, but once they asked you not to, that was it. The man stopped screaming and began to whimper once the shower was shut off. Oates sat on the edge of the bath and looked through the wallet.

"Who are you?"

"Detective Chief Inspector Oates, Metropolitan Police."

It frustrated Oates that this answer seemed to grant the man some comfort.

"Give me a towel."

Oates peeled the sodden bath mat from the floor and dropped it on top of him. The man arranged it over his groin.

"What do you want?"

"I want you to answer my questions," Oates said, "and then stay here quietly until I can get someone down to arrest you for sexual assault."

"Do you know who I am?"

"Hugo Travers-Brom. Seventy-five years of age, resident in Chelsea, London."

Oates tossed the ID down so that it hit him on the top of the head and bounced into his naked lap.

"How do you know Prudence Egwu?"

"Prudence... what?"

"The man who owns this house."

"I've got no fucking idea. The hotel I'd booked us into was double booked and I can't take her home with me, and she said she had a friend's place we could use."

"I'm going to go back out there now and talk to that young girl, and if she tells me a different story, I'm going to find the biggest, spikiest dildo in that bag of tricks and I'm going to come in here and I'm going to stick it up your pompous arsehole whilst I read you your rights. Now do you want to tell me anything different?"

"No, no I swear, it was her idea!"

Oates shut the door on him and went back into the bedroom.

*   *   *

"ARE YOU OKAY?"

She nodded.

With no clothes on it was difficult to tell her age, but she had the kind of face which makes a man read unlikely virtues.

"The key's over there," she said, pointing with a pink painted toe.

Oates undid one wrist, and got up and walked all the way around the bed to do the other one. She watched him go round. When she was released she lay there for a few seconds with an awful passivity. Then she sat up padded over the floor on her hands and took a cigarette from the backpack. The hand that held the light was untrembling. She should have felt uncomfortable with her nudity, but instead she used it to make Oates feel uncomfortable. Maybe it helped her keep her pride, he thought, not to rush to cover up.

"What's your name?"

"Casey."

"The man out there said you brought him here because the place you were going to use was full. Is that right?"

She nodded.

"I didn't mean to do anything wrong. I mean he's dead right, Mr Egwu?"

"How did you know that?"

"He's one of my clients. Well, he was. And not mine so much as Hector's, but he likes to do us together sometimes. Hector said he died."

"Who's Hector?"

"He works for my agency."

"And the new-young bloke next door..."

"Hugo? He's no pickle. He just pretends he is."

"I've seen his driving licence. It says he's seventy-five years old."

"Me too. He showed it to me like he wanted to prove it, and I knew straight away it was a fake, but I went all impressed." She giggled at the memory. "Guys like him want you to think they're really rich, so they pretend like they've had the Treatment. They talk about all these old movies and music and stuff. But the real pickles never talk about the old stuff. They talk way too much about new stuff and about new music. I prefer the ones who are pretending because they take you to nice restaurants and plays if they like you. One time I even went to the ballet. Have you ever been to the ballet?"

Oates shook his head. She was recovering too fast. The cost of developing a skin that thick was that nothing would get through. Not love, or remorse, or even self-sympathy. It dawned on him that he had not really rescued the poor girl from a crime, so much as interrupted a session. When the man in the bathtub had finished with her, he would no doubt have released her, paid her, maybe a little extra for being so rough, and they would put the next date in the diary. And she would have forgotten the whole thing as fast as she did now. For her own survival she had maimed herself, and he felt sorry that she had been forced to do so.

"The real pickles won't do that," she went on, "They say restaurants are for old people. And they always want to take you to raves in Peckham and meet your friends. That's how you can tell mostly. Plus their bodies smell different."

"What do you mean?"

"I don't know. But I've been with lots of them and they just do. You're not going to hurt Hugo, are you?"

"No."

"Oh." She looked out of the window, and when she looked back some door in her mind had broken open and the years had piled in on top of her. "I don't mind if you hurt him," she said, and for the first time she pulled the sheet around her to cover herself.

It was funny, Oates thought, how a world which made the old look young made the young look old. In the horror stories vampires drank the blood of virgins to keep them alive, and the Treatment was the same, but with longer straws. The image of the Great Spa appeared as a vast, swollen bubble filled with those distant drinkers, and a long curly straw protruded and kinked its way through the London sky to lodge in the white neck of the girl in front of him. There were so many, millions upon millions of straws arching over London, reaching under doors and through keyholes. Like a mosquitoe's proboscis, you never even felt them going in. Straws in Lori, straws in Mike, straws even in little Harry; his family portrait a clutch of St Sebastians martyred to a faith that was not their own. The meek would never inherit the earth, because the rich would never die. The new-young suckled themselves to eternal health in their golden summer.

Hugo Travers-Brom Esq. was lucky he was a faker, as Oates felt an overwhelming urge to kick the crap out of one of the new-young. He pictured Prudence Egwu with his hand on his fucking globe. It made him almost sorry to be the one who had to find his assassin. But find him he would.

"But Prudence Egwu didn't need to pretend?"

"Mr Egwu wasn't pickled. He was old, like really old. He had all this baggy skin here and his ears were big." She couldn't help but glance at Oates's own ears when she said it. Her words surprised him, and he thought of the portrait downstairs in the study. The man in that picture looked old, not far off Prudence Egwu's chronological age. How recently had it been painted?

"When was the last time you saw Mr Egwu?"

She shrugged. "I don't know. Ages. Like, three, four weeks ago. Can I go now, I have another client to meet soon."

Getting the Treatment three weeks before his death? That was more than coincidence. That was hubris.

"Will you do me a favour first?" he asked.

"Sure."

Oates left the room to let the girl get dressed, and walked downstairs with her. On the hall security monitor he called up the footage from the break-in, and scrolled through to the face of the young man standing on the doorstep.

"Yeah, that's Hector."

"Can you tell me where I can find him?"

She shook her head.

"How did he contact you to tell you about Mr Egwu's death?"

"Helen has a secure message board. We were chatting about another job."

"No phone number, email, anything?"

"No. Hector's his work name. We never use our real names. He hangs out sometimes at the skate park on Portobello Road, you know, under the motorway. Or I think I saw him there a couple of times."

"Do you want to come down to the station? We have a unit and a safe house, no one will know you're there and you can think about what to do next."

"Like what?" she said, genuinely interested, not in the notion of going to the safe house but of what this old policeman thought she could do differently.

"Like go to school, or something."

"No. But you're nice. If you ever want to see me you can. I have loads of policemen so it's okay. But you have to go through Helen or I get in trouble, okay? Oh, wait!" Her eyes widened, and she turned and ran back up the stairs. She was gone for a couple of minutes, and he was about to shout up after her when she came back down holding Hugo's wallet.

"I'm never going to see him again," she said, "and he owes me like a ton of tips. That's okay, right?"

Oates stood back from the door and let her go past. She ran by him, stuffing the stolen wallet into her backpack, its pink sides bulging and clinking with their hidden load. She stopped and shucked the pack up onto both shoulders before heading off, her thumbs hooked in the straps. In that leafy street, she could have been another daughter at the private day school on Holland Park, come back home in the afternoon to pick up a forgotten text book. She turned and waved to him just before she passed out of sight. Oates felt himself about to cry. He smashed his fist a couple of times into the wall, and the pain chased that fugitive weakness back out of him.

Flexing his hand, he headed back upstairs. As he reached the first landing he smelled smoke, and heard, for the second time, a muffled screaming from the bedroom. He took the next flight three at a time. Casey had torn one of the pillowcases into strips and balled them up with some crumpled pages torn from an investment magazine on the bedside table. She had stuffed these into the cracks along the underside of the locked bathroom door, along with the lighter itself for the fluid kick. The face of some stern CEO was just crisping as he reached the top of the stairs. The fire-alarm started its high pitched scream as Oates stamped the life from the little conflagration.

In the toilet, Hugo was on the floor. He had levered himself out of the bath in his attempt to reach the flames, but the chain that clasped him to the water pipe had been too short to reach. The handcuffs had cut into his wrists, giving him sister scars to the ones on Casey's wrists. He was breathing through the sodden bath mat, and Oates opened the window to disperse the smoke.

"She took my wallet."

"Yeah."

"She tried to kill me."

Oates leant down and unlocked the handcuffs. With his hands free Hugo curled into a fleshy ball like a poked anemone. Oates squatted by him on the damp floor.

"If I was you, I would hope that nothing ever happens to that girl. I would hope she invests in a good pension, and lives to a ripe old age, and dies surrounded by grandchildren in a sunny retirement home. Actually I would hope she marries a millionaire and gets the Treatment and lives forever. Because if anything ever does happen to her I'm going to give Helen Girst the notion that it was you. And if she takes that notion there won't be a place in the world she won't find you. You're free to go."

Oates took his damp coat off the towel rail and went back downstairs. He returned to the study and tossed back the last of the whisky. Before he had time to think, he turned to the security panel, called up the video of himself running up the stairs and Casey running down, and wiped it. Then he shut down the cameras so they wouldn't record Hugo leaving. He would say he'd done it by accident, scrolling through to last night's break-in.

As a soldier Oates had learned the necessity, and later the pleasure, of placing oneself in the hands of a higher authority. He had been a wild young man, and he privately thought the army had saved him from self-destruction. All that mattered was obedience to the system, faith in a wisdom greater than your own, and the ability to take the piss out of both. The Army was like a wife back home whilst you drank in the pub with your mates – you'd complain about her, but you knew you'd go to seed without her, and you'd be happy to go home to her, even if she bawled you out when you got back. In the months and years after they came back from the desert, many of Oates's old comrades had stumbled, and clutched for the institution, and finding it gone had pitched over the precipice into chaos.

Oates had been lucky to find the police when he did. The stark white lines of the justice system bounded him like the edges of a football pitch; within them he could foul, he could cheat, he could win and lose, and when the ninety minutes were up he could jog off the field and be with his family again. For all his rough play, he stayed within the law, or at least the rough consensus on what constituted the law that existed between him and the other officers (and indeed criminals) whom he respected. It was the only thing that allowed him to act as he did, free from the fear of self-reproach.

Letting Hugo go was uncharacteristic. It was not a breaking of the rules of the game, but an action taking place outside of the game entirely, with no reference point beyond its own morality.

The thought made him feel queasy. He wondered whether he should call in the whole incident, put out a warrant for both of them, and dismissed the idea. It would be impossible to explain why he had not arrested them in the first place. If he could not properly articulate the reasons to himself, he was unlikely to be able to do so for John, or the competent solicitor he sensed lodged politely but firmly between the pages of Hugo's address book.

As he stood on the cold doorstep he felt again the troubling sensation he had had within the spa when the fat PR had made him dress up as an anachronous version of himself, a doubling of self-perception. He thought for one hallucinatory moment that he could hear his own voice talking to him, whispering in his ear about the love of his life, and he realised with relief that he could, and that Lori was calling him.

"LOVE OF MY *life. Love of my life–*"

"Answer."

"Hello my love. Where are you?" she said.

"I'm just in Notting Hill. Do you need something picking up?"

"Have you heard on the news?"

"No, I've just been working. What is it?"

"They say there's going to be more trouble tonight. The school's going to close early, can you pick up the boys?"

"Of course. But I'll have to go back out again. What time can you be home?"

"Don't leave them alone. I'll be back as fast as I can."

"Alright. But..."

"Don't leave them alone."

"Alright."

"They can bloody wait for you for a change."

"I won't leave them."

"I love you."

"I love you too."

"They're saying on the radio it's going to be bad again tonight."

"Don't worry. They're always saying that."

Hugo came downstairs in his sodden clothes, holding his coat in his hands. He pushed past Oates without looking at him and strode off shivering into the cold with his head down. Oates had one last look around upstairs, fished one of Casey's cigarette butts from the ashtray on the bedside table, and went to retrieve his car.

He had no doubt that Casey was telling the truth when she said she had a lot of policemen on her books. Helen Girst's agency was one of the criminal institutions which existed with one foot in the law. The situation was tolerated because the Met simply didn't have the resources to police every crime in the city, and where they couldn't police they had to trust to self regulation for fear of something worse. The Girst Agency paid tax, didn't take slaves, didn't drug its employees to keep them docile, and didn't allow violence against its girls, unless the violence was consensual and properly compensated. Over time however, tolerance had morphed into something approaching collusion, and Helen Girst had shored up her alliance with judicious freebies. There was no way he could force her to give information on one of her boys, and if he tried he was likely to get his heels nipped by someone higher up the food chain.

He had the feeling that whatever Hector had stolen from Prudence Egwu's house, it wasn't likely to be with him for very long. Hector was no criminal, his incompetence on the video had shown as much. He was doing someone's bidding. Someone who knew that Prudence Egwu was dead an hour at most after the police knew it themselves. Possibly even before. Someone with a knowledge like that could greatly help Oates with his enquiries. Perhaps he could make Helen understand that the boy might need protection as much as Oates needed help.

What he lacked was the time to convince her. Ali was slowly cooking in his warm summer custody, and although Oates had no intention of charging him he needed all the time he could get to question him about his sponsor. Soon he would either have to be released or charged. Whoever the real killer was, they must suspect by now that Ali had been fingered for an Eddy, and they would be trying to get in there with threats and lawyers and counter-offers.

The trouble was he couldn't ask someone else to follow up on Hector through official channels. One look at Helen Girst's file, one word in the wrong ear would cast the hulking shadow of her protection machine, and maybe even frighten Hector to ground.

BACK IN THE car he called Grape.

"I need you to do something for me."

"Ask."

"I need you to find someone."

"Who is he?"

"He's a prostitute."

"Eeeh, well I never…"

"Pack it in. He works for the Helen Girst Agency, his work name's Hector. No idea what his real name is. He's a good-looking boy, I'd say half white half Chinese, about five foot ten, and in for a world of trouble if anyone finds him before me."

"Cats don't play fetch. If I start digging around for the police…"

"I don't want to bust him. I told you, I just want to talk to him."

"It's not much to go on."

"There must be a review on the internet, or a post in the chatrooms, the clubs, something."

"I tell you what home slice: you tell me why you're after this dude and I'll get him for you."

"He broke into Prudence Egwu's house last night."

"And?"

"And he stole some papers."

"What papers?"

"Question one on my list when I find him."

"And you want me to find him because he's one of Madame Girst's boys, and if you start digging around on the office computer you're going to piss people off?"

Smart girl, he thought.

"Call it outsourcing. Maximising resources at a time of budgetary cutbacks."

"Alright, daddy-oh. But if I do this thing for you, I want an exclusive when everything comes good. You download to me and me alone, deal?"

"Okay."

Oates heard the sound of Grape spitting.

"Spit shake on it?"

Oates took one of his hands off the wheel, spat in the palm and waved it in the air in front of him.

"I can tell you're really doing it. That's rank. I'll see what I can do. End call."

THEY NEVER LET parents into the school buildings, so despite the cold the kids were lined up in form groups on the wet tarmac of the playground when Oates arrived. Looking at the children he was reminded of the films and photographs of kids he had seen from the Blitz, standing with little bundles of possessions and signs hung around their necks on station platforms.

It had taken him an hour to collect the car and get back out to Putney, and with a little prick of guilt he estimated that about three quarters of those forlorn figures had already been spirited back to the warmth of their homes. That put him and Lori in the bottom quarter for parenting skills. It was an area in which he sensed the school already viewed them as deficient. He felt this more as a slight on Lori than on himself, as in his case they were probably right.

Harry's form teacher in particular had taken against Oates, largely, he suspected, because he was a policeman, and Mr Prendegast had the look of someone who might have been on a few protest marches in his time. It was the little goatee beard, and the jumpers. Sometimes Oates even wondered if he might once have given Mr Prendegast a sharp knock over the head in the running street battles he had dealt with as a fresh recruit, but Lori told him he was just being paranoid. He hated the idea of his lateness justifying the teacher's bad opinion. Oates could just imagine him polishing up his prejudices, taking a perverse pleasure in his cold wait as each departing child confirmed his judgment of little Harry Oates's father.

He parked down the street, and walked along the mesh fencing of the playground, trying to pick Harry's form from among the depleted huddles of children. When he finally spied him, it was worse than he had thought. Harry was the last boy left from his class, standing there beside Mr Prendegast, who had his arms folded across his parka. The teacher clocked him at an awkward distance, too far for a proper greeting and too close to ignore, so Oates half-raised his hand and jogged the last few paces to his son.

"Sorry to make you wait, Frank."

Mr Prendegast smiled, and blew ostentatiously into his cupped hands.

"Oh, that's quite alright, Mr Oates."

"You'd think the school would make an exception today and let you wait in the gym."

"Rule are rules, Mr Oates. I've had my flu shots this winter so I'm sure I'll be fine."

"Still, I guess this is an unexpected holiday for you guys."

"Hardly a holiday. But now that you've come for Harry, at least I can start home."

"I'm sorry. Like I said."

"That's quite alright, quite alright. We're here to help. Anyway, I expect you're busy today, with everything going on."

"Not so much for our lot to do. No murders last night."

"Yet! Thank God. It's a terrible shame for the city. But what can you expect, when things are like this. For the young, I mean."

Oates happened to agree, but he wasn't about to give the man the satisfaction of showing it. Besides which he had the idea that Mr Prendegast's sympathies would last exactly as long as the riots stayed clear of his street. The moment one of those masked boys got within Molotov-flinging distance of his new electric robocar, he'd be calling for the rubber bullets and the water cannon. Harry was standing between them, not looking up but staring over the playground. The only acknowledgement he had given his father was to take one of his hands, and as he held it Oates noticed how cold his fingers were, and felt another prickle of guilt under his collar. Mr Prendegast must have sensed his weakness, as he pressed the point.

"I'm sure you agree with me, as a parent. You can't abandon the youth to unemployment and despair, then be surprised when they riot."

At that moment Mike, who had been playing football at the other side of the playground, flung himself at his father's thighs and started tugging at his holster.

"Mum says if they come to our house, dad's going to smash their skulls! Smash, smash, smash!"

Mr Prendegast looked down at the boy with undisguised dislike. Oates wanted to lift him up and kiss him.

"Come on Michael, what did we say about trying to understand other people's problems?" Mr Prendegast said.

"Smash!"

"I'd best get these two home," Oates said, lifting his eldest son off his feet with his free arm and turning him upside down. Mike squealed in delighted outrage.

"And I must get back to my wife. She'll be wondering where I've got to. Good luck."

"And to you. Oh, and if you do run into any trouble this evening..." Oates set Mike back down on his feet, reached inside his coat, and pulled out one of his cards, "just in case you can't get through to the police."

Mr Prendegast plucked the proffered card with thumb and forefinger. As he slid it into his top pocket, his expression put Oates in mind of those intrepid Victorian explorers who would force themselves to ingest some foul local delicacy so as not to offend their savage hosts. The two men shook hands, and Oates led his sons back to the car.

"SHOTGUN."

"You went in the front with mum this morning. It should be my turn now."

"Duh, that's the rules of shotgun."

"If you're going to fight you can both go in the boot."

Together: "No!"

With the threat of the boot hanging over him, Mike sullenly relinquished his claim to the front seat, and Harry climbed in beside his father. When the doors were shut both boys reached for their seatbelts without being told, and Oates thought, *At least we got something right.* The trip down to the school had presented itself to him as a simple interruption, a chore to be discharged to keep the peace with Lori before he got on with the real business of his day. With the doors of the car closed against the cold, and the car's old heater breathing musty warmth on him and his children, the trip now seemed a blessing, unasked and unexpected.

Harry was one of those children for whom abstract ideas could take on a kind of epic emotional significance. When his son turned his big-eyed curiosity onto him and asked one of his special questions, Oates felt like a bomb disposal expert faced with a set of identical wires. It was Harry's accidental viewing of a film on global warming (narrated by an animated polar bear) which had led to the enforced replacement of every light fitting in the house with vastly expensive low-energy bulbs, and it was on Harry's insistence that the plate of milk-soaked bread was left on the doorstep every night for hedgehogs. There being no such animals in Putney, or at least none sufficiently accommodating to present themselves at their doorstep, it was generally Oates's job to disturb the saucer of sodden bread after the boys were asleep in a simulation of hungry hedgehoggery.

The conversation they had had about why the man who begged for change outside Putney Hill tube station couldn't sleep on the camping bed in the TV room was one which still gave him nightmares. And as for explaining where Anna had gone to… well, at least he had been too young to really understand all that. Being that kind of boy, Oates knew Harry would have been worrying about the riots all day, and his son confirmed this by hugging his backpack to his tummy and staring out of the window in silence as they pulled away from the curb.

Mike was more straightforward. With most kids it's the disruption of routine which really brings a sense of disaster home. You can tell them the world is coming down, or that China has launched nuclear missiles, but it's not until their tea fails to appear at the appointed hour, or their favourite television program gets interrupted by the news that they start to get nervous. In the playground he had been excited, but his dad coming to pick him up in the middle of the day had begun to worry at him, and instead of babbling about his morning he was playing on his phone.

"What would you boys like for tea?"

"Will you be cooking us tea?"

"No, mum will cook you tea. I'm just wondering what you'd like."

"Will you be there for tea?"

"Not for tea. But I'll be back home tonight."

"Dad, Tony Stancliffe says we're going to be attacked tonight. He says the rioters will come for everyone with masks on."

"Why will we have masks on then?"

"Not us! The rioters."

"Oh, them."

"You knew that."

"No one will come by. And if they do we'll smash them. Right?"

Mike looked up from his phone and caught his eye in the rearview mirror. He smiled and went back to playing. Bhupinder called, but Oates ignored it. He didn't want to speak about the murder with his children in the car.

Harry, who had been silent all the way home, turned to him when they pulled up outside their house.

"You've got something there dad."

"Where?"

"Just by your ear."

Oates flipped down the mirrored sunvisor. He spat on his fingers, and rubbed away the spot of Hugo's blood which had dried on his cheek whilst the boys ran to the front door.

OATES LEFT THEM playing computer games in their bedroom and went to the bathroom. All along the shelf above the toilet was a series of books in combinations of primary colours. Each one was titled *A Beginner's Guide to...* and then a different theory or artistic movement: psychoanalysis, modernism, romanticism, Plato, Keynes, Shakespeare, psychogeography, jurisprudence. These were Lori's (as were the celebrity magazines on the cistern). She never spoke about the ideas she had read, and she never read further into them than the little primers. The books were arranged in the order of their publication, and when she had finished one of them she went on to the next, regardless of any disjunct in the subject matter.

When she had first started reading them, shortly after Mike was born, Oates had tried joking with her about them a couple of times, calling her "Professor", even taking up one of the books and reading sentences aloud in the silly voice of an Austrian academic. She had pretended for a while to find this funny, before exploding at him with a fury that at the time he thought was crazy. After that he tried looking interested and asking her serious questions, but she always declined to answer him.

It had taken years to understand. She had been so angry because Oates had mocked one of the most private things about her – a dogged determination to make sense of the world, and a faith that better minds than hers would help. Lori had been to university for two years before dropping out, which was two more years than Oates. It made him quietly proud of her, as she stood in the middle of the chaos of life, building the fire of her knowledge a couple of sticks at a time, so that the ever expanding circle of light pushed back the darkness. He felt that even though they never talked about the books, even though he had no idea what half the words in the titles meant, he and the boys were sitting by that fire with her. He ran his finger along the spines, tracing the journey of his wife's thoughts over the years with his finger.

When he thought about the people he loved, it was never the whole person that presented themselves for inspection, but rather some emblematic detail which contained his entire conception of the beloved. With Lori it was the little collection of volumes above the toilet, slowly growing.

She would be home soon. A measure of peace restored by the books and by the car journey with his children, he needed only one more thing to think clearly. He went back to the TV room and retrieved the bottle from the back of a drawer in the dresser. In his bedroom he lay on the bed in full uniform and stared at the ceiling with the glass on his chest.

When he heard the slam of the downstairs door it startled him. He rinsed the glass quickly in the bathroom sink, and popped a couple of brushes in it. So as not to worry Lori he inched a mint caterpillar of paste onto his finger and scrubbed his gums. He put the tube in the glass beside the brushes and flushed the toilet. He kissed his wife on the cheek as she entered, and to avoid any conversation about when he might be home he pretended to be speaking to John on his earpiece. He mimed apologies to her and bowed in their tiny hall, and she smiled and courtseyed, and called for the boys.

BACK IN THE car he checked his phone, and there was a text from Grape: *Found your boy.*

The Apollo House Hotel on Haggerston Road. Hector's street was in Hackney, just north of the bridge over the old canal that ran down to Victoria Deer Park and no more than a ten minute detour. He could pay Hector a visit on the way back out to the Great Spa.

It wasn't safe to leave the car in the streets too far east, so Oates parked in customer parking under the shopping mall at One New Change, and headed up towards the Kingsland Road on foot, taking the bridge over the canal. These were the neighborhoods that would give up their sons and daughters for the ranks of the riots, and also the neighborhoods that would most likely be destroyed. Although Oates's pride would not allow him to change out of the tell-tale boots and the shin-pads which came beneath the hem of his raincoat, his common sense made him tip the collar and fold the breast to stop the wind from getting in, or the shape of the standard issue body armour from getting out. Unless you looked close, you couldn't tell he was a policeman.

His big figure trudged down the street, puffing steam. The still grey water of the canal reflected the evening sky and the orange bulbs of the streetlights, and chilled the cold air. There would have been ice on the water if it had been clean stuff, but the million secretions of East London dissolved in it and kept it from freezing.

Along the Haggerston Road the houses knew their place, and rose no higher than the second storey. Oates walked the long channel carved in the mirrored terraces, above which was the illuminated henge of the financial headquarters in Canary Wharf, the names of the banks hanging like a divine judgment over the two-up two-downs. The Apollo House Hotel was composed of a couple of houses knocked together, with one of the front doors bricked up. Oates stood at the end of the garden path, and looked up and down the street.

The pavements were empty, but in the early gloom he could see one car parked with the lights on inside. The car was filled with smoke, turning the air milky in the refracted light, but Oates thought he could make out three figures, two in the front seat and one in the back. A faint pulse of bass reverberated from the car's interior. He was debating whether or not to go over and knock on the window when the car drew out into the street, and drove off. Oates peered for the numberplate, but he couldn't make it out, and turned his attention back to the building in front of him.

The name was spelt in a neon pink frown over the unbricked door, with a couple of the teeth blacked out. No estate agent's euphemism could have done anything for the outside of The Apollo House Hotel. Oates had been to many boarding houses like this in the early days of his career, delivering news of deaths and taking statements. Once upon a time, this was where the council put you when the waiting list for housing grew too long, and they had to park you with the private landlords. It was better than the streets, which is where you'd end up these days, but not much. The outside promised suffering, and the inside delivered.

He stood on the pavement for a moment, and wondered what one of Helen Girst's boys was doing in such a dump. A session like the one he had interrupted at Prudence Egwu's place would cover a month's rent at The Apollo House Hotel, with change left over for the razor to slit your wrists. You had to pay good money to do things like that to people without their going to the police. It meant that Hector was either a spender or a saver. Only an addict could spend such big wads of cash that quickly, and only addiction would re-order the priorities so thoroughly that living in the boarding house would seem a fair exchange for the indulgence of some other pleasure. But Helen Girst was famous for checking her charges, not just regular urine and blood tests but spot checks for track marks between the toes, under the eyelids, for anything that the body processed too quickly to catch.

That left gambling or saving. He'd know when he saw him. An addict's attention was never complete, as the inner life was entirely consumed with the prospect of satisfaction, and in talking with the police instinctive craftiness had to do the work of intelligence. A saver, by contrast, would commandeer every spare neuron to the defence of the pot.

The house was too old to have a keycard lock. He pushed the bell, and no sound emerged. He banged with his fist on the door. A shape emerged, shuffling behind the frosting of the safety glass. The door opened on a chain that Oates could have snapped with a firm push, and a wrinkled face appeared at the level of his belly button.

"Is Hector in?" He showed his badge.

"There's no Hector here."

"A young lad. Asian."

"No Hector, no."

She shook her head.

"I'm not here to cause trouble. His mum's sick."

The eyes assessed him from the bottom of a lake of polluted experience.

"We know he's staying here. I don't know what name he's using."

The eyes in the crack stared at him for a few seconds, trying to get at the truth in him. The door closed, and he was about to kick it in (he was just listening for the shuffle of the old lady out of the door's inward swing) when he heard the sound of the chain sliding across.

The entrance hall of the boarding house made good on the threats of the cracked front garden. A patch of mould had grown across the ceiling. It felt colder in the hall than it had outside. Oates could see his breath. The doormat was covered with leaflets advertising pizzas, pawnshops and chances to enter the Treatment lottery. One of the shiny lottery flyers was addressed to an Adrian Chong. Oates heard a sound behind him, and looked up.

A child stood in the doorway to the kitchen. He held a dirty rag against his mouth, and swayed from side to side at the waist whilst watching Oates over the tops of his knuckles. Oates put his own hands up over his face, and concocted a mad grimace before flinging them open. It was something that had never failed to make Harry smile when he was a toddler. The child in the doorway just watched. Then a mother emerged behind, a tall black woman in a towelling robe, holding a steaming wooden spoon in her hand.

"What's his name then?"

The woman stared at him. The sound of a hiss on a stove came from behind her.

"I've got three of my own," he said.

"Fuck you," she said.

The child waved at Oates, and he waved back until she pulled the boy back into the kitchen. The old woman reappeared.

"He's gone out."

"Well you won't mind me looking then."

Oates stepped quickly past her, and caught the boy he recognised as Hector leaning over the banister, listening for their conversation.

"Hello Hector. Or is it Adrian?"

"Does Helen know you're here? Does your boss know you're here?"

"No one knows I'm here but you and me. I just want a little chat."

"You call Helen. You want to speak to me about anything, you call Helen, she'll make everything straight."

Oates began to mount the stairs slowly, his hands held out in front of him. Hector cast his eyes back over his shoulder at the safety of his bedroom.

"It's not illegal. You ask Helen."

"I'm not here about your private life, Hector." He sniffed the air. Hector watched him suspiciously. "How long you been in this place then?"

"Two years."

"Bit of a shithole, isn't it? No place for kiddies. I saw the little one downstairs."

Hector's face softened for a moment. "Liam."

"Is that right, Liam?"

"Yeah."

Oates continued his ascent whilst they spoke, until he was close enough to grab Hector through the banisters if he tried to make a run for it. The boy was scared, and his fear made Oates relax.

"The council stick you here?"

"Yeah, they put me here."

"You got lucky. Single healthy young bloke on the benefit could be on the streets."

Hector sniffed, and wiped his nose on the back of his hand.

"Isn't that right?"

"Maybe. Don't know."

"You are on the benefit? Right? You know I can find that out, with a phone call. But you won't mind that, because you're declaring your earnings. So you won't be worried about me calling up your benefits officer. Checking your tax returns. Calling immigration. Checking out the terms of your student visa. You're here on a student visa, right? Really having a good root round. Because you've got nothing to worry about. Isn't that right?"

Hector looked momentarily panicked. A saver then. A saver keeping together every scrap he could so that the day he left this place, he knew he'd never have to come back.

"We've got you on tape from Prudence Egwu's gaff. There's a camera on the porch where you took off your mask."

Hector looked at him in shock, finally understanding why he was getting this visit. He tensed up for a moment, and then his shoulders slumped.

"Okay. It's in my room."

Good boy.

Oates followed him up onto the landing, where Hector motioned him towards his bedroom. The moment they opened the door, Oates understood why Hector hadn't wanted him upstairs. The landing was as cold and damp as the rest of the house, but the door to Hector's room was fitted with a shiny new brass lock. Up close Oates could see that a new steel frame had been fitted, and the door itself was panelled with metal under the whitewash. If you wanted to break into Hector's room, you'd be best taking a sledgehammer to the wall.

Inside, the room was cosy and filled with the tiny red lights of electrical equipment, glowing in the teenage dinge like embers spat from a winter fire. The light in the room came from the glow of the computer screen, a fish tank filled with tiny bright blue fish and a length of Christmas lights wound like an electric cornice around the ceiling and down through the fronds of a palm tree sitting under a gro-lamp in the corner. The walls were covered with posters for the same films and bands that the goth kids at Oates's comprehensive had loved thirty years before. The Venetian mask which Hector had worn during the robbery was mounted above the bed. Blondie played on the stereo, and a stick of incense burned in a holder beside the fish tank. The room smelt of patchouli, dirty clothes and semen.

"You here about Mr Egwu, yeah?"

"Yeah."

"Oh shit! I knew that was trouble, I knew it." Hector cast himself down on his bed, and held his head in his hands. "Look, I didn't even know he was dead."

"You told Casey he was."

"That was later! I have news alerts set up for all my clients. Sometimes they like to talk to me about stuff in their lives, you know? I didn't know when I went to his house. All he said to me was he knew the house would be empty last night and I had to go in right away. I said to him, 'Look, mister, I have clients, you know, I can't just be running off after you every five minutes'. But he said it had to be then or not at all."

"Who's he?"

"Chris Rajaram. I mean that's why you're here, right?"

"When did this Chris Rajaram first contact you?"

"I don't know. Like six months ago. He wanted me to find some stuff in Mr Egwu's house."

"What stuff?"

"Some science stuff. It was really hard to find it at first, because he has all these hundreds of files. But I had to look for the ones that talked about the Tithonus Effect, so I looked for that and in the end I found it."

"What were you supposed to do?"

"Well, first I told them he had this big safe in his study where he kept all his papers. Then I was supposed to break into his safe, but that was super easy because his code is his birthday backwards. Who still does that? Then I was supposed to photograph it, I mean the pages in the files, and send these guys the photographs. Mr Egwu likes me to sleep over sometimes, but he's a super deep sleeper. Sometimes he snores and I have to go sleep in the guest bedroom anyway, so even if he woke up it would be okay."

"And how do you know it was Chris Rajaram who wanted you to do this?"

"I didn't know who it was until last night. I'm not supposed to know. Normally it's these encrypted instructions on this website. But then last night some guy just called me from a mobile, so I checked him out. He wasn't even ex-directory, you know?"

"What time last night?"

"12:27."

"12:27?"

Hector slid his body forward on the bed, the better to access the pocket of the tight jeans he wore. He disgorged a phone, scrolled quickly down the screen, and offered it face out to Oates. The received call record showed the exact time.

"I'll need to take that."

"Okay, sure. I've got like three others."

"Is there anything else?"

"Hey, no! Look, I don't want any trouble. I work to pay my fees, you know?" Oates rolled his eyes. "I do. You go check, look, look."

He grabbed Oates by the sleeve and pulled him towards his desk. Sure enough before the computer screen was an open textbook, a notepad filled with cramped handwriting, the wrapper of an energy bar and all the detritus of domestic scholarship. Oates was unsure why it was that Hector thought this proof of his studiousness would help his cause, but his utter conviction that it would was infectious. He stood there nodding in satisfaction over the display.

"Alright, so what happened?"

"When?"

"I mean, you were supposed to photograph the folders, but you stole them."

"Oh, I forgot the camera. And the one on that phone's shit, it doesn't even work anymore. I dropped it in the toilet at this party. I had to get it out with a plastic bag, it was disgusting."

"And you gave the folders to Chris?"

He shook his head.

"No, no. He broke the deal. I mean the deal was I send him a sample, and he sends me a down payment, then I send him the rest, then he gives me the balance, right? Only I send him the sample and he says I'm taking the piss, like making a big joke on him."

"What sample did you send him?"

"I don't know. Some pages from the middle."

"Give me the files."

Hector lifted his mattress, and pulled the two manila files from the space between the stained underside and the springs strung across the frame. It was the hiding place which saved him. That was the same place that Mike kept the violent Manga comics which were technically contraband, but which Oates and Lori had decided should fall into the parental blindspot. Oates lived in troubled anticipation of the moment when he looked under there and found something worse. He wasn't about to arrest a boy with no more gift for subterfuge than his own child. Oates took the files.

"So are you going to arrest me or what?"

"No, I'm not going to arrest you. If you testify against Chris Rajaram when we find him, and with your cooperation so far, we might be able to get around the burglary."

"I can't do that!"

"Well if you can't do that then you go down for burglary."

"No, no I can't. If Helen finds out I was going to rip off a client..."

"Oh."

"Don't you have witness protection or something?"

"You don't need witness protection. We'll talk to Helen. I'll talk to her myself, alright? I promise. She doesn't like trouble any more than you. You might not be getting any more work, but you won't wind up in a ditch either. How does that sound?"

Hector nodded. He stuck out his hand for a comrade's handclasp, and Oates took it, feeling a little ridiculous.

"Alright then. Don't do anything stupid like trying to leave London."

"I won't."

"And thank you for your help."

"Yeah, no worries."

The landing was cold after the dense fug of Hector's room. The door at the other end was open a crack, and Oates thought he could make out the glint of an eye watching him from the darkness. He waved, but there was no acknowledgement, and he started back down the stairs. In the kitchen, the young boy was eating a bowl of pasta, his feet swinging several inches off the floor.

WITH THE FILES tucked under his arm, Oates walked back to One New Change, the shopping mall sitting opposite St Paul's Cathedral, stealing the elegant renaissance reflection to decorate its sheer glass flanks. A cordon of police had formed around the entrance to the mall, round plastic shields clasped to their arms. It was the first real sign he had seen of the police reaction to the disturbances. It reminded him of his own early days on the force, but it was a strange kind of rioting – the traditional targets, the police stations and the public buildings, had been left largely untouched, but the shops were the subject of a furious assault.

Oates looked for a face he knew among the mass of officers, but the accents of the men and the numbers on the shoulders of their boiler suits told him they were from a northern force. They had been bussed in to master the capital, and there was in their manner a brittle excitement that made them laugh and call out bad jokes to one another. In the normal course they were made to feel inferior to their southern cousins, as if the crimes that really mattered all took place in London, and they were enjoying both their authority over the moneyed citizens and the grudging need of their metropolitan colleagues.

Oates knew the dangers of having men on crowd control with something to prove, and he was grateful that Lori and the kids were nowhere near the City, where the majority of the outside forces were concentrated. Their loose line was permeable to men and women stepping out from the offices around St Paul's, but when a group of poor-looking kids approached, the cordon sealed, and they were turned away with jeers. In this way, the police barrier seemed almost an extension of the policies of the management company that ran the mall, making explicit a principle of exclusion that had previously operated only on the level of frowning staff and overly attentive security men.

The kids moved away down the street, but they did not disperse, and they were making phonecalls in the gloomy afternoon, their cheeks illuminated on one side with the glowing screens. Oates could picture those calls, the voices summoning up the hatred and discontent of the inner city, calling them to war. A couple of police horses stood, their breath steaming white in the darkness.

One or two of the policemen nodded to Oates as he crossed the line. Inside the shopping mall, beneath the blast of warm air which lay in welcome behind the sliding glass doors of the entrance, another world was waiting, as separate in its way from the outside as the summer of the Great Spa from the freezing London suburbs. The shops were decked for Christmas, a rich sparkle to dazzle the eye. The overdose eyes of the billboards rolled slowly in their sockets.

Oates was just looking for signs to the parking bays when he felt someone tugging at his sleeve. He turned around, and saw a girl standing beside him. She looked about fifteen years old, and she was so small that her face was quite upturned when she spoke to him.

"You're the guy who was looking for Hector, right? Listen, please, I need to talk to you."

"Who are you?"

"I'm a friend. It's about what Hector gave you. Look, it's important, can you please just come with me?"

The girl was looking over her shoulder, so palpably agitated that Oates allowed himself to be led by her to an alcove under the escalators. There was a boy of about the same age waiting for them there, and as they drew close he produced a pistol from the inside of his coat. It was a homemade plastic gun, what Oates called a pronta-pistol. Some bent software engineer would be employed to crack the safety codes on a stolen 3D printer, and start knocking out crude weapons. You had to remove the protective casing to do the hack. As a result they often looked like all-year round ski-instructors, these backstreet armourers, because they would get tan lines around their safety goggles from the UV light used to cure the liquid polymer.

A pronta-pistol wouldn't have the punch to make it through his body armour, even fired point blank. The chambers only held a couple of rounds, and the firing mechanism was prone to snap. Up this close, he'd likely only get one shot in. To slow Oates down he'd have to hit him in the arms or the leg below the knee, and to stop him he'd have to shoot him in the head. Oates was against the wall, tucked away in this little cubby hole off the main drag.

"We're not going to hurt you," the girl said, and she was quite calm. Her agitation had been an act. Not so her friend. The snubbed tip of the barrel had a slight quiver in the air, like the raised nose of an animal.

"Not with that you're not," Oates said, gesturing to the pistol.

"Give us the papers Hector gave you."

"What papers?"

"Just give us the fucking papers, man," the boy said.

No shoppers back here. A stray bullet ought to find a wall to bury itself. A part of his mind felt a kind of abstract pleasure at the speed of this analysis. In the second or so after he saw the gun, he had decided he was going to make this kid wish he'd left it at home.

"These papers?"

"Give us the folder, and we'll let you walk away."

"Alright then," Oates said, "I'll flip you for it."

The girl started to protest, but he held up his hand, and with the other reached into his pocket. The boy made a strained noise, and gestured with the gun, but Oates shook his head. He came up with a fifty pence piece, and held it in front of them like a conjurer fixing their attention. The boy glanced at the girl.

Oates tossed the coin in the air and threw his gaze after it, and cried, "Call!" The boy's eyes followed it involuntarily, and Oates's arm was already coming in a great swing between them, and it knocked the gun skittering across the ground. The girl grabbed the folder from his hand, and shoved him as hard as she could in the chest. Oates's body was still turned from the swing, and coming from below the girl's push was enough to throw his balance. There was a cleaning trolley parked behind him, and he went down, flailing at the air.

She screamed "Run!", but the boy lunged aside and went on all fours for the sliding gun. The direction of Oates's swipe had carried the weapon away from the cubby hole and back into the trample of the shoppers' feet, and now he saw the danger, but all he could do was draw his own gun. He knelt up amid the spilled rubbish and popped it from his thigh pad, but the boy was already on the gun. He picked it up and ran crouched with the gun turned backwards from the wrist, looking over his shoulder. He fired, the shot flying wide over Oates's head.

Oates steadied the gun and fired twice. The sound sent some people scattering, but some just stood and watched, holding colourful bags of shopping. It was if they thought they were watching the gunfight on TV, with no more danger to themselves than a spilled bag of popcorn. The boy fell forwards, the bullets buried in his back. Oates pulled himself up, staggering a little on his right leg. He felt the war joy surge up in him, the gun in his hand more real than any other single thing in his life.

The girl was running through the atrium and he shouted at her to stop. She sprinted on, parting two shoppers with a shove of her shoulder. She had the papers clutched in her right hand, and they flapped like a bird being held by the legs as she ran. He raised his gun again, but the marble floors were thronged with shoppers, their sense of danger deadened by the calm music and pleasantly familiar brands. For a second he felt his finger quivering on the trigger, but her youth kept her safe. In another second she was gone, and the files with her.

He walked over to the boy lying face down on the marble concourse, his blood pooling silently around him. The spinning lights of the adverts reflected in the crimson puddle. He shoed the gun away from the body. He spun the boy over and saw in his eyes that shocked animal expression which had made Oates an atheist at the age of nineteen in the desert. He reached inside the boy's pocket, and pulled out his wallet. The wallet was empty except for a single printed business card. It said, *Dwayne Jeffries, born 11 June 2016, died in the cause of Mortal Reform, 21 November 2035.*

For a moment he felt as if he was about to be sick, and he stood with his hands on his knees breathing heavily.

M.R. The symbol springing up all over London. The Mortal Reformers.

A spook from counter-terrorism had come in to give a training session on the Mortal Reformers. Oates remembered it particularly because Anna had had one of their posters on her wall. He'd spent the whole session staring at the bloke, thinking about what he'd do to him if he tried to arrest his daughter. Then he'd gone home that evening and made Anna take it down, leading to much talk of fascism, free speech and who was living under whose roof.

Oates wasn't much interested in politics. It was a hangover from life in the army, where it had been helpful not to inquire too deeply into the motives of those giving the orders. Anna was though. Because of her, and because of what was on her wall, he had listened closely to the briefing.

The spook had given some background to the movement in his lecture. The decision to label the Mortal Reformers a Proscribed Organisation under the Terrorism Act had been a controversial one. He ran through the handful of MPs who had previously been members of the political wing, and had now been dismissed, triggering a rash of byelections. He projected flowcharts showing the party structure, key supporters, sources of support and fundraising.

The core of the movement was a student thinktank that predated the invention of the Treatment, called the Centre for Policy for Inter-Generational Fairness. They weren't much in thinking up snappy names, but they set out to highlight how increasing longevity screwed over the young. Longer and larger state pensions, more expensive end of life care funded by taxes, and the eldest holding on to jobs and real estate for periods without historical precent, all at a time of rising birth rates and youth immigration. Oates hadn't ever really considered any of these things, but he could trace their effects into riots and crime he dealt with on the streets. The CPIF had been making some headway and gathering some influential friends in government, right up until the Treatment came along.

The Treatment had exacerbated all the problems which CPIF had sought to combat. It also strengthened the resolve of the powerful to resist any change. When death had been inevitable, the thought of relinquishing some of their privileges had been acceptable. After all, you couldn't take it with you. With eternal life before them, they saw no reason to give anything up. You still couldn't take it with you, but what if you didn't have to go?

As the reform agenda failed, the revolutionary voices within the movement started to get a better hearing. Fringe elements had attached themselves to the CPIF – neo-Marxists focused on capital accumulation in the hands of the undying, Malthusian Green extremists obssessed with population explosion, religious fundamentalists decrying the perversion of God's will. They brought with them a heritage of direct action and protest in contrast to the CPIF's methods of lobbying and persuasion. The organisation changed its name to the Mortal Reformers. Between the prevailing economic conditions, the support of music heroes, and the atmosphere of wordy political theory, students flocked to them. The more the government tried to shut them down, the more attractive they became to the real-young. Anna had been one of them.

The boy on the ground was about the same age as Anna would have been. The girl who he had been about to shoot had looked like her. But it couldn't have been Anna, because she had been killed on the road two summers before.

It had been the darkest time of his life. Oates had heard the phrase survivor guilt, but he had never considered before its application. It had never troubled him in the war because they had all lived with the threat of death. Oates knew that if death came for him he would not begrudge his mates their survival, and because he attributed similar sentiments to his comrades, his mourning for them was a clean fellow-feeling. For Anna, he felt only guilt. He looked over the crime scene photographs taken after the accident. The driver had had a heart attack at the wheel, and wasn't prosecuted.

On the street where Anna had been hit the cherry trees were in bloom, and their blossoms had blown into the blood pooled by the roadside. Oates would touch the glossy surface of the photos with his finger and feel nothing but self-reproach. It got into every nook and cranny of life, so that to make a sandwich was to eat in spite of her death. How dare he be hungry, with Anna dead? How dare he take out the rubbish, with Anna dead? It was a betrayal to fix the leaking tap in the bathroom, because with Anna dead the leaking tap should have had no meaning, and to give it meaning placed it on a parity with Anna in the order of significance. What kind of monster fixed a leaking tap, with his daughter in the ground and the man who did it still free somewhere under the London sky?

A couple of weeks after it happened, he'd been clearing out her room. No sense in leaving her stuff in there, when there were charity shops who'd be grateful to have it. He'd found the Mortal Reformers poster he'd made her take down from her wall. She hadn't thrown it out, as she'd promised to do, just hidden it under her bed. He'd unrolled it in his lap. It was a picture split lengthways in two – on one side was a shot of an upmarket London street, the kind where people bought investment properties. It was nightime, but not a single light burned in any of the windows. The owners were off in other houses, in other countries. On the right hand side were ranks of rough sleepers sheltering under the curve of a brick tunnel. He had looked at the picture for a while, and then stuck it back up on her wall. He couldn't bring himself to touch anything else.

Oates had not realised how impossible it had become to discuss death until the need to do so had arisen. In the crematorium they'd had no service, and she was in the oven and up the chimney faster than cooking a microwave dinner. The next family were already waiting when they came out. They had the urn sent on. He couldn't even talk to Lori about it. He had never considered the evolving mortal taboo in relation to himself and his wife, but if he had he would have assumed that as with the rest of society's ridiculousness, the two of them would close the door on it when they got into bed together. But when Anna died he discovered it was not so.

Grief, even in the privacy of the home, even in the privacy of the head, was unseemly. The only acceptable response was to pretend as quickly as possible that the person who had died had never existed. They were an unperson, like rebels disappeared by some despotic regime. To talk about them was dangerous, as if it brought the threat of death closer to the person you were talking to. Only in private memories were the dead allowed an existence. He had withdrawn into these memories, moving away from the living members of his family to spend time with his dead daughter.

Lori said nothing to him about all this at first. His silences grew longer and his temper shorter. He came home drunker and later. The night she finally tried to talk to him became a confrontation. He accused her of not feeling anything, and she said she wished she had never married him. They might have come to blows if their shouting hadn't woken Mike, who was suddenly standing sleep-fuddled in the door to the kitchen. The two of them were ashamed to find themselves in the midst of the strewn cigarette butts, the empty bottle, the smashed glass and all the debris of domestic conflict. Oates had whisked him up in his strong arms, and the two of them kissed him, and when he was back in bed they kissed each other.

All this rushed in on him as he looked at the dead boy. It was an importunate deluge of irrelevant emotion, like a burp in church, like hiccups in a eulogy, brought on by the sight of what he had done to the boy, and his horrible memory of the brief moment of exhilaration he had felt returning fire.

A police Sergeant and a couple of bobbies had joined the security men in the circle. One of the shoppers was holding a camera phone up over the heads of the police, filming the body with Oates beside it. The repairing of this rift in the social fabric, this sudden eruption of violence, was already underway. The ambulance was being called, the officers were forming a cordon around the victim and moving people along, and soon the body would be lifted, photographs would be taken, and then a man in overalls would come and scrub the area with a mop, and within the walls of One New Change it would be as if Dwayne Jeffries had never existed.

"You shot him," the Sergeant observed.

"He was shooting at me."

The big man nodded slowly, as if that was only to be expected.

"You'll have to wait for the internal investigators now then."

The thought of spending any more time in the midst of these shops with their twinkling Chistmas lights was unbearable.

"I can't wait."

"Internal investigations need to be called in whenever there's a shooting."

"I'm not stopping, Sergeant. You've got my number, and my governor's Superintendent John Yates, Metropolitan police."

The Sergeant hesitated, and Oates could see him weighing up whether or not to escalate his attempts to detain him.

"You'll need to talk to security about how best to get the ambulance in here," Oates said.

"We've enough to be getting on with with those boys outside…"

"And stop those fucking people filming."

"Alright. But you're supposed to wait for internal investigations, end of."

Oates walked away from the little pile of death, and headed for the stairs. The Sergeant watched him go for a few paces, then turned and started shouting orders to his men. Quite a crowd was forming, and Oates had to push his way through them. At the back, he thought he recognised a couple of the kids who had been repulsed from the entrance by the massed ranks of the Yorkshire constabulary. They had found another way in. Most of their faces were black or mixed race, and Oates had a thought, rising for a moment above the others – Dwayne Jeffries looked like a mixed race boy, but dark enough to be black if that was what you wanted to call him. And that's what the press and the lairy boys from the estates would want to call him. The Superintendent was going to love that. Oates tried to focus only on the practical repercussions of what he had done. He could feel his conscience making a space inside him for the guilt.

How had the girl known what he was carrying? The only person who had known of his mission was Grape. But why would she have betrayed him? And to whom? If someone wanted the contents of Hector's file bad enough to shoot a policeman for it, the simplest thing would have been to go and take it. Grape had given him Hector's address herself. Oates's mind turned to the smoke-filled interior of the car he had seen parked up on Haggerston Road. If it was a stake out, it fit with the youth and the punkish incompetence of his robbers.

On the road he tried to call Bhupinder back, but the phone went straight through to voicemail. The walls of the Great Spa admitted no signal. Bhupinder must have been coming all the way out through the gates to call him. How many calls had he missed?

Driving through London, the clouds were low and the river ran high. It had been a mistake to close down the schools. Some of the groups of kids hanging out on the Shoreditch High Street might otherwise have been in class, and they already had their hoods up. They milled in groups of five or six, laughing and playing on their phones, circled by outriders on BMXs. They were children waiting for the shops that excluded them to become a playground. The police had no luck – the rain and the wind might have tamped the riots down, but the rain had stopped.

The supermarket was still open, and there was a queue outside the cinema full of shop assistants and teachers using their unexpected half-day. There was no violence yet, no break at all in the lawful pattern. Some of the men and women excused from their offices even lent the city a carnival atmosphere. But he could feel people waiting for the sun to go down like the audience waiting for the lights to go down in a theatre.

He pulled into a petrol station east of the Limehouse Link and bought petrol from a man behind bullet-proof glass. He got changed into the seventies suit in the toilet and stuffed his armour and his gun in his duffel bag. He straightened his tie in the pocked metal mirror. For a fraction of a second, he caught a glimpse of Dwayne Jeffries's face in the distorted darkness over his shoulder, the eyes rolling in mortal bafflement. All that soul rubbish given the lie as the blood and breath disappeared. Born 11 June, 2016. The same year as Anna. *You would have shot me, you little bastard, but I got there first. Now fuck off.* He tried to be firm with himself, but the harsh words sounded hollow. He didn't want to have killed the boy. Lori would make it alright for him. But he couldn't see her again until the Egwu business was done with. The toilet was lit in blue neon to stop junkies from finding their veins, and it made his face look old.

SEEN BY THE light of day, the Great Spa seemed less mysterious, but somehow no less threatening than it had in the small hours of the morning. In the dim sunlight the coloured bulbs glowed but faintly, and Oates could see brown streaks on the white flanks of the dome, and something which might have been a hawk or a falcon circling the pinnacle. The benthic calm of the floodlit plains around the perimeter became merely grubby: a fly-tipper's paradise. The dome had shed that weird aura of the organic, and assumed instead a massive mundanity. Its dirty gigantism, its belittling of the private dwellings which surrounded it now seemed more like the fascist or communist architecture of the mid-twentieth century, mongrelled with the shopping malls of the twenty-first.

Yet it was not until Oates had driven off the motorway and turned into the drive of the Great Spa itself that he became aware of the most significant change. He drove past the turning to the service entrance that had deceived him on his first approach, and passed on towards the reception area he had left that morning. He was still perhaps a mile from the gates when he was brought to a halt by an impenetrable queue of traffic. Where last night there had been only the orderly desolation of the wasteland, now there was chaos. One or two of the vehicles he saw were news vans, another was a tow truck trying to rescue a spavined Mini rolled off the road by its owners, but the majority seemed to be the kinds of ordinary families Oates had passed on the road streaming out of London.

He wound down the window, reached up and stuck the detachable siren onto the roof of his car. The light alone did nothing to clear the way, so he switched on the wail. It seemed at first as if this too would be ignored, but gradually, with a bad grace the cars clogging up the approach began to nudge aside. Robocars were programmed to shift out of the way automatically in response to a signal from the siren, but they were hemmed in by the old fashioned manual vehicles in the crush. Even with the light and siren some drivers still seemed to begrudge him his wing mirrors, and it took almost fifteen minutes for him to reach the manned checkpoint and the barriers that separated the road from the private carpark within the steel ring of the fence, where the guests' cars were arranged in their neat grid.

The guards, who were standing with their guns outside the barrier, paid no attention to his approach, and when he gestured to the man in the booth to lift the pneumatic arm and lower the mechanical teeth at the entrance, the man shook his head and waved at the crowd. Oates turned off the siren and got out, leaving the car parked on the road. The guards were arguing loudly with a couple of men, and one woman who held the bundle of a baby in her arms. Just out of sight of the security men, a boy with his trousers pulled down and his shirt held up to his nipples in both hands was peeing against the corner of the gatehouse.

Oates took his badge with him and flashed it at the guards as he passed the barrier. He walked up to an older man who seemed to be in charge, speaking into an earpiece some feet behind the checkpoint.

"Who are you?"

"DCI Oates, Metropolitan Police."

"If you're here for the murder just head on through and they'll see you at the desk."

"What's going on here?"

"Some of them have relations in the spa, or they say they do. They want to be let in to stay with them tonight, or pick them up and take them further outside London. The news people are here because someone tipped them off about the murder, although now they're starting to talk to the people stuck in the jam, and the rest of them, buggered if I know. I think they just saw a queue and joined the back."

Oates turned to look back down the long file of cars. People in London were frightened, they wanted out of the city for the night, but not all of them had somewhere else to go. The rich could be relied upon to take care of themselves. The security here was obvious enough. If you couldn't afford a motel and you didn't want to spend another night in your flat with the lights off, hoping no one tried to rob you, then parking up under one of those gun towers must have seemed an attractive option. Although bad tempered, there was no sign that the drivers were ready to force their way into the carpark, but nor were they leaving; the cars had simply begun to drive away from the barriers and over the hard shoulder, out around the edges of the fence. They clustered for company around the chainlink like old horses put out in a field.

"Where's Charles Golden?"

The guard tossed his head in the direction of the reception. "He's holding a press conference with some of your lot."

"Who?"

"I don't know. Some bloke, must be a bigwig, he turned up with enough bloody people. Now, if you don't mind," and he gestured back to the growing crowd around the barriers.

Oates hurried on towards the lobby. Why hadn't he been told about the press conference? And who was this important man? He felt a niggling sense that he should never have left the Great Spa. The thought of the missed calls from Bhupinder rose to make him queasy. Things were clearly moving out of control.

OATES DID NOT have to look far. Inside the automatic doors of the reception there was an unruly scrum of press and police dispersing from a conference room. Inside this room ranks of plush cushioned chairs were arrayed in front of a trestle set with water jugs and microphones. The people not in uniforms wore identity badges on their chests, and Oates saw the names of pretty much every major news organisation he could think of. The reception area was outside of St Margaret's proper, and Oates in his seventies suit got some odd looks from the journalists.

His worst fears were confirmed when, pushing his way upriver against the bodies streaming out into the lobby, he saw Superintendent Yates and Charles standing in conference behind the trestles. The Superintendent was dressed in his normal uniform from the waist up, but on his lower half, which would have been below the level of the trestle during the press conference, he was wearing a pair of bell-bottoms.

Charles saw him first, and beamed.

"The prodigal returns!" Charles said. "I'm so glad to see you've taken to your suit."

"There you are, Inspector," John said, "Good of you to join us. I believe you know Charles."

"What's going on? There's a tailback outside the gates all the way to the motorway."

"It seems we underestimated the interest our little incident would generate," Charles replied cheerfully.

"A few press, alright," Oates said, "but there must be four hundred people…"

"We had some senior bods from some of our competitors staying at the spa. I advised against it, of course, but Miranda rather likes to rub their noses in our success, and to be fair to her they'd get their spies in through the back door if you didn't welcome them through the front. You can't make calls or send messages from inside as you know, but some of them cut their stays short this morning. Very odd, as our guests are generally extremely reluctant to leave. I'd say they've been calling in favours, wouldn't you?"

Charles waved to someone standing behind them, and made to move off, the smile of a fresh greeting filling his sails. Oates took his arm and held him.

"You and I need to talk."

"Of course, Inspector, of course, but you wouldn't begrudge me a few minutes in the service of order."

Charles looked not at Oates but at the Superintendent. The Superintendent gestured with his hand for the PR man to pass freely, and Oates released his arm. As Oates watched him go, he realised that alongside his mounting consternation as he passed the ranks of massed humanity outside Avalon's gates, there had been a compensatory schadenfreude at the thought of Charles's smooth manner being engulfed by the chaos. In this, Oates was mightily disappointed.

Not only did Charles seem undisturbed by the crisis, he had actually supped from the febrile atmosphere around him and stored it as raw energy. Perhaps he had lived for too long in Miranda's shadow, and the public relations nightmare engulfing Avalon was allowing him to make his own bid for power. Certainly her absence from the conference room felt significant. Miranda was the queen of the spa as it was, but Charles was the master of the spa as it appeared, and the balance in the relative importance of these two states had shifted radically in the few hours since Oates's departure.

Had he been alone he might have grabbed Charles by the collar and pushed him up against the wall, but with John there he felt he had to keep his cool. It was a bad thing, to think of his superior as a protection for the Great Spa rather than an ally in his investigation.

"Thanks for keeping control here, sir," Oates said when the two of them stood alone, "I don't want to sound ungrateful, but what are you doing here?"

"I received a call from the senior management of Nottingham Biosciences informing me that you had given orders for the entirety of the guests to be removed from their... therapy in the new buildings," John said, "Is that correct?"

"I wanted all possible witnesses interviewed."

"For Christ's sake. I told you this was delicate."

"Have you been in there?"

"Why do you think I'm wearing these ridiculous trousers? I have also seen the guest list. There are three current members of the House of Lords and an unobtrusive gentleman listed as a businessman whom MI5 informs me is a member of the Standing Committee of the People's Republic of China. I have of course informed the management here that we will not be disturbing any guests who were unconscious during the crime."

"What do you want me to do, John? Do I investigate or am I an errand boy come to pick up the suspect?"

"I should very much like you to investigate, only I understand from Bhupinder that you felt it was more important to return to London than to attend to matters here. A casual observer might think that an odd choice, though I myself have no doubt that you had the best reasons, both for being absent and incommunicado. Please don't think it any more than a formality if I ask to know what they were."

"Prudence Egwu's brother disappeared a few years ago. Minor worked the case. You might remember it, sir, he was working under you at the time."

"I am aware, Detective Chief Inspector, of the details of my own career. You found him in the pub, presumably."

"I did."

"And did you join him for a drink?"

Oates looked up at him quickly to see whether he was joking. John was one of those men with whom jokes and deadly seriousness jostled along in the same crowd, and if you got them mixed up the consequences could be dire. He was not looking at Oates, but smiling rigidly at someone on the other side of the room.

"I did what I felt was appropriate in the circumstances to get the necessary information."

"This was information necessary for the understanding of a high profile murder investigation of which Minor has no possible knowledge, taking place in a different part of the country, for which you were responsible and which you left to the care of a Sergeant?"

He was not joking. Oates elected to stay silent. John knew perfectly well why Minor's involvement would have been worth a look, and why the very fact that the murder was high profile made it more important to discover the nature of that involvement, but if he was pretending not to there was nothing Oates could do. He could hardly accuse his superior point blank of having overseen a case involving potential impropriety. He began to feel claustrophobic as John's enquires surrounded him. The room was hot with the packed bodies of the recent conference.

"And what information did you glean?"

"Minor said there was nothing odd in the original investigation, but he did mention that a number of accusations were made against Nottingham by Prudence Egwu with respect to the disappearance of his brother, a fact neither Charles nor Miranda thought worth mentioning."

"I was also aware of those particular accusations, and I did not consider them worth mentioning either. Is there anything you learnt in London of any actual relevance to the case?"

"I stopped off at the victim's house on the way back out here. There's been a break-in. Someone lifted some papers from his office. I think they might have been related to his own investigations into his brother's disappearance."

"Ah yes, Mr Egwu's house. I have been speaking to the tech team who arrived, and they tell me they found the place in a bit of a state. They had hoped the security tapes might shed some light on the events, but apparently they have some unfortunate omissions."

"That was me, sir. I was trying to retrieve the whole period from when I came in and I accidentally stopped the thing."

"Really? Apparently you may also have accidentally wiped the back up. Quite extraordinarily clumsy. I think perhaps when this case is a little more settled I would be interested to hear more about the circumstances of that particular mishap."

"Yes sir."

"They also tell me that they discovered a glass of whisky on the desk in Mr Egwu's office. Tell me, do you think we should have it tested for DNA in an effort to catch the perpetrator of the break-in? Or might that be a waste of time and resources?"

Oates had conducted enough interviews himself to know that if the only thing you could say was incriminating, it was best to stay silent. It was a testament to how badly the discussion had gone that he was grateful when Charles bounded back into view.

"I'm so sorry, Inspector. Now what was it you wanted to talk to me about?"

Oates looked at John, who raised an eyebrow and smiled tolerantly. Oates felt utterly disarmed. It would be difficult to pursue a line of questioning in front of John which John had just declared irrelevant. But if he missed the opportunity now, the fact that Charles and Miranda had concealed their knowledge would stale.

"I wanted to ask if you had ever come across Mr Egwu or his family prior to his stay at St Margaret's," Oates said.

"Ah, you're referring to our little falling out over his brother's disappearance? Well, John can tell you all about that. We'd buried the hatchet some time ago, if that's not an unfortunate expression in the circumstances. One of the benefits of being a monopoly. You can be as cross with us as you like, but if you don't want to die you still have to make nice and give us your money. I thought that was common knowledge. Besides, between you and me if you add up all the people in the world with an axe to grind against Miranda, Nottingham wouldn't have a single customer left!"

"How long ago did you 'bury the hatchet'?"

"Well, I can't speak for Mr Egwu, and since he can't speak for himself I suspect his own views on the matter will forever remain a mystery. But we have never borne him any ill will, not even at the time he was making his unfortunate allegations. Capability was a great colleague and friend to all of us, and Prudence having lost his brother, the stress he was under, it was quite understandable he might lash out. It was all some time ago…"

"But Prudence only had the treatment very recently. In the last month or so. Isn't that true?"

For the first time, Oates sensed a brittleness at the edges of Charles's bonhomie. He smiled tightly. "I'm afraid I really can't tell you. As you know, Inspector, I am a humble PR man, and my kingdom stretches only as far as the carpark you see outside. If you want to check Nottingham's clinical records I suggest you speak to her majesty. Now I don't wish to be unfriendly, but as you can see the barbarians are still very much at the gates."

"Of course, Charles. Thank you for your time."

"Don't mention it, Superintendent! Inspector Oates, I'm sure this is merely au revoir."

The two policemen stood in silence. Oates felt the blood heating his cheeks. His hand was still sore from hitting the wall in Prudence Egwu's house, and he flexed his fingers, using pain to bring himself back under control. Charles had interrupted their conversation before he could give a full account of the afternoon's events. He had said nothing to John of his visit to Hector's place, or the subsequent shootout at One New Change. As the two of them stood together, he decided he wasn't going to say anything more. Partly he knew that if John found out about the shooting, he would take him off the case. He would take his gun and send him home to wait for internal investigations. That wasn't going to happen – he had made that decision when he had left the scene. He would pay for it later, of course, but that didn't matter now.

But there was something more, something for which the simple practical point of wishing to continue the investigation could not account. He had told John enough already to make a clever cop suspicious, and John was a clever cop. He was actively resisting any line of enquiry which led away from Ali, and the simple explanation which had been proffered by the authorities at the spa.

"I want to interview Ali Farooz again," Oates said.

"Of course. Do you mind at all if I sit in?"

"I've formed a rapport with Farooz. I'll get more out of him if I speak to him alone."

"Fair enough. Presumably you won't object if I observe from outside the room. Or is Mr Farooz camera shy? I wouldn't want to upset what is clearly a delicate relationship."

"Of course not, sir."

"Good. Well, we've set something up in one of the cabins in the maintenance complex."

"Ali's been moved? I specifically asked Bhupinder not to move him and not to let anyone in to see him."

"I'll tell you an amazing thing about orders, Detective Chief Inspector. The closer one is to one's inferiors, the more likely they are to be obeyed. A pity you had such pressing business in London."

THEY MET BHUPINDER inside, and Oates found his subordinate couldn't look him in the eye when he gave them an update. Seeing Bhupinder's glum look, Oates stopped being cross with him and started being cross with himself. There was nothing Bhupinder could have done to resist John's orders once he was in the spa. He should never have left him alone. He told them that Ali had been transported out of the main part of St Margaret's entirely, down to the maintenance complex that Oates had seen clustered along the tunnels at the spa's edge. The easiest way to reach these rooms was from the outside of the dome, but given the chaos at the gates it would probably be preferable to approach from within. Because of the Great Spa's unique geography, the journey was quicker by river than by road.

A blue-suited groundsman took Oates and the Superintendent down one of the side streets that wound around the walls of St Margaret's to a small dock, shady beneath the trees. When Oates had departed that morning the first classes of the day were beginning, but the double-time in the spa had pulled its weird trick, conjuring a long sunny evening from the domed sky. A bleached beer can floated in the water beside the punts, and Oates could see the glint of fish in the water. Among the wooden boats was a small launch. Oates and the Superintendent climbed into the bow, and he was gratified to see that even John's dignity couldn't survive the rocking of a skiff on the water. When the porter hopped in by the engine, the shift in gravity almost threw the Superintendent into the river. He sat down heavily, and looked around to see who had noticed.

As they pulled away from the shore, the chug of the engine sounded outrageous in the still twilight. They moved off upriver under the stares of the students lolling in their punts, or sunbathing along the banks. They headed in the opposite direction to the one Oates and Miranda had taken along the towpath that morning.

On his first arrival in the spa, Oates had wondered how anyone could enter into the self-deception demanded by the project without feeling ridiculous. He felt that for himself it would have tripped embarrassment in him like a circuit-breaker, shorting the suspension of disbelief. As they moved down the river in the light of the setting sun however, he found that the challenge was not to suspend his disbelief, but rather to keep reminding himself that what he felt and saw was not real. On an intellectual level, he still thought the entire idea of so many powerful people taking a month to play make-believe would have been merely ridiculous, had the expenditure of money and effort required not rendered it obscene.

But the sun on the skin was not interested in the intellectual, any more than the sound of the wind in the trees, or the laughter of a girl he heard somewhere on the towpath beside the canal, out of sight.

These were influences that did not announce themselves at the door of the conscious mind, but slipped in through the secret tunnels in eyes and ears and nose, so that even as Oates was condemning the whole scene, he caught himself thinking how lovely it would be to bring the boys here for a swim. This was how the spa achieved its effects – it made traitors of the senses, and through them the emotions, and only when those two were conquered was it strong enough to advance on consciousness. Oates hated the spa and everything it stood for, and yet he found himself trailing a wrist in the cool water. He pulled his hand out, and looked up to see the Superintendent watching him, a faint smile playing around his lips.

As they moved further up the river they came to an isolated stretch of slow-flowing green water, where the trees grew thick along the banks and dipped their branches beneath the surface. Oates tried to match his conception of the spa's external dimensions with its internal geography, and decided they were in one of the long arms stretching away from the dome in either direction. The arms had been less than half the height of the main dome, which meant that the ceiling of the cavern in which he travelled was no more than four hundred metres above his head. He craned his neck back and shielded his eyes with his hand. There was nothing but the purple ozone of the sky, shading into pink the colour of a seashell at the horizon. Over the peaceful fields, swallows traced their intricate trajectories.

They passed a herd of cows grazing in a broad field. One of them had fallen into the water and was unable to climb back out onto the steep bank. Several of its fellows stood waiting for it on the solid ground, chewing in placid sympathy. The groundsman spoke a spell into the mike in his cuff as they went by, and as the boat neared the next bend in the river Oates saw a green Land rover speeding over the field towards the distressed animal. As it bumped to a halt, a man climbed out holding a boltgun.

They had been travelling for perhaps twenty minutes when they finally came to a halt beside a low jetty. There was a second groundsman waiting for them there. He hailed his fellow and caught the tossed line as they idled to the planks. He offered his hand to Oates. Oates ignored it and clambered onto the grass unaided. The Superintendent took the proffered hand, and thanked the owner with exaggerated courtesy. They walked about two hundred metres from the bank to a fence, and as Oates watched he noticed the most extraordinary thing. Hanging suspended as if in thin air there was a neon-green sign bearing the legend 'EXIT' in capital letters. Its presence in the air was such an affront to logic that Oates blinked to try to unsee it. When he opened his eyes however the sign remained; even in the depths of this dreamworld, fire safety regulations were strictly applied.

At the fence one of the groundskeepers stopped. He put out his hand, and the fence and part of the view beneath the exit sign swung open to reveal the concrete corridor beyond, the walls painted an institutional green. The air in that tunnel was a couple of degrees cooler than in the field, and the sound of distant machinery was audible somewhere down the length of it. From more than five feet away, the walls simply refused to disclose their presence. Just as he was about to pass through the door, Oates thought he detected a flicker in the spire of a church topping the trees in the distance, and he noted how the dead leaves and a crisp packet were piled against the bottom of the fence with a symmetry inconsistent with its visual dimensions. Still as he stepped through the door, he felt he was walking through a hole in the universe.

Inside the corridor with the summer field closed behind them, the sound of machinery was loud enough to make you raise your voice. One of the porters told them they were near the turbine house that kept the river gently flowing, and the sounds in the walls came from the giant drill-shaped pumps churning the water. Oates excused himself to go to the toilet, and once inside a cubicle he pulled a fifty pence piece from his pocket. His hands were shaking a little when he flipped it the first time, and it slipped through his fingers and plopped into the streaked bowl. He ran his fingers through his hair and stared for a few seconds down into the foul water. He reminded himself that he didn't really believe in luck, and went back out to where the others were waiting without having completed his ritual.

They had set up an interview room complete with a camera so that the Superintendent could watch the questioning from outside. Ali Farooz was waiting there, and when Oates came in he greeted him as casually as if the Inspector had just popped out for a few minutes at the end of their last interview, and was now returned. This caused in Oates a momentary disorientation. The discrepancy between the events of the last couple of hours in his own life, and the changelessness implied by Ali's greeting was unsettling. He felt a weird conviction that nothing had happened to him at all – that he had ceased to exist the moment he left Ali's room, and was popping back into existence now on re-entry. It was an absurd idea, but it enthralled him, and he knew it would pass not with rational thought, but with the lapse of time.

To gather himself he sat in silence for a few moments at the little desk between them, and pretended to study the custody log. Ali waited. They had moved further into the building so that the sound of machinery was deadened by the supervening walls. Despite the silence, Oates thought he could still feel some deep subsonic vibration in the ground as the giant turbines built the summer river a turn at a time.

"So then, Ali. I trust you've been looked after."

"Yes thank you, Inspector, I have been most well looked after."

"Has anyone been in to see you?"

"Lots of people. They have been very kind. I have seen a doctor and a lawyer and some of your friends. And one of my friends brought me a change of clothes and my toothbrush."

Ali smiled politely. Oates nodded. He got the message. Whoever had been in to nobble Ali, it would be no easy matter to identify him. The message could have come from anyone. If Ali had seen him coming, there was no point in being subtle.

"I know you didn't do it, Ali. Whoever killed Prudence Egwu was right handed."

He gestured to Ali's left hand, and Ali moved it under the table.

"Now I think you know who killed Prudence Egwu. I'd like you to tell me who that was."

"Why would I say that I had done something which I had not done?"

"Come on, Ali. You're not stupid. You've been in this country half a decade. You're telling me a clever man like you, a political man like you, doesn't read the papers, watch the news? You know what an Eddy is don't you?"

"Yes. Yes I know what is an Eddy."

"Well that's what I think you are."

Ali stared a him for a few seconds in disbelief. Then he leant back in his seat, and burst into a rich, deep laugh. The boom of it filled up the room as the mighty pumps did in their distant atrium.

"What's so funny?"

Ali's laughter was almost hysterical. He doubled over in his chair, and shook his head. He squeezed tears from the corner of his eyes. Oates wanted to get up, walk around the table and smash his head. All the respect, all the strange affection he had felt for the man at the conclusion of their first interview was for a moment subsumed by rage at being laughed at. He thought again of the young man he had killed a few hours before. He felt angered on Dwayne Jeffries' sbehalf.

"Please Inspector, I do not mean to make fun. Only you see I have spent altogether in my life some time in rooms like this one, answering questions. In the first part of my life, it was policemen trying to make me to admit to things I had not done. They put pins under my nails and they kick me until I say I had done all kinds of things. And now in this country, I am being told to deny the crimes to which I have confessed." He was still breathing hard from his laughing fit.

Oates didn't want this man's history. He didn't want to be mollified by the fact of his suffering. He wanted the truth. He wanted the truth from him as a hungry man wants the meat from an animal. He couldn't give a shit what happened to him after the truth was out of him. He could be discarded, and Oates could get back to his family. He stayed silent and stared at Ali.

"Even let us say you are right," Ali said, "I would not know who had done this thing. I would know only who had invited me to take the blame."

"And who was that?"

"If someone lies to the police, that is an offence, is that not so?"

He looked at Oates, waiting for an answer, and Oates nodded his head and folded his arms across his chest.

"That is what they call wasting police time, yes? Perverting the course of justice? And for an offence such as this, one could also go to prison for some time. Only when one got out of prison, there would be no reward at the end. Let us say that a man does what you are suggesting, and accepts that he will take the blame for something in return for something else. Well, if he cannot any more take the blame, he will not anymore expect his payment. But that does not mean he would want to go to prison just for the hell of it."

"We can make a deal, Ali. If you tell us everything and tell us now, I will do everything in my power to make sure you get off."

"If there was a man with the power to offer such a thing as eternal life, that man would also have the power of death in him. Would you not say this?"

Oates did not reply. Ali watched him for a few seconds, and nodded slowly at this confirmation of his thinking.

"And would you not further say that if this man was betrayed, he might take the trouble to find out who had done this thing, and to pay him back?"

"We can protect you, Ali."

"I tell you again what I told you before. I really did go to see Mr Egwu like I said. I really did go up and see him after dinner."

"This is a one time only thing, Ali. If I walk out of this room now, you won't have another chance to tell the truth and get credit for it."

Ali said nothing, but raised his palm to Oates, as if all the answers he might seek were written in the dark lines of the unexpectedly pale skin. Oates pictured the scene as it would appear to the Superintendent on his little coloured screen. He reached around to the back of the camera, and switched it off. Then he went over and locked the door.

"Have you ever heard of something called the Tithonus Effect?"

"I have heard of this, yes. This is the thing these people come here to make better."

"What do you know about it?"

"I know nothing."

Ali looked down and away from him, and Oates was certain that he was lying. He leant forwards across the table, and gripped his lapels.

"I killed a boy today. He wanted to get hold of some papers on the Tithonus Effect. Why would anyone die for something like that?"

Ali did not seem at all surprised. There was no resistance in his torso, he simply allowed his shoulders to be pulled forwards over the table.

"I am sorry, Inspector. I do not know anything about it. Only this one thing. When I was at first school, the teacher she used to tell us about Hell. She say it was a burning lake of fire and we would go there if we were bad. And the worst thing about Hell, it is forever. She told us to imagine the wing of a butterfly, brushing a ball of steel as big as the earth. The time it would take to wear away the ball of steel with the butterfly's wing, that was not even one million part of the time we would spend in Hell. When she told me, I had nightmares for months. My mother, she even complain to the school. I used to lie awake in my bed at night, thinking about it. This Tithonus Effect, I am thinking it is Hell. And the people who go there, that is where they deserve to be."

The handle to the door turned, and finding it locked, a firm knocking followed. Oates stood up from the table, and flicked the switch to turn the camera back on.

"We'll find this guy, Ali. And when we do he'll throw you in as part of his plea-bargain."

"That is the way things go for people like me, would you not say, Inspector?"

Oates unlocked the door, and stormed out past the waiting groundsman. He slammed the door behind him, leaving Ali alone in the room with his hands folded before him on the desk.

*   *   *

"Someone's got to him. I need to find out who spoke to him, who moved him down here. All that stuff about perverting the course of justice, he's smart but he's not a bloody lawyer. Someone's been in to put the frighteners on…"

"I find that highly unlikely," John said, watching the still figure on the monitor, "All the conversations he has had since being brought down here have been recorded. And I didn't hear him say a single thing a man couldn't pick up from watching the news and crime drama on the television."

"You asked me to handle this, sir, because you wanted to know whether or not he was an Eddy. And I'm telling you I think he is."

"I asked you, DCI Oates, because I value your judgment, but I do not think it infallible. Whilst you were pursuing your own investigations in London, Sergeant Bhupinder was engaged in the rather more old-fashioned process of actually interviewing witnesses. Stuffy and conventional I know, but we aren't all blessed with your levels of intuition. It appears that one of the guests saw Ali walking up to Mr Egwu's room shortly before the murder took place. He couldn't sleep and was smoking a cigarette out of the window."

"He's already said he went up there, first to carry the case then to argue with Egwu about the money."

"This witness further indicated that he heard the sounds of an altercation some moments later. The timings coincide with the scenario put together by the Oracle. You know how I loathe the predictable, but I don't think we should be seeking out originality even at the expense of the truth, do you?"

"I want to speak with this bloke."

"Which bloke?"

"The one Bhupinder interviewed. This witness. I want to hear it from him."

"Why?"

"To satisfy my curiosity."

John shook his head.

"He's no longer staying at St Margaret's."

"Why did he leave?"

"Because he wanted to and there was no reason to stop him. If you must know I suspect he's one of the people we may have to thank for the circus outside."

"One of Nottingham's competitors?"

"Yes. He works at another bio company."

"What does he do?"

"I don't know exactly."

"What's his name?"

"Chris Rajaram."

The answer shocked Oates into a momentary silence. He had pushed the events of the afternoon to the back of his mind, but the mention of the name of Hector's employer created a sudden nexus. Could this Chris Rajaram have killed Prudence Egwu in an effort to conceal the theft of his accumulated research? For a moment, he had the unpleasant sensation that he was shaping external reality, that the link he had forged in his mind had somehow infected the real world.

"I want to speak to him," Oates said.

He and John stared at one another. Oates could feel an old alliance on the point of dissolution. They had worked together on and off for the best part of a decade. Though John could be supercilious and sarcastic he was basically a decent man. They had always held one another in mutual respect. But Oates could sense in both of them a reckless desire to tear down that relationship, and to throw up in its place a new and profound enmity. What was the reason? Standing there in the maintenance rooms of the Great Spa, it felt like nothing so much as a fascination with what might happen. It was kin to the sensation that seized Oates at the top of high buildings, the whisper of how easy it would be to step into the air. Finally John looked away and shook his head.

"Speak to him then, hear the story for yourself. But I want you back up here before tonight, I want Ali charged and taken down to London. We're going to need every man we have on the streets tonight. The Commissioner has cancelled leave and men are being bussed in from everywhere from Cornwall to Yorkshire."

"And if I'm not satisfied?"

"If you're not satisfied, Detective Chief Inspector, I will want to know why. So I know what to tell my own superiors." Oates thought again of Minor's last words to him in the pub: "It's you as should watch your back!"

"Did you ever fancy having the Treatment yourself, sir?" he asked.

Quite unconsciously, the men had squared up to one another. Oates looked down, and noticed their fists were closed. He thought for a moment he had gone too far. He hadn't actually accused a senior officer of corruption, but he had come as close as made no difference. To his surprise, a grin spread across John's face; not the ironic smile which was its habitual resident, but an expression broad and boyish.

"I rather think one lifetime is enough, wouldn't you say?"

"One can seem like a lot."

There was a knock on the door, and the porter was waiting outside to escort them back to St Margaret's. The two of them took the launch back along the river. This time the beauty of the scenery held no distractions, and Oates was grateful for the sound of the engine on the way to the main body of the spa. It removed any obligation to speak. He couldn't be certain of anything in this place. It interfered with the frequencies of his self-belief. His nose had got bunged up in the summer fields. Was he being as perverse as John's exasperation implied? He had no particular wish to help Ali after his behaviour in the interview room, but his desire to see the right man punished penetrated deeper than personal prejudice. If this Chris Rajaram was involved in the murder, Oates would run him to ground.

Was Ali clever enough to be double-bluffing? That would have been an incredibly dangerous tactic to adopt, but if he had been caught virtually red-handed perhaps it had seemed the only option. Perhaps he even planned to revoke his confession at some point prior to the trial, claiming he had been paid, but was unable to identify the parties who had made the offer. If that was the plan, a testimony from an investigating officer to the effect that he had doubted the man's guilt to the point of defying a superior would be a valuable thing. Oates tried to remember the exact words he had used in the interview room, and how useful they would be to a defence team trying to take that line.

The doubts multiplied inside him like the worlds inside opposed mirrors. He clung to the idea of interviewing Chris Rajaram. His confusion could not be complete, so long as there was an identifiable gap in his knowledge still to be filled. With that interview outstanding, the crisis of a decision on whether or not to charge Ali Farooz could be postponed.

He and John barely said goodbye to one another when the launch nosed back into port. There were things they needed to settle between them, whether John was intending to stay, how many men might be needed for operations in London, but the inertia of the silence proved impossible to disturb. There were other conversations to be had within St Margaret's, but Oates found he could not face them. His overriding desire was to fix in place the guilt or innocence of Ali Farooz – not only for the purposes of his investigation, but for his own peace of mind.

Back outside the main gates, Oates's car was where he had left it. The confrontation around the barrier seemed to have ended, but the flow of cars away from the tarmac and onto the grassy wasteland was gathering pace. All around the darkening fields, interior lights created warm little worlds where men and women huddled companionably in their car seats. In one or two places, he saw tents were mushrooming. It was if a travelling circus had descended on a village green, filling it up with lights and strangers, caravans and wonders and crime. It was nearing dusk when he turned the car, and he had the headlights on as he drove back into London. As before, he alone appeared to be travelling that way.

CHRIS RAJARAM HAD certainly called Hector from the Great Spa shortly after the murder. Hector bothered Oates, because the boy was an incompetent. The idea that the head of a rich corporation would choose someone like him for industrial espionage just didn't sit right. If that was what you wanted there were men in London who could get in and out of a house without leaving so much as the ghost of their breath on a windowpane.

The only advantage he could see in using Hector was that he was a male prostitute. A man in Prudence Egwu's position would never report a crime in those circumstances. And that was the only possible explanation for employing Hector as the means of effecting the theft – the crime would go unreported. Seen in that light, the choice of Hector was strategically brilliant. Chris would at one stroke have secured his prize, and protected himself from the possibility of investigation.

But why bother going to such lengths if you were going to stab the man to death? It would have been enough to accomplish the theft to know Prudence Egwu was staying in the Great Spa, and that his house would therefore be empty. In fact, if Chris was after the research papers which Mr

Egwu had accumulated, the murder would have been a huge inconvenience – he must have known that with Prudence dead the police would eventually search his house, and might impound and examine any papers they found there. The fact he had contacted Hector directly was proof of a plot disrupted. He had not profited from the murder, he had been forced to accelerate his plans because of it, and the bungled late night visit from Hector was the result.

Finally, there was the nature of the murder itself. Oates had watched those blows fall and retract on the screen of the Oracle. Oates had used a bayonet before; he knew how hard it was to get the blade back. The thing slipped in easy enough with a quick thrust the way it had in training, but the dummies had no ribcage, and the serrated blade of the knife got stuck. In the end he'd had to put his foot on the dead man's shoulder. Whoever had killed Prudence Egwu had done that thirty times. That wasn't murder for profit. That was the fury of madness.

The offices of United Sciences were on the fifth floor of a building near the Old Bailey. His police pass got him into the underground carpark, where he changed between the doors of his car. The lift opened into a marble hall. He pushed open a set of glass swing doors etched with the company's name and asked for Mr Rajaram at the front desk. He felt the receptionist's manner tighten ever so slightly at the sight of the uniform, her spine straightening by a couple of degrees, her smile a few millimetres wider.

She asked his name, and Oates gave his name and rank. She asked if he had an appointment, and he shook his head. Her fingers paused for a moment over the computer in front of her, hovering in the air whilst she took in the uniform, the stance, the attitude which Oates had traipsed in from his long day of murders and gunfights. She excused herself for a moment, and conversed with someone on the other end of a telephone in a voice too low to catch. When she came back, she showed him to a seat, and told him someone would be down in a minute to collect him, and would he like tea or coffee?

Oates sat on the soft leather sofa in front of a vase filled with orchids. Beside him there were three men in suits with briefcases. They had been talking tactics when he came over, but his presence extinguished their enthusiasm.

On the wall of the reception room was a painting exactly like the one he had seen in Prudence Egwu's townhouse. He cast about for something to distract him whilst he waited. There was a pile of broadsheet newspapers on the table in front of him, and he recognised the pink pages of the *Financial Times*. He picked it up, and immediately threw it back down. He crossed his legs, but the low seat was uncomfortable, and he slid forward on the shiny leather. Two of the businessmen beside him were studiously ignoring this display, and pretending to study laminated folders they had brought with them, but the third was watching Oates, his cheeks reddening in the silence.

"Anyway," he began, speaking louder than he had been before Oates's approach, "I think we should be pushing for full reliance. On the disclosure report."

His companions started up from their folders. One of them muttered, "possibly, possibly," and smiled in a placatory way before returning to the page. The speaker, however, was not so easily perturbed.

"It's, what, a couple of million more in terms of exposure. And you're not telling me they don't have the insurance. If it's a professional liability issue, they shouldn't even be at the table. They shouldn't even be in the room!"

"Well, we'll find out when we see them."

"Yes, but I think we have to be up front that this is a show-stopper. We won't accept anything less…"

Oates plucked up the *Financial Times* from where he had thrown it, and spread it open on the table in front of him. He removed his gun from its holster, and checked the barrel, dirtied with the recent discharge. He disassembled the firing mechanism, laying out the pieces one after another on the spread newspaper. Each one made a muffled click on the glass beneath the paper as he set it down. He removed the small oilcloth he kept in a pouch by the solid gun housing, and laced it through the bore. He lifted it to his eye, and winked at the painting through the clean hole. The man continued to talk, but his eyes were watching the slow assemblage of lethal components spreading oil over the pages of the *FT*.

Taking the gun apart helped Oates to calm his mind. He was so engrossed in the coming together of the gleaming gun, that he was startled to find the woman from the desk standing over him along with a slightly older lady in a skirt and blouse. The lawyers were gone. With a smile and a sweep of her hand, the receptionist passed him into the care of her elder. The latter introduced herself as Mr Rajaram's personal assistant, and invited him to accompany her.

MR RAJARAM WAS concluding a meeting elsewhere in the building, and Oates had a few moments alone to take in his office. The family photographs faced outwards on the surface of the desk like a defensive pallisade, a protection against any questioning of this man's practice or priorities. The wife was pretty, the children smiling, the frames plain and heavy silver. Mrs Rajaram was white, and a couple of inches taller than her husband, with the distant beauty of a fashion model. She had also undergone the Treatment, so that in the family portrait the couple looked like the older siblings of their own children.

The flat monitor of the computer was turned away from him, but Oates watched the screensaver photographs scrolling past in the reflection of the window behind the desk. One of them was taken in the interior of an epic church, the kind so big that the altar spreads tv screens like great wings on either side, filled with a twinned image of the pastor sweating in close-up. Another photograph showed Chris standing outside a hut on a dusty plain, his arms around two black men in khaki shirts. The black men were smiling. The images hung outside in the dark of the London evening. On the wall above the desk was a wooden cross. Oates had been waiting perhaps ten minutes when the smoked glass door behind him opened, and Chris Rajaram himself surfed in on a wave of business.

"Don't get up, don't get up! I'm sorry to have kept you waiting, Inspector."

"No problem. I was just admiring your office."

"It's a lovely view, isn't it? We're very lucky."

"That's something you don't see much anymore," he said, indicating the cross.

"Oh, you'd be surprised. The churches are heaving, not just at cult but the Catholics, even dear old C of E."

"Cult?"

"The Church of the Present Resurrection. We like to call it cult, because everyone else does," he laughed good-naturedly, and threw himself down into his chair with his arms behind his head.

"Isn't that the group that believes that the Treatment comes from Jesus?"

"No, unfortunately not! My job would be a great deal easier if Jesus held the patents for the Treatment. The Treatment comes from Nottingham Biosciences, sadly. But we believe in the human face of God. God was made man, and there's no reason that the beginnings of the afterlife should not also come through man. The Treatment is the beginning of His kingdom on earth, the first of the elect. The press has the tendency to pick up on the more fantastic elements of our faith. Personally I think it's a lot less controversial than, say, cannibalism in the Catholic mass."

"I don't know anything about that."

"If you're interested you should come along some time. We're open to all, not just the new-young. The Treatment is a message to us to try and build His paradise here on earth. Get a head start on the New Jerusalem. It's Him saying, I'll be here soon, I'm on my way, get out the bunting and the paper cups!"

"How do you do that?"

"Small things. Some charity work, some trips to schools. Inviting promising young people from disadvantaged backgrounds to come and work here, and other companies like it in the City. I'm sure you make your own contribution to building a better London."

"I wanted to ask you a few more questions about what you heard on the night of the murder."

"Oh yes?"

Oates flipped his notepad, and waited with pen poised.

"I did try to tell your colleague everything."

"I know that, Mr Rajaram."

"Chris, please. I'm happy to be a witness you know. In court or anything. Diary permitting, obviously."

"Thank you."

"So, do you just want me to tell you again, or what?"

"Tell me again."

"Okay. As I told your colleague, I went to dinner in halls, and I came back to my room around 9:30."

"9:30pm Spa time?"

"Yes."

"Was that your usual routine?"

"I wouldn't say I had a usual routine. I'd only arrived at St Margaret's about a week before."

"Was it your first time?"

"Yes."

"You were in the other centre for the first fortnight?"

"Yes."

"Did you bring Mrs Rajaram with you?"

"No."

"Why? If you don't mind my asking."

"Not at all. She wanted to spend some time with the children."

"So you came back to your room alone?"

"All alone."

"What did you do?"

"Read a book."

"What book?"

"Uh... Boswell's *Life of Johnson*. Does it matter?"

"For homework?"

"No."

"For pleasure?"

"Yes."

"And what time did you call Hector?"

"I'm sorry, who is Hector?"

"Hector is the male prostitute you paid to steal documents from Prudence Egwu's house shortly after he was found murdered."

Chris bounced on his chair. Oates folded his notebook shut.

"I'll be honest with you, Mr Rajaram. Chris. I don't think you killed Prudence Egwu. I think that you might know why someone would want him dead. I think that the touchcard records will show you exiting St Margaret's to make a phonecall very shortly after the discovery of Prudence Egwu's body. I think that you have probably been very careful in your communications with Hector to date, doing everything in conversation via an intermediary with nothing written down or recorded, but this one time you will have been aware of the opportunity and the need to move fast, and I would guess that overcame your natural caution. I've got Hector's phone in my pocket with the call log. As I said, there's a lot of guesses in there. If they're wrong, you've got nothing to worry about. But if they're right then the sooner you tell me the whole story, the sooner I can be out of your office."

"I'm afraid I can't say anything further without a lawyer."

"You can do that. I can't formally interview you without your lawyer if you want one. But what I can do is arrest you. And I can do it now, and I can call up a few other officers in uniform from downstairs, just to make sure we all get safely to the patrol car."

Oates sat back, and allowed the image of Mr Rajaram being escorted in handcuffs past the smart receptionists and the kind of lawyers who won't settle for anything less than full reliance to sink in.

"It's amazing how hot the press are on this Avalon murder. Still, you'd know all about that, wouldn't you? I think they'd be very interested to hear that a director of a rival company was helping us with our inquiries."

Chris opened his mouth to speak, a look of outrage gathering momentum in his brows. Oates knew exactly what was coming. There was a class of British men and women to whom the police force was a dog chained in the yard, trained to bark at strangers only. They were the same people who were always amazed when they were arrested for being caught with cocaine, who were offended when they got towed for parking on double yellows. Question whether they thought the law should apply to everyone the same, and they would look at you like an idiot for asking. Apply the law to them, and they were amazed.

Then Chris closed his mouth again, and the rage vanished. He smiled at Oates, and stood up. There was a bowl of fruit on the desk, and he picked from it three oranges. He stayed standing behind his desk, and began to juggle them.

"Do you know where I learned to do this? On a company bonding weekend Human Resources sent me on. Circus skills. Me and the rest of the board, and some of the senior execs. Total waste of money, but now I know how to juggle."

"I'm not interested in the theft of some documents, Mr Rajaram."

"Chris."

"You're not even under caution. I'm interested in who killed Prudence Egwu. Just tell me what you know and I'll be gone."

"Alright. I don't know who killed him. And I don't know why anyone would want him dead. Look, we've had Hector working for us for some time, but I only saw Prudence Egwu at St Margaret's by accident. When I saw him I arranged for one of my employees to contact Hector and to tell him to go ahead, that the house would be empty for at least a month. And it would have been fine, only I came back from afternoon classes to find that someone had killed poor Prudence, and there were police all over the spa. I knew they would search his house eventually, and would take things as evidence. There might never be another chance to get the data. So I called up Hector myself, and told him it had to be now. The rest of it, everything I put in my statement, it's all true. I saw that guy going into his room at about 3am, and I heard a scuffle. I have trouble sleeping you see—"

"We understand that Prudence Egwu was reconstructing his brother's research."

Chris became guarded once again. He was waiting to discover how much Oates knew.

"Specifically, his research into the Tithonus Effect."

"You're aware of it? Well, it's bad. And it's becoming more pronounced. The human soul has its own trajectory you see, independent from the body, and independent from the faculties of intellect. The Treatment can restore and preserve your brain function at the level of a healthy twenty-year-old, but it can't re-invigorate the soul. When you cease to be excited by and take pleasure in life, you begin to have to do more extreme things to achieve stimulation. Also your capacity for empathy diminishes. We have seen some extremely bad cases here from clients who have received the Treatment from Nottingham, some of them bordering on psychopathy. When you consider the positions of power generally occupied by the new-young, you can see the danger."

"And Capability was working on a cure?"

"Capability Egwu suffered from this very badly. As a key developer of the Treatment he was one of the first to experience it, and also consequently one of the oldest men alive. I knew him very well, Inspector. He was a member of our church. He was an extremely active philanthropist, and he contributed a great deal to the lives of ordinary Londoners. But he also suffered from the depression which often seems the dark companion of genius. The Tithonus Effect exacerbated that depression and made him quite unstable. There were others in the church closer to Capability than I was, and I came to understand from them that Capability was working on a cure for the Tithonus Effect. From what we can tell he was very close to the completion of his research when he disappeared."

"And you wanted that research for yourself?"

"Not for myself, exactly."

"But you paid Hector to steal it."

"We became aware that Prudence was making progress into his brother's disappearance. We made him a very fair offer for anything he could recover of Capability's work, but he wouldn't hear of it."

"And you don't like hearing no. Hector says he sent you a sample of what he stole from Prudence Egwu. A couple of pages from one of the files."

"That is correct."

"What was in them?"

"It was a joke. A prank of some sort."

"So tell me the joke."

"It was a series of articles about something called Sudden Accent Syndrome. When people get a bump on the head, and wake up speaking with an Australian accent. Or they get hit by a car and then they only speak French, or German or something."

"Can I see these articles?"

By way of answer, Chris rose from his desk and walked over to a large metallic chest of drawers in the corner of the room. His quick fingers danced the code, and he pulled out a couple of pieces of paper.

"You thought it was a joke, but you didn't throw them away."

Chris shrugged. He scooped a stapler off the corner of his desk with a flourish, and neatly clicked the corner of the pages together, before setting them on the desk in front of Oates. His movements still held a residue of the Great Spa, a kind of physical exuberance which was oddly incongruous with his suit and the office setting.

"Is there anything else you want to tell me?" Oates asked.

"Like what?"

"Earlier today I killed a boy. He had a gun and I shot him. The girl he was with knew I'd been to see Hector. Do you know anything about that?"

"No, Inspector. I'm afraid I don't know anything about that."

"He knew he was going to die. The boy. I found a card in his pocket, dated today, saying he was going to die." Oates hadn't meant to say anything further. Vocalising what he had seen on the card, it sounded unreal. He was acutely aware that if he had heard someone else saying it, he would think they had cracked. Chris, however, merely nodded and looked thoughtful.

"Well, if something like that happened to me, I would assume it was a message. Have you taken life before? Do you feel guilty?"

He did feel guilty, horribly guilty, and tired. Not just for the boy in the shopping mall, but for a lifetime of violence. He had killed six men that he knew of, maybe more he didn't, tracers fired in the night that might have punctured some frightened stranger on the other side of the shifting line. At the time each one had seemed, not justified exactly, but normal. In the course of something he should be doing. The thing was, though, that over time his views of what was normal, of what was right had changed, but the deaths had stayed the same. The dead never changed, they just hung around at the edge of your conscience, waiting for a gap to open up so they could come in and trash the place. Oates stood up to leave, and Chris came around the desk to shake his hand.

As their flesh touched, Oates felt the urge to crush his fingers, to slam his face into the desk, and there was another problem. His taste for violence hadn't gone away, it was his capacity to deal with the after effects that had worn out. He was like an alcoholic with a damaged liver. All of these thoughts coalesced around the man opposite as their hands clasped.

"Something I've always wondered," Oates said, not letting go of his hand. "How do you act like you do, if you really believe in God and the Bible and all that stuff?"

"What do you mean?"

"Stealing. Lying. Just making money, even."

"This may be difficult for you to believe, Inspector, but I have devoted a great deal of thought to that very question. Jesus is no fan of monopolies. It does us no good. We would have taken this technology, and we would have opened up the market. Lowered prices, democratised the process, maybe even brought the Treatment within reach of the average consumer. And my conscience tells me that is something God would approve of."

Somewhere at the edge of perception, there was a scent that made Oates's soft palate tense up. He felt the pressure of the other man's proximity, and remembered Casey telling him the new young smelt different.

"So you would have given it away for free?"

"No, not for free. But cheaper than our rivals."

The two men gazed at one another. Chris's eyes were open and honest, and he did not look away.

Oates had encountered the same guileless sincerity in professional criminals. When he had first joined the police, he had conducted himself under a false premise; that other human beings are basically similar to you. He thought of criminals as people who had buried the guilt which their crimes would have inspired in Oates had he committed them. If something was buried, it could be dug up, and he had considered that process of excavation to be part of the job.

Later, he had to accept that some people were simply incapable of recognising their own guilt. It had driven him mad, as a young officer. He had longed for the moment of catharsis, when the impact of remorse finally broke through upon the conscience of the perpetrator. He carried the suffering of the victims of the crimes he investigated inside himself, and he wanted to pass the knowledge of that suffering on to the criminals. But some of them refused to accept it, so slowly it built up inside him, silting up the channels of his faith in man.

Chris was the same. The truth of his nature sat between them like a bill in a restaurant, and if he wasn't going to pick it up, Oates would have to. He could never force Chris to see himself as he really was. You could drag him by his hair and his chin to the mirror, and he would see only a victim of brutality. It was Oates's consciousness of that sense of victimhood thirsting for justification which helped him to rein in the anger that had threatened to overwhelm him. He let go of Chris's hand.

"You'll be hearing from us about the break-in," he said, turning aside to pick up his raincoat.

"I understand. 'As you sow, so shall ye reap.' Listen, Inspector, I don't know your first name."

"Oates is fine."

"Well, Oates, would you do something for me?"

He went to rummage in one of the drawers of his desk. Oates waited in front of his chair, his coat folded over his arm. Chris thrust something into his hand.

"Take this. I'll pray for you."

It was a leaflet for The Church of the Present Resurrection. *Whosoever liveth and believeth in me shall never die – John 11:26.* It was conceived as a genuine act of charity, and in that assumption it became an act of violence. Chris Rajaram wielded his sincerity like a bludgeon.

Oates crushed the leaflet in his fist, and a memory came back to him – the leaflet he had removed from under his windshield that morning. He dropped the scrunched up ball of paper on the floor, and as he left he felt the pitying gaze of the criminal upon him. Some of that pity might even be justified, for Chris seemed more content in his abominable certainty than was Oates in his torment of doubt. He was shaking with rage.

The receptionist wished him a pleasant evening on the way out. The lobby television showed a shot of a street with a car burning. Figures in hoods stood at one end, and figures in helmets at the other. A banner ran underneath them in yellow, with the words 'Unconfirmed reports of a second fatal shooting by police in East London'. Oates wondered briefly what could have happened, before realising the story was about him. He stopped and stared at the television. Seeing the words on the screen brought the reality home to Oates more firmly than the actual experience had done. It gave him the sick dream-lurch of realising you are naked at the important meeting, that your teeth are falling in to the sink.

As he stood in the lift, he looked at the first of the articles Chris had retrieved from the cabinet. It was a printout from a medical website detailing the case history of a young Norwegian woman, Astrid L., who had been struck on the head by shrapnel during an air-raid in 1941. When she awoke from a brief coma, she spoke her native language with a heavy German accent, and she found herself being shunned by her own people as a German spy. The second was a newspaper clipping about a Hindi-speaking boy from an Indian slum in the 1990s who had suffered from severe migraines, and had awoken one morning to discover that he spoke only English, despite never having learned it. A local sadhu had proclaimed him the reincarnation of a famous American scientist. He shuffled quickly through the other pages, and they were all the same.

He could see why Chris had thought Hector was playing him – the last article was printed out from a website called *www. talesoftheunexplained.com*. But it wasn't in Hector's interest to have cheated his employer. The boy Oates had met would just have wanted to get the exchange over with as fast as possible. If the wild stories really did represent a part of the research which Prudence Egwu had managed to reconstruct from his brother's work, what did it mean? Had the famous scientist been a crank? He could have checked the articles against the rest of the contents of the file of course, if he had still had it.

The carpark beneath the offices of United Sciences was in the basement of the building, and so focused was he on thinking about the case, he didn't see the man sitting in the passenger seat of his car until he was fishing the keys from his pocket. The man was waiting for him. The light above the rear view mirror was switched on, but the angle of illumination gave no more than an impression of the contours of his features, lighting the nose and wrinkled forehead and poking black holes for the eyes. Oates took out his gun, and pointed it at the man through the windshield. The man raised his gloved hands, and put them on the dashboard in front of him. He drummed his fingers once, but otherwise remained quite still. Oates walked around the car keeping him covered through the glass, and with one hand he opened the passenger side door.

"Get out."

His voice rang oddly loud on the bare concrete walls. The man swung his legs over the seat of the car and stood up, taking the opportunity to stretch out his back. In the harsh fluorescent lights he looked not only older than Oates, but old. His vertebrae cracked. Oates heard laughter, and looked up to see a young couple twenty metres away, loading presents into the boot of their car.

"Turn around."

The man put his hands on the roof of the car and spread his legs without being asked. In a holster at his side was a police issue handgun. Oates took it out, and found that the safety was on, with a round in the chamber. He tucked it into the waistband of his own trousers, and searched the stranger's pockets. In a little leather folder in the inside breast was a police ID. Oates spun him round and held the picture beside his face. He was so utterly without expression in the flesh that the resemblance between him and the formal photograph was almost comical.

"Eustace Morrison, Internal Investigations. You didn't wait for us at the shooting."

"I was in the middle of a murder enquiry."

The young man loading his car dropped a parcel, and the woman shrieked again with laughter. The man looked over at them with the camouflage of a friendly smile on his lips.

"Could we speak in your car, Detective Chief Inspector?"

Oates nodded and Morrison stubbed out his smile like a cigarette as he sat back down in the passenger seat. Oates walked around the car and let himself in. He pulled the gun out of his waistband before sitting down. The two men sat beside one another, staring forwards.

"You're here to arrest me for leaving the scene of the shooting?"

"No."

"Alright."

Oates gave him back his weapon. Morrison checked the round was still in the chamber and the safety on, and popped it back into his holster.

"We're aware of your investigation. In fact, it has crossed over into another investigation we've been conducting for some time. Specifically the disappearance of Capability Egwu, and the involvement in that case of Superintendent John Yates."

"John?" He checked the rearview mirror. "I don't know anything about that."

"You know a good deal more than you think."

Oates laughed out loud. From the midst of his confusion, to be told he knew more than he thought by this arrogant stranger was too much. Morrison showed no surprise at his laughter. Oates had the feeling there was nothing on the earth that would surprise this man.

"It was Yates who deleted the photograph of Capability Egwu from the police file on the case," Morrison said. "Someone has gone through a similar process with respect to images of Capability Egwu stored on the internet, with the passport agency, with Cambridge University and anywhere he worked where he might have had an identity card."

He spoke so quietly that Oates found himself leaning in towards him. Up close, he smelled slightly of peppermint.

"We assumed that Capability Egwu had disappeared with the connivance of both Nottingham," Morrison continued, "or possibly rogue elements within Nottingham, and of senior figures in the Metropolitan Police. The attempts to expunge his image would suggest that he underwent some degree of reconstructive surgery."

"Do you have any photographs of him at all?"

"We have some from our own files."

"Why would he have wanted to disappear?"

"According to the profiles we prepared on him, Capability Egwu had a paranoid fear of being controlled."

"It's not paranoia if they really are out to get you," Oates said, and sat back in his seat.

Morrison ignored him. "There is tremendous interest in keeping the proprietary technology connected with the Treatment in Britain. Anything which could lead to that technology being transported abroad comes within our purview. We advised Capability to think of himself as part of the heritage of our country. We asked him to keep us informed of his movements. He failed to do so on a number of occasions, and we were in the process of considering how to proceed."

"And he got away from you?"

"We were unable to locate him, although we are fairly certain he remains in the country. When we failed to locate Mr Egwu himself, we shifted our attentions to the task of trying to reconstruct his research."

Whilst they were speaking, Oates was trying to fathom what it was that gave a man who actually looked old so much more authority than the new-young, even the most senior among them. Chris and Miranda were both of them the heads of international organisations. Everything in their manners and the way they were treated by others trumpeted their dominance. And yet in conversing with them, Oates never doubted the supremacy of his own will. By contrast, he felt himself being overmastered by the investigator.

The difference in effect could be partly explained by the residual significance of appearance. Oates was old enough to remember when most important men had looked like the one beside him, and those who looked young were green on the inside too. But that was not the whole story. Morrison had the stillness of absolute power. Oates intuited he could have arranged for the Treatment had he wanted it. It was the implied choice which lent him the extra authority. Here was a man who was comfortable with his own decay, with the fact of his own death, moment by moment. The others bore the scars of their fears on their flawless faces – they were terrified of their mortality. That was why Oates could look down on them.

Morrison reached into the footwell, and when he came back up he was holding a toy motorcycle in brightly coloured plastic, the spokes picked out in shiny metallic paint. Mike must have left it there on the way to or from school. Morrison handled it with what in another man might have passed for absent-mindedness.

"You're not just in internal investigations, are you?"

"You were a soldier, I believe, before you were a policeman."

"So you're what? A spy?"

"I am a civil servant. The boy you shot was a member of the Mortal Reformers."

"Yes."

"The girl who stole the documents from you is known to us. We believe she lives and operates from the slums in the Underground tunnels beneath the Strand. We want you to attempt to retrieve those pages."

"I just killed her friend and almost shot her in the back," Oates said. "Why would she talk to me?"

"Because the Mortal Reformers will know that Hector sent out a sample of his materials, and will infer that you collected it from the offices of United Sciences. We believe they have been watching Hector for some time."

Oates thought back to his walk down Haggerston Road, and the smoke-filled car with the three figures.

"The Mortal Reformers are as keen to secure the research and all copies of the research as we are."

"What do they want with it?"

"That's not your concern."

"If I'm going to negotiate with them, I need to know what they want."

"We don't know what they want to do with it. We assume they intend to use it as a bargaining chip. They have a number of demands and some key operatives in custody."

"The boy, he was carrying a card. It said he was going to die today."

"That frightened you, did it?"

The two men stayed staring straight ahead.

"The agents of the Mortal Reformers fill out those cards whenever they go on active service. It helps them to create an air of mystery, which in turn helps them recruit among the real-young. If he'd survived today's mission, he would have thrown the card away, and filled out another one tomorrow. Don't be embarrassed. It's a simple enough trick, but we only figured it out ourselves the first time we caught one alive."

"What happens if I tell you to put that toy down and get the hell out of my car?"

"We're not mobsters, Detective Chief Inspector. But you shot a boy in front of an early evening crowd of shoppers in the midst of social unrest. If you feel unable to cooperate with us, you must expect that the findings of the report into the shooting will be unsympathetic, and will most likely indicate prosecution to be in the public interest."

He spoke with the candour of a doctor taking pains not to patronise a patient. He had the air of a man who has spent his life doing things he does not enjoy, not by compulsion but by choice. There was a wedding ring on the hand that fretted with the toy motorcycle, but something told Oates that this was a piece of camouflage no more real than the smile he had assumed for the couple loading their presents. He had the feeling that he was glimpsing an alternative destiny, looking at the kind of man he might have become without children.

"It's up to you, Detective Chief Inspector. I won't insult you by trying to pressure you further. You know the context, you know the consequences. I've left an earpiece in the glove compartment if you need to contact me." Morrison made to leave the car, but stopped himself. "Oh, and of course, we need to take a copy of the pages."

"What pages?" Oates asked.

"The pages you collected from the offices of United Sciences."

"No."

"As I said, we need to take a copy."

"You don't get anything until I know what's waiting for me at the other end."

Morrison leant forward in his seat, and squinted up at the lights overhead. Oates tightened the grip on the gun in his hand.

"Alright," he said at length, and opened the door. The greasy breeze running down from the street passed into the car, and Oates was grateful for the cold.

"One more thing," Oates said.

"What is it?"

"What did you give Grape? What did you do to her, what did you offer her to set me up?"

"Excuse me?"

"No one knew I was going to see Hector except Grape. The Mortal Reformers were there already, I get that. But you weren't. So why did she tell you?"

"Ah, I see. We did not speak to Grape. Grape does not exist."

"She's one of your agents?"

"Grape is any number of our agents. She is a fiction, a personality protocol and a voice modulator. We use her to keep tabs on some of the more idealistic members of the intelligence and law enforcement community. After the death of your daughter it was felt that you would be more accommodating to a young woman you perceived as being in need of protection."

He set the toy motorcycle with great care on the dashboard. He lowered the small plastic kickstand so that it stood upright. For a moment after he took his hands away, he held them palm out in front of the little toy, warning it to remain upright. Then he got out of the car and walked away under the lengths of strip lighting. Oates thought about getting out of the car and shooting him dead. Before he could make up his mind however, as Morrison neared the fire exit to the stairwell, a father with his children pushed it open, and he held it for them. When he disappeared through the door, it was as if a stone had been dropped into the deep sea. Oates had a feeling he could spend the rest of his life looking for the man who had called himself Eustace Morrison, and he would find no trace of him.

Oates spent some time getting to know the threat that had been made. He had no doubt of the spook's sincerity. No one was powerful enough to invent a crime from nothing to frame a senior officer, but Oates could make out the ambiguities of the incident into which a hostile investigator could poke his fingers, the angles of his vulnerability. Why had he shot the boy in the back? Why had he escalated a situation in a crowded shopping mall which led to an exchange of gunfire?

Had he been drinking? There was the pint in the pub (had it been a couple?) and the glass in Prudence Egwu's house. Why had he not waited for the internal investigators? Why had he disobeyed a direct order from John? Why had he allowed the situation to disintegrate at the Great Spa to the point where John had to step in? Had not his whole conduct that day been a chain of erratic decisions and criminally negligent actions, leading inevitability to the tragic death of a promising young man? Anyone shot by the police turned out to have shown promise, even if their actual achievements up to the point of their death were mostly in the field of violent crime. He could see himself conducting the questioning of the hypothetical perpetrator of such a sequence of calamities, and it would not go well for them.

For himself, he would not have cared. But he could imagine how things would be for Lori and the boys, being the family of a man partly blamed for inciting the city to burn itself down. Then there was suspension, the possibility of prison. They wouldn't get by for long without his salary, such as it was, and then there would be the hostel like the one in which he had found Hector, and Lori would be the woman standing in her dressing gown in the cold doorway with nothing to defend herself against the city but the strength of her bitterness and a steaming wooden spoon.

His mind drifted back to the nights in the barracks at Camp Fortitude, waiting with his hands behind his head, staring at the ceiling between patrols. Some of his squad had photographs of their families pinned above their beds, but Oates had a picture of his motorbike, and had been grateful for it. Some soldiers only made it through because of their families, but for Oates it had been the other way around. He had only made it through the desert because there was no one waiting for him back home. Every risk he took, every decision he made, he made for himself alone. If Lori and the kids had been back home then, he would have felt them clinging to his feet as he ran, slowing down the decisions which, in battle, are made immediately or not at all.

Now here he was in battle once again, only this time the photographs hemmed him in. In the end, loving shows weakness of character, because it means you can't get by on your own. A real soldier, a real policeman, must be able to get by on their own.

Grape was the proof of it – he hadn't been betrayed by someone else, he had betrayed himself. After all the middle-aged women he had seen diddled out of their savings by nothing more than a photograph on a dating site and some voice modulation software, he had fallen for the idea of someone he wanted to believe in. He remembered how proud he had been at identifying her accent, and pinpointing her in his imagination to one of a couple of Hackney estates. He found it hard to admit, but he had even daydreamed about meeting her. Of pulling over to help out some girl in distress on the midnight pavements, and recognising the voice in the thank you. His motives had proved as transparent as that of a dog staring at food on a table.

The image of himself and his suffering being discussed dispassionately in a room full of professional men and women, their faces green with the verdigris of a screen glowing in the dark, came to him with extraordinary clarity. He was not special or unpredictable, he was not a creature with independent agency, he was nothing but a bundle of emotional needs awaiting manipulation. He had loved his daughter, and that love had exposed him. He felt an intense hatred for Grape, for the person he knew did not exist, and then another wave of grief washed over him.

Darkness proper was in the city streets now, the dome of St Paul's Cathedral illuminated on the skyline. Lines of riot police stood shield-locked in front of the Old Bailey. Groups of men and women with hoods up and bandanas over their mouths jeered at the evening commuters and tripped at their heels. The city was changing hands. The diners in the restaurants at the top of the skyscrapers would be able to watch the pitched battle in the streets beneath like Roman aristocracy cheering on the clash of gladiators. But when dinner was over, they would have to pass through the battle on their way home. Masked figures and uniformed figures wandered in the traffic. Oates headed west to the address that Eustace Morrison had given him.

His EARPIECE STARTED to sound. "*Number unknown, number unknown.*" He didn't want to speak to anyone, but he was aware of the possibility that Bhupinder might try to call.

"Answer."

"Hello, have I got Detective Chief Inspector Oates there?"

"Who's this?"

"Oh, I'm terribly sorry to bother you. It's Mr Prendegast. You know, from Michael's school."

"Oh yeah. Hi."

"I just wanted to know if you and your wife were free the Thursday after next. Sheila and I are organising some Christmas drinks. I was hoping you might be able to come."

Mr Prendegast cleared his throat. Oates pulled over to the side of the road, and sat in the bus lane with his emergency lights blinking. He rubbed his eyes with his gloved hand. Something in the teacher's voice kept him from hanging up.

"I'm don't know, Mr Prendegast. Lori has our diary."

A fire engine screamed past, extending an invisble hand to rock his car gently on its suspension.

"Oh, that's quite alright. I understand, it's just the same with me and Sheila. Where would we be without our better halves, eh?"

"We'll call you about it tomorrow."

"That would be ideal."

"Goodbye."

"Oh, there was one more thing, while I've got you."

"What is it?"

"Well, there's a man in our garden. In the back garden of our house."

It was then Oates knew what was strange about Mr Prendegast's voice. He was almost whispering.

"What?"

"There's a man in the back garden."

"What's he doing?"

"He's smoking and looking over the back wall into the street. Only I've tried ringing 999, and our local police station, and the number our community officer gave us for noise complaints when number 39 started throwing parties. Only none of them seem to be available at the moment. And you very kindly gave me your card."

Mr Prendegast cleared his throat. Oates heard another voice, querulous in the background, and the teacher said: "Alright, alright Sheila. And we can hear chanting. Coming from the High Street."

"Are you in the ground floor, basement, or first floor flat?"

"First floor. We don't know the people in the basement, there's a lovely Asian couple on the ground floor."

"Get your family together in one room. It's too late to leave the city, you'll attract more attention in your car. You need to stay away from the windows."

"There's bars on the basement windows. I remember the agent making a point..."

"Good. Can you jam your letterbox shut?"

"I think so."

"Jam it shut, and gather your family and your neighbours in the flats above and below in one ground floor room. Get yourself and your family dressed in warm clothes and get together everything you might need if you have to leave the house. I mean insulin shots and inhalers, not photo albums. If you have packing or insulation tape, place it over your windows in a cross. If you have a fire extinguisher or blankets in the house, bring them with you. Keep a radio with you and listen out for instructions. The disturbances last night were limited to looting and arson. Remember that, there's no reason why anyone should try to hurt you unless you give them a reason. Keep the lights on in the room and if anyone approaches, all of you make a lot of noise. Bang your sticks and shout. If they keep coming, don't try to fight back, just get out. Agree on your exit routes back and front, and arrange a place to meet if you get split up. Mr Prendegast, it's important to realise you're on your own. No one will come until tomorrow. Mr Prendegast?"

"I'm here."

"Remember, they're just kids with masks. If you can handle Harry five days a week, you can deal with this."

Mr Prendegast let out a burst of laughter, brought up short by embarrassment. Oates heard his wife say, "What is it, what does he say?"

"Thank you, Detective Chief Inspector. Good luck tonight."

"And you, Mr Prendegast. I'll see you in school on Monday."

"Quite right. See you in school."

"End call."

A man in a suit ran past the window of Oates's car, heading for the Embankment tube station. Oates sat in his car and watched the traffic. He thought of Mr Prendegast, alone with his wife and his neighbours, frightened but ready to stick by the people he loved. All over London he knew there would be little scenes like that. Oates was a father and a husband too. He wasn't going to leave the city again tonight without his family.

THE END OF Fleet Street was closed off with police barriers. He took the right up Kingsway, and cut back down through Covent Garden, working his way along the narrow streets until he reached Trafalgar Square. The evening air was hazy with condensation, and the lighted globe at the top of the Coliseum hovered like a ghost on the shoulders of the white marble statues bearing it above the rooftops of London. The roads around the West End were full of cars that had reached their destination. Young men and women filled the front and back seats, and shouted from the windows, rolled down despite the cold. It was as if all of London supported the same football team, and that football team had won the treble.

The air was filled with shouts and whistles, and the music of car stereos. He saw a four by four parked in the stationary traffic with two girls sitting on the edge of the open sunroof, passing a bottle of sparkling wine between their smoking lips. As he pushed back south the street seized up like a long muscle in the cold, and he mounted the pavement. He nosed slowly through the throng of pedestrians, and whilst some of them shouted and slapped the bonnet, others cheered, and one girl exposed her breasts to him. At the police barriers at the entrance to Trafalgar Square he held out his warrant card.

"I need to get through. It's an emergency."

"Sorry, sir. We've closed down the square and no one's to come through, not them lot or us."

"Who's in charge?"

She shook her head.

"You won't be coming through here."

He spun the wheel away from her, and gunned the engine. The officers scattered, and Oates had a few clear metres before he hit the milling crowd of protestors already in the square. One of the policemen drew his gun, and the female bobby who had stopped him slapped the pistol down with her hand. Oates saw her in the wing mirror as she began to speak ominously into her radio. He jammed his hand on the horn, and the crowd made way for his beat up car. The atmosphere was friendly, the presumptious friendliness of a drunk at the bar, with the same sense of incipient violence.

Some of the men and women were wearing hoods, or had scarves tied over their faces. Someone had spilled fuel over the water in the fountain, and had set it alight, so that a low liquid fire blossomed in the stone tub. Advertising lights from the nightclubs lanced the sky, projected with huge rooftop spotlights on the underside of the clouds. With their strange symbols and garish colours, they looked like beacons calling on competing superheroes to come and save the city.

An enterprising group of communists had set up a makeshift stall, and were selling face masks and hammer and sickle t-shirts by the bus stop. And t-shirts with something else printed on them, something which made his heart lurch... Oates strained to look, but the gap through which he had seen them closed as swiftly as it had opened up.

A boy was spraypainting a Mortal Reform symbol on the flank of the bronze lion at the base of Nelson's Column. Oates imagined the great green beast shaking its mane, stepping off the stone pedestal and catching the hooligan's head in its mighty metal jaws.

The vividness of the vision startled him, and it raised a sense of déjà-vu. It was kin to the feeling he had had in St

Margaret's, when the summer evening had seduced him into suspending his disbelief in the charade of a river. It was the feeling that fantasy and reality could swap places whilst your thoughts were elsewhere. The protests were transfiguring the city in the way of a deep and sudden snowfall, making the familiar strange.

As he pushed deeper into the square, he came into the midst of a group dressed in identical t-shirts. As if he had summoned the image from his own mental recesses, the face of Dwayne Jeffries suddenly surrounded him, pressing in on his windows. The ghost of the boy he had killed was there on every side, smiling in a school photo. Oates almost screamed before he realised that this was not a horde of avenging spirits, but a picture printed on the bellies of the people in the crowd. Another symbol of protest for the disaffected people of London, mounted on a t-shirt. They were chanting his name. Oates was willing to bet there wasn't a soul in all that riot who felt the boy's death as much as he did himself. He gripped his sanity with both hands as the car inched past the many faces of his victim.

On the other side of the square, the police just waved him through. The cordon here was not so tight, and although the policemen Oates had nearly run over were less than a hundred metres away, with the chaos in the square they might as well have been on the other side of the world. Consequence was slow to make its way through the packed streets. Oates actually found himself gasping for breath as the grip of the crowd relaxed, and he came through onto the empty road.

Oates left the car down one of the side streets leading off the Strand to the Embankment. With the Trafalgar exit shut down and the blockade at Aldwych, the Strand itself was relatively quiet. The tubes were still running, and office workers were heading down towards Charing Cross Station. A family were arguing with a policeman about tickets they had got to see *Cats*, and how were they supposed to get to the theatre with the streets all shut off they would like to know? He saw a group of Japanese tourists with their guide standing on the station drive, deep in discussion. They looked to be deciding whether to observe this fascinating collective expression of the English culture at first hand. One of the more intrepid husbands in a green raincoat had gone over to stand on a transformer box, and, steadying himself with one hand on a lamppost, held his camera above his head to take aerial shots of the interior of the square.

He looked at the address the spook had given him, traipsing up and down the Strand for want of numbers on the doors. He walked past it several times before he spotted it, because it wasn't like any club he had ever seen. It was nothing more than a metal door, the kind to be found on old fashioned lifts, where the metal panels fold into one another like a concertina when pulled across. It was covering the entrance to the disused Strand tube station. He looked between the metal slats, and made out chinks of light in the interior. He banged on the door with his fist. Nothing happened. He banged again.

"We're closed."

"Police."

"Piss off."

"Open the door."

"Come back in a couple of hours."

Oates kept hammering his fist against the gate. No one came, but in his frustration he tried to force it open, and found it unlocked. Inside the sliding metal gate, the tiled hall of the former tube station was bathed in the warm light of a huge globe suspended from the ceiling. At the bottom of the milky glass he could make out the shadows of dead insects. The walls were tiled in green and white, and the old wooden ticket booth still stood in the corner. Behind the glass stood a tall, broad transvestite in heavy make-up.

"My name's Florence Agogo, but you can call me Flo. What can I do for you, mister…?"

The voice was soft and penetrating. Very different from the gruff sound that had told him to piss off, but he was pretty certain they had both come from the same mouth.

"Detective Chief Inspector."

"Aren't you a big one. Have you come to protect us from all those ragamuffins outside?"

"I'm looking for a girl."

"Will I do?"

"This one."

Oates held up the photograph the spook had given him. Flo gave an enormous sigh.

"So romantic, running about the city looking for your sweetheart on a night like this. It's enough to warm the cockles of a cynical girl's heart."

"Don't fuck about."

She stared at him through the glass, and pursed her glittery lips. Oates held her gaze.

"Alright, let's see it."

Oates handed her the photograph through the little partition. She had to scrabble a bit to get her scarlet nails between the edge of the photograph and the smooth metal surface of the counter. When she had it, she held it up the wrong way round in front of her face, and looked at the blank backing.

"Never seen her before. She's a bit plain mind."

Oates punched the glass of the booth and cracked it. Flo gave a theatrical scream and pressed her hands to her fake breasts.

He punched again and radial cracks spread to the corners of the glass. The third punch smashed the glass and Oates shoved his fist through, the jagged edges cutting at his wrists as they rolled up his sleeve. He grabbed for her, but she dodged and Oates got a fistful of wig. It came away in his hands, revealing sparse brown hair combed flat beneath a tight flesh-coloured net. Flo screamed again, snatching for the hairpiece, which was tangled now in the fingers of Oates's glove, and glittering with shards of glass. Oates was shouting too.

"Take a closer look. Take all the time you need."

"Can I help you, sir?"

The voice was loud but calm. Oates turned without removing his hand from the glass to find a smartly dressed man standing in the centre of the lobby behind him. Flo stopped struggling.

"Florence, perhaps you'd like to take a few moments to tidy yourself up."

"She started it, Mr Ingram," Flo said, pointing at Oates.

"We can't have you greeting the guests like that."

"No, Mr Ingram."

"Why don't you go through and take a seat at the bar," the man said to Oates. "We're still setting up, I'm afraid, but we should be able to manage a drink. Whisky, yes?"

Oates removed his hand from the glass with a great deal more care than he had thrust it through. He was bleeding from several cuts around the wrist, and he rolled his sleeve down to staunch the blood. The man led him across the marble floor of the ticket office and down into what must once have been the lobby. This area was filled with plush leather seats around a low stage, with a small bar at one side. On the stage were two women in ballerina costumes stretching and making simple turns. Their movements showed an uncanny doubling, and as he watched he realised they were identical twins. The place was getting ready for the night. Someone switched on music with a low beat. Oates took the whisky offered him. He showed the manager the girl's photo.

"Lara thought you might be coming round."

"She's the one who sent those kids after me?"

Mr Ingram nodded. "You killed a good boy out there."

"That good boy tried to shoot me," Oates said, "How did you know him?"

"They come into the club sometimes. I'll just find someone to take you down."

The man was gone for perhaps fifteen minutes. During that time Oates finished his drink, and called for another. The atmosphere in the club was like the backstage area of a theatre before the big show, and he found himself buoyed up by the infectious excitement. One of the barman, who wore a smart red waistcoat, was turning brightly coloured bottles over the back of his wrist, flinging them over his shoulder like a juggler and muttering: "Who's the best? Who's the best?" under his breath. A heavily tattooed man with snakes wound around his muscles walked down the stairs on his hands, jumping from palm to palm on each step. Someone's girlfriend sat on the stage, a skinny young thing smoking and trying not to look out of place.

There was no talk or awareness of the impending riots outside – though perhaps there was an extra charge in the air, a brittleness like that among the policemen swapping jokes with one another in their cordon outside One New Change. The feeling of self-conscious bravery that came with behaving normally in the face of impending disaster. It seemed to Oates a peculiarly English quality. It was almost as if they relished danger as an opportunity to prove their imperturbability, the way a bullfighter goes into the ring to walk with his back to the bull in his fancy clothes.

WHEN THE MANAGER reappeared, he was accompanied by a man chewing gum. The gum chewer stared at Oates in a way that made him close his fists.

"Okay, she will see you," Mr Ingram said, "Carlos here is going to take you down."

Oates rose from his stool. The manager appraised him at his full height.

"You are quite large. I hope you're not scared of small spaces."

He smiled at his own joke, and Carlos chuckled. He turned away without speaking, and Oates followed him from the bar down a spiral staircase sectioned off from the lobby by a red velvet rope. As they moved further into the earth, the air grew warm and close. At the first landing, perhaps twenty feet or so beneath the surface of the street, there was a small door marked VIP, and Oates caught the glisten of painted skin through the portal window. The staircase turned and turned down into the ground, and soon Oates had lost all sense of how many steps he had descended. He wanted to ask Carlos where they were going, but something told him that his guide would simply laugh at his querulousness, and he didn't want to give him the satisfaction.

With Carlos moving ahead of him, he was able to observe the way the front pocket of his sweatshirt bulged and bounced when he descended the steps. His hand seemed to find its way to the lump under the fabric every minute or so to check it was still there. Carlos was carrying a concealed weight he wasn't used to, and Oates was glad he'd cleaned his own gun in Chris's office. Take any opportunity to maintain your weapon and clean your socks. Army rules to live by.

The music of the club above faded and was replaced by the sound of music coming up from below. At last they came out into another space decorated with green and white tiles in the style of the entrance hall above. The platform of the old tube station had been transformed into a kind of shanty town, with a whole series of makeshift buildings standing with their backs to the curved wall and their mouths opening onto a thin strip of pavement along the yellow line that in working stations demarcated the safe distance the commuters have to stand from an approaching tube train.

The shacks were designed to create privacy rather than to provide shelter in the enclosed space, and so many of them were little more than fabric stretched over frames, like the screens around a hospital bed. Looking down the length of the station, Oates could see one such construction with walls made of grubby white sheets. Inside there burned an electric light, creating on the external wall the silhouette of a figure reading a book, distended to great size by its proximity to the lamp. Along with the strings of Christmas lights that crisscrossed the roof of the tunnel, there were lines of washing hanging in the column of air that moved steadily down the tube. Among the clothes were several different sets of uniforms he recognised. There was a nurse's blue smock, and a series of branded t-shirts from an upmarket coffee place.

The pavement was too narrow for two men to pass abreast, and so at regular intervals there were sets of makeshift stairs leading down onto the tracks. As the space against the station walls was domestic, the space between the tracks was commercial. It was like an old-fashioned market, rows of stalls hung with foods, clothes, hardware, books, magazines, coloured lights, Japanese fans, breathing masks, children's toys and live animals in cages and glass tanks. The music he had heard winding its way up the stairs was coming from speakers mounted on the corners of one of the stalls.

In the well closest to Oates's feet, a woman wearing dirty cycling shorts and a t-shirt cut off at the stomach was cooking crabs. She was wearing a single rubber glove, and she reached down and picked up a handful from a bucket of dirty water beside her on the ground, before tossing them on to the skillet, a corrugated sheet of metal sitting on a barrel of low fire.

They danced frantically for a few seconds, the woman herding them with a short paddle when they came close to escaping. There was a hiss of moisture almost as if the little animals were screaming, and then they died on their feet, turning brown and crisping. As Oates descended the steps, he saw that the fresh crabs moving in the filthy water were a nacreous translucent white, as if they too had existed for generations in the caverns under the streets.

They had been travelling down the tunnel for three hundred metres or so when Carlos stopped. Oates had allowed himself to fall back a little when the two of them had left the relative safety of the shanty town, and pulled up behind him. He leant against a concrete pillar and hooked the hem of his jacket away from his holster, ready to take cover and pop the gun if Carlos' shand slipped into the front pocket of his sweatshirt. Carlos went instead for the pockets of his trousers, and produced a long length of rag. It was filthy, and Oates expected him to blow his nose on it, but instead he hung it over his shoulder. He dug around again and came up with a white plastic cable tie.

"You must be bloody joking," Oates said, nodding at the cable tie.

Carlos frowned. He had obviously been looking forward to telling Oates he would have to go blindfolded and tied up, and was irritated that Oates had pre-empted him. The two of them stared at one another. Neither moved. Oates could hear the drip, drip of water in the echoing hollow of the disused tunnel and, somewhere in the distance, the rumble of a tube train bearing commuters in the parallel universe of the city of London.

"Lara says you come in a blindfold with your hands behind your back or you don't come at all."

"What if I refuse?"

"Then maybe you don't come and you don't get to leave either," Carlos said, and pulled the stock of the pistol from his sweatshirt pocket, showing it to Oates. From what Oates could see, it looked a more serious prospect than the piece the boy had pulled on him in the shopping mall.

Oates decided to get the thing dealt with as quickly as possible. He put out his hands, with the wrists together. Carlos spat on the ground, and walked towards him, his heavy boots crunching on the gravel. Oates could feel the tension behind the bravado as he advanced, and the tickle of incipient triumph, as Carlos allowed himself a little foretaste of the pleasure he would feel at having an agent of the state to lead blindfold back to his comrades. When he was close enough he reached out with the cable tie. Oates jerked his wrists back suddenly, and Carlos gasped.

"Just playing," Oates said.

Carlos scowled at him, and went again for his wrists, meaning to grab them this time to stop him pulling the same trick. The movement created just enough momentum for Oates to seize Carlos's hands and yank him forward off his feet. He gasped as Oates lowered his head like a charging bull. Carlos's cheek bone met the intractable logic of his forehead with a crack loud enough to send back echoes from the ends of the empty tunnel. He sat down hard and curled into a ball, clutching his injury with both hands. The gun fell out of his sweatshirt onto the space between the tracks, and Oates picked it up.

"You alright?" Oates asked him.

"Ah, my face, you broke my fucking face!"

"Come here."

He took the back of Carlos's sweatshirt in one gloved hand and hoiked him upright. He picked up his chin with the other, and looked into his eyes. Both pupils were the same size, and when Oates shone the light from the torch into them they constricted. He had a lovely sunrise coming up on the left hand side of his face, but his nose was unbroken, and he could move his jaw up and down and left to right.

"You can head to the hospital for an x-ray after we're done, but you're fine for now. Put your hands behind your back."

Carlos did as he was asked. The headbutt had knocked ten years off him. If there was a hardened paramilitary core to the Mortal Reformers, Oates had yet to find it. He didn't fancy their chances against Miranda's army of groundsmen. He yanked the cable tie tight.

"On your knees," Oates said.

"What are you going to do?"

"I'm going to tie this blindfold across your eyes, and I don't want you kicking me in the balls when I do it."

"But... if I'm blindfolded, how will I be able to take you?"

"Fair point. Force of habit," Oates said, pointing to the packing tie. "We used a lot of these in the army."

With Oates now holding Carlos's gun in his back, the two of them trudged on down into the bowels of the city.

THEY BRANCHED OFF the disused tube tunnel into a service shaft. From there, Carlos indicated a metal door, the hinges rusted but glistening with fresh black grease. A short ladder led them down into the first of the sewers. A rill of foul water ran along the curved base, and coagulated lumps of fat and toilet paper clung to the walls. The air made Oates gag. The ceiling was so low he had to bend almost double, and still he scraped his bald patch on the dripping bricks. The heat of human enterprise in the city above had sunk into the ground, and he was sweating under his body armour. He wanted to wipe the moustache of perspiration from his lip, but with gloved hands filthy from the walls he didn't trust himself to touch his face. The beam of the torch jumped about in the blackness as he struggled to keep his footing. The pipe went on for perhaps thirty metres, but it seemed to Oates as if he had been travelling through that Stygian gloom for a good while when they finally came to the end.

The second sewer was broader. There was a ledge along the side, but the Victorian brickwork was still coated with grease, and it was all he could do not to slip into the murky stream below. From the smell and debris as much as his sense of direction, he reckoned they must be under Chinatown. He could hear the scuttling of rats in the dark. His guide was nimble and Oates struggled to keep up. At the back of his mind was the distant fear that if the man ahead contrived to lose him, he might never find his way back out.

He was more grateful than he cared to admit when they reached a new set of passages, different from both the nineteenth century sewers and from the service tunnels of the tube. The walls here were made up of the skinny bricks of Roman masonry. The floor beneath his feet was lined with slabs of good stone. The passage radiated the sheer age of London, the great history that made the riots above seem no more than the ancient city turning over in its sleep. In the distance, he could hear the sound of a river running underground.

"So you were in the army, yeah?" Carlos said to him. It was the first thing he had said since Oates had taken his gun.

"Yes."

"And you were in combat?"

"Yes."

"Where?"

"In the Middle East."

"Were you..."

"What?"

"S.A.S.?"

Oates almost laughed out loud, but managed to catch himself. Of course Carlos would want to think he had been defeated by some special forces ninja. *What the hell. If he wants to save face, and have a story to tell his mates which doesn't make him look a pillock, why not?*

"I can't really talk about it," Oates said, in the voice of portentous mystery he used when winding up Mike and Harry. "We did a lot of things that are... classified."

Carlos nodded, suitably impressed.

"I won't tell no one."

"Good."

The silence that slotted back into place after this exchange was almost companionable. Some minutes later, they came to a junction lined with fresh steel pipes.

"We have to stop here."

"Why?"

"There are guards on the doors up ahead. You need to give them a signal so's they know you're coming."

"What signal?"

Carlos nodded his head towards a large spanner leaning against the wall of the tunnel.

"Bang on the pipes. There's a code, I can do it but not with my hands tied."

Oates considered the request, and concluded that Carlos was sufficiently docile to be released. He had internalised the makeshift handcuffs on their long trudge through the sewers, and wasn't likely to try anything. Particularly not when he was unarmed, and in the presence of a lethal S.A.S. commando. Oates turned him round, and split the ties with a swift jerk of his knife. Carlos rubbed the red rings around his wrists and rolled his shoulders.

Carlos stooped for the big spanner. He brought the metal tool down hard on the pipes, sending a pattern of distinct strikes clanging around the corner of the tunnel into the gloom. Oates watched, gun still trained on Carlos but held light as a dowsing rod, ready to twitch in the direction of the gap ahead if anything emerged from the darkness. For a few seconds, nothing happened. Then someone beat on the pipes in answer.

There were two distinct sounds, one the original strike conducted through the air, the second the reverberations of the metal conduits. They mingled and masked one another, so that it was impossible to tell how far away the sentries were placed. They could be a hundred metres away, or just around the corner. Carlos gave the pipes a last hammer blow, as if for luck, and the two of them set off again down the tunnels.

It was the light he saw first. A curtain hung across an opening in the passage ahead, but it was full of holes, and little circles of light lay on it like coins on a table cloth. No one came out to meet them, but they could hear sounds coming from behind it. An indistinct mix of voices and machinery.

Oates could see how the posters and t-shirts of Dwayne had been produced so quickly. There were banks of printers down here, some larger presses for posters, and a couple of grubby photocopiers. Somewhere he was willing to bet he would find the 3D printer that had given the boy the gun that got him killed. Against one wall were stacks of placards attached to wooden handles, some bearing Dwayne's face, some bearing the faces of various politicians with devil's horns or similar adornments, some bearing slogans of Mortal Reform. One of the photocopiers was still spitting out warm leaflets. The automated motion was eerie in the empty room. The place felt not empty, but deserted.

The photocopying stopped abruptly. It had been masking a recorded voice emerging from speakers standing on a desk.

"The real mystery of modern democracy is that people continue to vote against their own best interests. Since the late 1980s in the United Kingdom, voters have continually given their support to parties promising low rates of taxation on the very richest, and have punished any party proposing wealth or land taxes, despite the fact that they themselves would not pay these taxes, and would benefit greatly from the improved public services such taxes would fund. This apparent contradiction can be explained when we consider the optimism and individualism propagated by consumer society. As children we are taught to believe in the inevitability of our own success, and as adults we vote to support not the class we are in, but the class to which we aspire and to which we feel we belong by right, if not in fact. Part of the difficulty in effecting democratic change exists because to do so involves an assault on this sense of self-worth. This sense of self-worth is no less potent for being based on a fallacy. The phenomenon is greatly exaggerated in the matter of the Treatment, for in voting against the interests of the new-young, the voter must accept not only the certainty of their own continuing poverty, but also the certainty of death. Failing to acquire the Treatment is, after all, the equivalent of accepting a death sentence. This is why we have come to believe that only direct action–"

Christ, not more bloody politics. Oates advanced towards the computer to shut it off. Carlos was still hanging back by the entrance. Oates was striding forward, reaching out for the switch, when the ground beneath him disappeared. He felt his weight shift instictively as his front foot came down on air, but it was too late. His momentum carried him forward, his arms flailed at the large greasy cloth that had been stretched over the hole in the floor, and in a panic he felt his whole big body plummet down into darkness.

WHEN HE CAME to, the first thing he saw was Carlos's face grinning down at him through the hatch in the roof. That suggested he had been only briefly stunned. He did a quick inventory of his limbs. He must have landed well, everything worked without too much complaint. He heard the sound of something skidding across the floor beside him, and turned his head. He was eye to toe with a steel-capped boot. Looking past it, he saw someone stoop to pick up the gun the boot had just kicked away from him. He could still hear the politics coming faintly from the speakers in the room above. Booby-trapping something you'd want to touch, that was a proper paramilitary trick. He chided himself for a lapse in his instincts.

The boots belonged to a tough looking woman in her thirties carrying a sawn off shotgun. There were a couple of other men in the room similarly armed. This was more like it. Oates actually felt grateful. He might have to come after some of these people one day if they kept going the way they were going. And if he made it out alive, of course. He didn't need the extra guilt of thinking they were all like Carlos and the kid he had shot in the mall.

The room into which he had fallen contained, in addition to the heavies, a bare mattress with faded stains, and a series of crates. Taking up almost the whole of one wall was an ancient map of the tunnels marked as the property of the Metropolitan Water Authority. Over the old blue ink of the pipe system, later hands had drawn in more pipes and conduits in red and black and green ink, crossing out some of the old tunnels, here and there scrawling words and dimensions and tidal timings in twenty different scripts. The whole thing looked like the art project of some particularly gifted primary school class.

In front of the map stood the girl who had stolen the file from him. She was wearing a grubby white vest and tracksuit bottoms, and towelling dry her wet hair.

"This the bloke from the New Change?" the tough looking woman said to the girl.

"That's him. He shot Dwayne."

"You're Lara, right?" Oates said to the woman.

"How did you know where to find me?"

"A man came to talk to me. After the shooting. He said he was in internal investigations, but I think he was a spook. He seemed to think I might be able to get that file back off you."

One of the blokes holding a shotgun laughed at this, but Lara didn't.

"He reckoned you were going to use it as a bargaining chip," Oates said.

"Just goes to show," she said.

"How do you mean?"

"They're all about the bargaining."

"Then why did you let me come down?"

"Hector sent a few pages from the file over to United before we got to you. We want them. We thought you might have them."

Oates heard a click behind him. He knew what it was without having to turn around. It could have been the hammers on one of the shotguns, but his money was on Carlos's pistol.

"There's no need for that," he said.

He stood up gingerly. His left ankle protested at his weight, and the knock to his head had rattled his brains. He pulled the pages from his pocket, and handed them to Lara. She took them, read through them briefly, and then removed a lighter from her pocket. She set fire to the corner and, when they were going, laid them down on the stone floor to burn out. As the fire died down, she looked quizzically at Oates.

"You don't seem that bothered."

"I'm not. I'm not here for the research. I'm trying to find out who killed Prudence Egwu."

"That's it?"

"That's it."

"It wasn't us if that's what you were thinking. I'd be speaking to your spook."

"What was in his research?"

"Right. Like I'd tell you."

"I think it might help me to understand why he died," Oates said. "I brought you what you wanted. Help me."

"Help you, yeah? Do you reckon we should snitch?" She addressed this to the other heavies.

"You hate Nottingham, right?" Oates asked.

She didn't contradict him.

"So help me to hurt them. If someone at Nottingham was involved with Prudence Egwu's death, I won't let them get away."

She looked around the circle. No one made any sign. She shrugged, and turned back to Oates.

"It was a process called MRT. Memory Replacement Therapy. About how to forget who you are. Capability Egwu was trying to find a way. You go to sleep one day as one guy, and you wake up in the morning as some new guy. He used to meet with the Mortal Reformers, did you know that? He helped us to campaign for inheritance tax changes, sentencing changes, all that stuff. Back at the beginning. I think he hated what he was."

"I don't understand, forget? Forget what?"

Lara walked up to him, and took his hands in hers. She looked up into his face, and spoke very softly. In part, she was addressing him as if he was an idiot, a child. But in the physical contact, there was an intimacy which existed alongside the mockery, a connection of his own disgust with hers.

"Forget who you are. Forget what you've done. If this thing had worked, they would have been able to escape it all. They wouldn't have to pay for anything anymore, not even in their souls. They'd get to live and do terrible things and get rich, and then at the end they'd pay to be someone young and new, with a clean conscience. With no memory of the things they've done. They wouldn't have to live with themselves. That's the last check left, that's the only thing keeping any last shred of fairness in this world. If Nottingham or anyone else had managed to put together Capability's research, that would be gone. Do you understand? That's why we were willing to kill you for it. That's why your spook wants it."

"But if what you're saying is true... why would Nottingham kill Prudence? Why wouldn't they just take what he had? It doesn't make any sense..."

And in that instant, he knew who had killed Prudence Egwu. It was like the light coming on in a room through which he had been groping his way, trying to identify the objects by touch, trying not to hurt himself in the dark. The intensity of illumination dazzled him, but as his mind cleared he saw all the facts of the case, sitting just where he had encountered them in the dark.

There was the photo album. There was Prudence Egwu's recent treatment, and his last minute arrival at the spa. There was Chris's testimony damning Ali Farooz, and there was Ali's confession. Ali Farooz, the man his head told him must be guilty, who his gut insisted must be innocent. The escape from conscience. The stories of the men and women who had woken up with someone else's voice. The search for eternal youth. Above all there was Superintendent John Yates, the jovial PR, and the white witch Miranda, presiding over her eternal summer.

He waited for the satisfaction, the joy that by rights should have followed this revelation. He waited like a groom at the altar; happy, expectant, then anxious, then joking with himself to hide the anxiousness. All through the longest day of his life, he had been tracking this solution. He had bullied, he had fought, he had threatened and bribed and calculated, he had killed, all that a killer might be brought to justice. Yet as he waited, he felt only the sordidness of the truth. The case, which had seemed to him different, was really just like any other. At the heart of it was money and selfishness. Oates felt terribly tired, and the urge to get back to his family filled him once again. He would see this thing through, but he needed to be with them, and not just to protect them. He needed their protection too.

"Listen, I'm sorry," he said as he turned to go.

"For what?" she said.

"For shooting your friend. For killing him."

"I didn't know him that well. He'd just come down from Manchester."

"The manager upstairs said he was a nice lad."

"He was. Do you mind if we get on now? This is going to be a really big night for us. Nottingham are going to remember this one."

CARLOS ESCORTED OATES back the way they had come. The journey seemed much shorter now he knew he was headed for the fresh air. At the old tube platform, he was shown to a water butt with a pump to clean the shit off his boots.

In the club the evening's entertainments had begun. A pre-op transsexual was dancing on the stage in front of a crowd of baying men and women in suits. The dancer was stumbling around to an aggressive rock track, drunk or simulating drunkenness, pausing to take deep swigs from a bottle of tequila he held in his hand. Skin pulled taut across his skinny sternum rose in the swell of the fake breasts, and his penis swung wildly as he danced. At the climax of the act, he squatted on the bottle to pick it up with his anus. The audience roared with approbation and disgust. He pulled it out from between his buttocks, drank a shot from the bottle, and spat it into the faces of the audience arrayed around the front of the stage.

"People pay for that?" Oates had to shout into the ear of his host to make himself heard above the uproar.

"People pay to be shocked. They pay to feel anything."

Flo was greeting guests at the door. She had restored her hair and make-up. When she clocked Oates she stuck her chin in the air and straightened her back, quivering a little.

"I'm sorry for frightening you," Oates said.

At the words of apology, she melted.

"You didn't frighten me, dearie."

"I was out of order."

"There's worse than wig-pullers out there, I can tell you. But thank you."

Oates smiled and put out his hand. She proffered her own and Oates kissed it on the knuckle.

"You mind yourself out there, officer. It's all going off. They're going to tear down the town," she said.

Outside the club, there was a small huddle of people hoping to be let in, the girls shivering in short skirts, the men acting nonchalant as if queuing outside was all part of the plan. The bouncer lifted the hook on a velvet rope for Oates as he left. Aside from the would-be clubbers, the street was empty though the buildings echoed with distant chanting. The damp wind blowing down from the West End carried the faint smell of peardrop boiled sweets, and it took Oates a moment to make the appropriate association – it was the aftertaste of tear gas.

He went back to his car, and was relieved to find it unmolested. He turned the key to start the heater and sat back in the front seat. He listened to the police chatter on his earpiece, trying to construct in his mind the clear path home. Trafalgar Square was properly sealed off now, and the Strand itself was closed at the Blackfriars end. Piccadilly Circus and Soho were swamped, with reports of glass fronts shattering all the way down to the Ritz, and the looters handing out truffles and champagne hampers from the ground floor of Fortnum & Mason to their compatriots in the street.

Oates could imagine the wild joy of the scene; even he, a policeman, could feel the thrill as the status quo tottered beneath the weight of temptation and privation. He believed that you should work for what you wanted, and that the law did more to protect the weak than the strong, but he felt the frustration of being constrained by that philosophy to an average life. Money had become an abstract ideal, and expensive goods the stuff of religious reverence. Even as the significance of riches increased, they were lifted away above the heads of Londoners, above the grasping hands even of those willing to stand on the bodies of others to reach them.

Those young men and women smashing their way into the stores must feel the way King Henry's soldiers had felt, breaking into the monasteries to reclaim the gold and jewels in the gorgeous crosses and kicking the monks up the arse. The trouble was you couldn't burn down the church without killing the people sheltering inside, and he thought of Mr Prendegast and his wife sitting with their lovely Asian neighbours and the strangers from downstairs, terrified in the darkness.

The disturbances spread all the way up to Marble Arch, where a police cordon bulged with the pressure of the riot. Outside of that, there were pockets of isolated trouble throughout the city, but the main areas of conflict were in Hackney, Tottenham, Brixton and Kingston. The Kingston riots had taken the police by surprise, and there wasn't the weight of officers there to engage the offenders. The water cannons and the horses were all deployed in the east.

Through the sporadic bursts in his earpiece, Oates heard the names of some streets he recognised – not his own street, but near enough to fill his mind with the image of masked men beating on the door of his flat, with Mike, Harry and Lori hiding together in an upstairs bedroom. He tried again to call his wife, but the call wouldn't go through; too many people ringing at once, the air thronged with the thwarted signals as every Londoner tried to contact their loved ones.

It took him ten minutes to assemble the new mental map of the city, with little images of the fires and barricades superimposed above the monuments and tube stations. He was about to drive off when his earpiece bleeped on the police frequency. It was Bhupinder calling from outside the spa.

"You need to get back here now, boss. Things are looking pretty bad out front. There's more and more people coming, and they're trying to get in to the spa. Some of the news people have got stuck and they want to get back to London for the riots, and we've had word from central that some of the troublemakers from the east might come out this way because they've blocked out the High Street."

"Alright. I'm on my way back now. I'll be an hour. Hour and a half tops. Can you keep everything under control until then?"

"I don't know. Maybe, yeah."

HE TRAVELLED ALONG the empty Strand, and took Waterloo Bridge across the river. Lambeth Palace Road was open, and although he saw a fire engine tearing along the other side with siren wailing, he also saw a couple jogging on their way around Archbishop's Park, and a family taking photographs of the police gathering on the north side of the river. There across the dark water was the Palace of Westminster, silent and peaceful in the night, and the face of Big Ben glowing like a second moon in the starless sky.

On Prince of Wales Drive along Battersea Park, the peace almost made him doubt the chaos he had seen in the West

End. The lights were on in many of the big Georgian houses along the park. The screens of televisions appeared through the windows, some of them showing the riots on the rolling news, others films or football. He saw a family sitting down to dinner in their front room, curtains open.

He slowed the car, and felt himself begin to calm down. Perhaps it really was coming down worst in the east of the city. In the park itself, a low mist clung to the ground. There wasn't a soul in sight on the long paths lined with lamps, or on the AstroTurf hockey pitch shining under the floodlights. Even the bare branches of the trees were motionless. The lights at the end of the drive turned red as Oates approached, and he pulled to a stop at the deserted crossroads. He waited there with the engine running in the silence. Then from a distance, but approaching rapidly in the still night, he heard the beating of hooves.

The traffic lights turned green, but he did not move. A police horse with no rider came galloping down the Albert Bridge Road. It was saddled, stirrups jangling, and the plastic visor to protect its eyes had been yanked across its face, so it ran half blind. Its neck dipped and rose with each stride as if it were moving through water. Oates was afraid as he saw it coming that it would break its own legs on the concrete in its headlong dash. Its tail was on fire, a terror it could never outrun. It passed so close to Oates's car that he could see the swell of the veins in its neck, and the sheen of sweat on its flanks. The heat and light, the sudden frenzy of trailing sparks imprinted itself for a moment on his retina, and then receded into the London night. Having passed him at the crossroads, the horse ran on towards Clapham. Oates put his car in gear, and drove on down towards Putney Hill.

HE FOUND THEM sitting in the kitchen with their bags packed. Mike was playing games on his phone, Harry was sat holding the naked action figure which he liked to carry round with him when they were at home.

"Dad!" Mike said, and ran over to clasp his knees.

"Lori, I'm so sorry."

"You're here now," she said. "We knew you would be. Didn't we Harry?"

Harry nodded.

"Come on then boys. Who's for an adventure?"

Mike cheered. Lori kissed him on the mouth, and as she did so Oates realised she would smell the alcohol on his breath. He pulled away from her and said, "Quickly, let's get them in the car."

She didn't move, and reluctantly he stopped and looked at her. Without saying anything she nodded, and handed him one of the cases from the floor. She pushed past him into their bedroom, and as she passed she brushed her fingers over the broad shoulders of his body armour, and he knew then he was forgiven without even asking. It was that as well as seeing Mike and Harry that made him certain he had made the right choice in coming home.

"Where are we going?" she said when they were sat in the car.

"Somewhere safe. I've got to finish this job I'm on."

"Oh, Rob, no."

"It's alright, it won't take long. It's at that spa, Avalon. They've got lots of police and security guards there, and I can bring you in with me and park you in a room whilst I finish things off."

"Will it be safe?"

"They've got politicians in there, captains of industry, all sorts of top brass. You'll be safe."

Lori nodded to herself.

They floated along the highway in the darkness, the lights turning the pages of the shadows as they passed beneath them. As they drove in the darkness with the wet road glistening under the tyres, the journey started to feel more like a destiny to Oates. The low metal barriers on either side of the three lanes ran him on towards a fate immense and inevitable. He recognised the feeling, and tried to fight against it – if he went into the spa with the smell of destiny still on him, he was likely to act like a character in the legend of his life rather than a policeman doing his job. The dramatic action was always the wrong one to take, the portentous thing the wrong one to say. To ground himself he looked into the back seat, where the boys were now curled up asleep.

"I was thinking," he said, "that maybe after Christmas we could go away for a bit. Just you and me."

"Where would we go?"

"We could go back to Spain. You always liked Spain."

"I liked Spain when I was twenty years old."

She looked out of the window. Her breath created a pulse of condensation on the glass. Oates felt the pressure of his foot increase on the accelerator as the car drifted on.

"Besides, what would we do with the kids?" she said.

"They could stay with your mum. You know she'd be happy."

"She can't be chasing after Mike."

"She's always asking."

She turned to look at their sons in the back, and Oates could tell from the expression on her face that she was hoping to find them awake, and so to avoid the conversation. But they were both sound asleep. Finding no refuge she stared ahead and frowned.

"They're out cold," he said.

"I don't know. I'd have to see about work."

"You've got days saved up."

"I'd have to see."

"Only I think we need to talk about some things." It wasn't until he said it that he realised his conversation had been heading towards this point. It worried him a little, how he found himself more and more doing the things he realised he was already doing.

"I started thinking about her again," he said. "About Anna."

"Were you alright?"

"I was in the end."

"Good. My poor love."

"We never talk about her, you know."

Lori said nothing.

"I miss her," Oates said. "I miss remembering her."

"When she was here she made me happy. Now she's gone she can only make me sad. Why remember her? It can't do her any good, and it doesn't do us any good either."

"You have to remember people. Otherwise it's like they weren't here at all."

"Isn't it better that way? That way you're both of you free."

"You're not free. You don't mean anything that way."

"I loved Anna as much as you did," Lori said, "Sometimes it was like you were trying to make me feel guilty by being in so much pain. Like you felt I should be in more pain than I was, or I was a bad mother or something. Well I'm not a bad mother, I'm a good mother. But you can't be a mother to the dead. When someone's gone they're gone and that's it."

"I can't help thinking about her."

"What's come of all your remembering then?" Lori asked. "Has something good come of it? Have you done anything for Anna or for you or for the rest of us with all this thinking?"

The cat's eyes flying under the wheels had taken on a hypnotic rhythm. Oates found he had to wrench his eyes away from them to look at his wife beside him. Lori had her forehead pressed against the glass, through which the city appeared darkly.

"Because it's been pretty shitty for me, Rob. You spend more time digging up the dead than you do with your family."

Oates did not reply, but after a few moments he put his hand on his wife's leg. It lay there alone until, to his great relief, he felt her cold fingers come for it. Oates drove on, trying to keep from changing gear so that he could keep his hand there. Bright billboards appeared in the distance, approached through the darkness, grew and passed.

The traffic was heavy with refugees as they skirted around the top of London, and the journey took longer than he had expected. Their destination crept up on them. After more than an hour of driving, there was the dome of the Great Spa again, the vision greeting him as it had that morning in the dark. Only this time his approach was from the M25 itself, and Oates could see the fires burning around the perimeter on the plain, like the watch fires of some nomadic tribe in the desert. The Great Spa was the most state-of-the-art thing in England, but with those fires of human encampments around the base it looked like some ancient temple, built with technologies that had vanished from the earth, worshipped now by a race of men who together had come to an erroneous consensus on its significance. Oates could sense Lori's silent awe beside him. A face appeared between them over the gearstick, still innocent with sleep.

"Are we there now dad?"

"Yeah, we're there."

"Oh good."

The tailback of stationary traffic which had greeted Oates on his first approach had increased, and stretched now all the way to the exit from the M25. Whilst they were still on the motorway the siren cleared a path for them in the conventional way, but as soon as they turned off and into the sphere of influence of the spa itself it ceased to work. It was as if the suspension of the conventional order within Avalon that Oates had remarked on that morning, that he had to some extent set in motion by his acceptance of John's order to respect the spa's rules, had begun to spread outwards as the riots in London weakened the claims of the conventional hierarchy.

Many of the cars along the stretch of road had simply been abandoned, and others had found their way over the verge to become stuck in the muddy edges of the fields, or to prowl around the chain link fence. After a few seconds stood with the siren howling impotently at the back of an empty van, Oates pulled the wheel over and drove off the road. Lori put out her arm instinctively across the space between the seats to protect the boys from their father's recklessness.

"They've got their seatbelts on," he said, but she didn't reply, and she didn't move her arm.

The gentle bumping of the old suspension on the hummocks of grass woke Mike. They drove right up to the perimeter fence, and then moved along it to where a car had tried to ram its way through into the interior. Security and a few policemen were clustered around the breach, and it was here Oates parked the car.

"Stay in the car. I'm going to go and find one of the security guards and get us all inside. You'll be safe in there. I'll leave Bhupinder to look after you while I go and finish off this case."

Oates went for what seemed to him the most senior man, the one shouting orders at his colleagues. He was one of Miranda's special forces goons done up to look like a caretaker. He came at him holding up his badge.

"I need to bring my family in."

"No chance."

Oates drew his gun, and held it down at his side. The caretaker looked at it without expression, put both his fingers in his mouth and whistled. In answer, one of the searchlights atop the neighbouring guard tower fixed them with its gaze, flinging long shadows behind them. Oates couldn't look up to see past the glare, but he could imaging the butt of the rifle snug to a broad shoulder, one eye closed and the other socket to the sight.

"You can wave that around as much as you like. I've got my orders and no one comes in or out of this place except on Miranda's say-so."

Oates looked behind him at the guards in the shadows, and then at the gunman in the tower to the right. He holstered his weapon.

"I'll park them up in the car under the watchtower. If anything happens to them, I'll come back out here and shoot you dead."

"That's your business."

He walked back to the car, where Lori was peering anxiously up at him through the windshield. He shook his head quickly as he approached.

"I'll be fifteen minutes. Take my gun. It's loaded, this is the safety, okay? If you shoot at someone, expect to miss."

"I love you, Rob. Come back to us quickly, okay?"

"I love you too. I'll be as quick as I can."

HE WENT BACK to the caretaker. There was screaming and the sound of a shot being fired as Oates approached.

"Warning shots. Over their heads," the caretaker said by way of explanation, and Oates looked back over his shoulder into the darkness, back to where Lori and the kids were holed up in the car. He wondered if by bringing them here, he had placed them in more danger than they would have been in at home. The Great Spa had seemed an obvious haven, but when enough people thought they'd find salvation in the same place, they destroyed it by their gathering.

He remembered the way his children had been when he left them that morning, sleeping in their darkened bedroom, safe under the fake stars. He trusted Lori to look after them. She was a resourceful woman. She might not know how to use a gun, but she would know when to use it, and that was more important. He couldn't let his resolve crumble now, when he was so close to the end. When he had finished his business with Miranda, he would come back and collect them. He followed the caretaker back to the gap in the perimeter fence. A couple of men had wheeled the car off the bent stanchions and in to the space between the dome and the fence, but their efforts to repair the damage had been unsuccessful. The wire mesh itself was pressed almost horizontal to the ground, but still intact, its crown of barbed wire glinting in the arclights. The posts were set into the ground with concrete, and had buckled. They would need heavy machinery to clear the wreck, let alone repair the damage.

Oates and the caretaker climbed awkwardly over the flattened barricade, and the armed guards on the other sides held the barbed wire down with their boots as they hopped onto the grass inside the perimeter. The walk back around to the carpark at the front of the building took about five minutes, and all along the way Oates could see glimpses of disturbances out beyond the wires. From the guard towers, the arclights moved like fingers through the dark, stopping suddenly to pluck a single scene in their bright beams. He saw one alight on a ring of cars arranged around a primus stove about a hundred metres out in the fields, over which a huddled figure had hung a kettle. It wasn't clear to Oates what was the purpose of illuminating this moment, unless it was simply for the edification of a distant spectator, like a spotlight in a theatre. No command came from the tower, and the man by the kettle simply held his hand up in front of his eyes, until the beam of light grew bored and recommenced its restless movement.

When they arrived at the gates, Oates understood where the warning shot had come from. The masses were now pressed up against the guns of the security staff, held in parallel between them to hold back the people pushing to get in. Some of them were refugees, some of them were protestors. There were people carrying banners for Mortal Reform, mixed together with Nottingham employees and newsmen. Along with security, Oates could see men in police uniform. John had diverted some of his own men from the riots in London to protect Avalon.

He went in through the double doors, and the porter told him that Miranda was waiting for him in the headaster's lodge. He didn't offer to change his clothes, and he wasn't asked. He moved through the reception area, with its conference rooms and marble foyer, and passed through the airlock into the spa itself.

BEING INSIDE ST Margaret's for the first time in his proper clothes gave him a feeling of empowerment. The old-fashioned suit had been a slave costume, the symbol of the capitulation of the rule of law to the interests of the rich, and the heavy body armour of his profession made Oates feel as if his own priorities were on the rise. Hived off from the chaos of the winter night, the peaceful summer morning in the school seemed like the purest complacence. Neither scream, nor gunshot, nor news bulletin could penetrate the shell, and so the inhabitants continued their lives in blissful unawareness.

Only the groundsmen showed any consciousness of the events unfolding on the outside. They were alert. They still smiled in their avuncular way at the students filing back from a late weekend breakfast in the dining hall, but they were more numerous than before, and were placed like sentries. Oates noticed three of them standing outside the college gates, and glimpsed a fourth on the roof behind the ornamental crenellations.

As he walked across the main court, he heard the sound of music coming from one of the open windows, borne on the warm breeze. It was Demis Roussos, singing his long ago hit.

The heat of the day was coming on, but the flagstones were still pleasantly cool, and when Oates rang the bell of the headmaster's lodge he could smell the scent of the flowers rising from wooden tubs that flanked the door.

One of the blue-suited men came to answer.

"Detective Chief Inspector Oates?"

"I'm here for Miranda."

"They're expecting you. Upstairs."

"They?"

"Miranda, Mr Golden and the Superintendent."

"Where's Sergeant Bhupinder?"

"What? Oh, the Indian bloke. He's gone back to London. They're having a bit of trouble down there, in case you hadn't heard."

They stood staring at one another for a moment, before the groundsman nodded his head and pursed his lips as if to say, *Well here we are then*, and exited the hall. Oates mounted the stairs to find that the door to the room where he had had his first briefing on the workings of St Margaret's was open. There they were, the three of them. Miranda was standing by the window, gazing out on the interior of the court. She must have watched him coming all the way across. John was beside her, and Charles sat sprawled at one of the desks, his legs open and his heels on the floor, his toes pointing at the ceiling. He was playing cat's cradle with a rubber band.

"How was your trip to London, Rob?" It was John who spoke, but he seemed to speak for all three of them. Oates had the impression of having entered upon a consensus, as if some weighty matter had been discussed between great minds, and they had only that moment come to a difficult but total resolve.

"It took a bit longer than I thought to get things sorted."

"And have you got them sorted now?" John asked.

"I reckon I have."

"Well, perhaps you could tell us?" John looked at Miranda, a smirk on his lips. But she was staring straight at Oates.

"Ali killed Prudence Egwu."

"I told you that myself four hours ago," John said.

"Ali is Capability Egwu, Prudence Egwu's brother."

Oates had not admitted it to himself, but he was terrified to see the effect of this statement on the assembled group. It seemed such an incredible thing to say out loud, and the implications were almost greater. To say such a thing was not only to assert the existence of a technology which belonged to the realms of science fiction, but also to accuse his boss and two powerful figures of conspiracy. He half expected to be greeted with outrage, incredulousness, hilarity, and he would almost have welcomed such a reaction, for he would prefer his own madness to the world's.

No such reaction came. John was looking at him with something close to pride. It was the look a father might give a son who stood accused of beating another boy in the playground, the requisite condemnation of the act mixed with implicit approval of the powers behind it.

Charles's hands continued to toy with the rubber band, but his eyes regarded Oates with a similar respect. There was not a trace now of the idiot jollity which was his default mood. The esteem he accorded Oates was expressed in part by this new seriousness, and in doing him the courtesy of dropping the charade of matey incompetence. His slovenliness however was no act, and he stayed slumped. Only Miranda's expression remained inscrutable.

"You see, Miranda? You asked for a clever policeman, and I sent you one of my best." John said.

She ignored him, and continued to stare at Oates.

"How did you come to that conclusion?" she asked him.

"It was Ali really," Oates said, "Everything pointed his way. Only thing was, he was left handed. The killer was right handed. I had him for an Eddy. The evidence against him kept piling up, all except DNA. When someone bribes an Eddy and has access to the crime scene, they plant blood, hair. With Ali there was nothing, someone had done a clean up job. Why would someone want to do that? It didn't make sense, not until I started to look into Capability's research. Capability Egwu had found a way of forgetting your sins. Forgetting everything about yourself. Changing everything, even your accent. Even your dominant hand. This research was the future of the Treatment. So I started thinking, what would make Prudence Egwu come visit the people he holds responsible for his brother's disappearance? Why was it that every time I spoke to Ali, I was certain he was giving a false confession, but every time I looked at the evidence, it pointed to him? Why wouldn't you want any of your Eddy's DNA at the scene? It all came together when I spoke to the Mortal Reformers. The point of MRT is, you don't know what you've done. You forget your sins. Ali seemed guilty because he'd done it. He seemed innocent because he didn't know he'd done it. Nottingham couldn't have it getting out that their shiny new therapy has homicidal mania under the side effects. So they sorted the best cover up they could - send the real man down so there's no loose ends. But don't leave him with any of the real secrets. And there wasn't any DNA because you knew we'd screen for the victim's and you couldn't risk us noticing the similarity between the two brothers. But if you were going to manage all that, you'd need a bit of help from inside the investigation. Isn't that right, sir?"

John glanced over to Miranda. She gave the slightest of nods.

"About twelve months ago someone called us saying they'd seen Capability working right here in Avalon," John said. "Working in the staff canteen. As you yourself realised, the involvement of Minor in the original investigation into Capability's disappearance created the potential for embarrassment. It was enough to make me take a personal interest in the case. I came down here to speak to Ali Farooz, and he flatly denied being anyone other than who he was. His paper trail was in order. I could see a resemblance, an uncanny resemblance really, between Ali Farooz and Capability Egwu, so I could quite see how the woman who called us had made a mistake."

"It's amazing how backwards the field of reconstructive surgery is," Charles said. "It had a rather illustrious start in military hospitals after the First World War, but by the turn of the twenty-first century it had become really no more than a way of fending off old age. The Treatment rather blew that out of the water. We did our best with Ali's face, his nose and so on, we destroyed every photo we could find of Capability, but there's only so much one can do." There was a defensiveness in his attitude, and from the way Miranda stared stubbornly out of the window, Oates sensed he was trying to score points in an old argument.

"I took a routine swab for saliva to tick the box," John continued, "and I thought nothing more of it. Before the results had come back, I got a call from Charles here. He explained the situation and between us we came to an arrangement."

"I thought you said one lifetime was enough."

"Oh, more than enough," John said. "But that's exactly what he offered me. One lifetime. And then another. And another."

"But why did Prudence have to die?" Oates said. "Even if he worked out where his brother was, why did you let him in?"

"That was as much a surprise to us as to you, Inspector," Miranda said. "We had been keeping an eye on Prudence for some years. We were aware of him digging around. Indeed Charles here was especially tasked with oversight of his activities."

"You can't protect against that sort of thing," Charles said. "No one can. Clearly as grand fromage it's your right and privilege not to risk chipping a nail on the practicalities–"

Miranda held up her hand palm out, and Charles pulled the sides of his cat's cradle wide apart. The elastic quivered, stretched white between his fingers. Oates thought that he might storm on, like some rogue musician striking up a solo in defiance of the conductor's final gesture. But the new influence which Charles had wielded all afternoon was in abeyance, as the focus of events had turned away from the periphery of the spa and back to its dark heart. He simply shut up, and went back to fiddling. John gave a little cough of embarrassment, and actually chanced a private smile at Oates, as if the two of them were partners, the last refuge of reason in this topsy turvy world.

"For whatever reason, Prudence was able to conceal from us the extent of his success," Miranda said. "We're still not quite sure how much he knew, but he clearly identified Capability's location, and had pieced together something of the process with which he had engaged. He further succeeded in undergoing the Treatment under a false name, and in gaining access to St Margaret's under the same alias."

Oates thought back to the register – Prudence Egwu's name had been the last one appearing on the matriculation book, and Grape had not been able to find him registered as a guest. If Prudence Egwu had snuck in under an alias, they must have stuck his name down as soon as they realised who he really was. It must have taken them time to update their computer records.

"And then Ali just killed him?" Oates said. "I mean, what, Prudence confronted him and claimed to be his brother? You don't kill someone for that."

Miranda seemed displeased by the question. Charles continued to play with his toy. Even John took a momentary interest in the boards between his shoes. Oates intuited that they didn't really know. Whatever had happened in that room in the boys' quarters, it was still at least a partial mystery, and the unknown element threatened them. It was Miranda who answered.

"Our theory is that Prudence made Ali realise who he used to be. He showed him photographs, and personal effects – the album, his trunk, that knife – and it broke through the protective layer of the MRT. You can't really delete the past you see, you can only replace it. It's like painting over the colour in a room. If you strip the new paint off, the old stuff's still underneath. You must understand, Capability wasn't very happy with the person he used to be. He was prone to depression, a condition which the Tithonus Effect markedly exaggerated. He also had substantial... doubts. About the Treatment, about the morality of our business. Everything. Towards the end of his last life, we were concerned for his mental stability. He was spending more and more time in church. His research into MRT had become entirely personal. He viewed it as his salvation."

"It was a bloody good thing he volunteered to play guinea pig," Charles said. "When you've got Mortal Reform t-shirts appearing on stage at Glastonbury, the last thing you need is the chap who worked on the invention of the Treatment coming out and saying the whole thing's evil, or he wants to die, or he's seeing Jesus and Buddha at the end of his bloody bed."

"Thank you, Charles," she said, but this time he wouldn't be silenced.

"For the last year or so I had to do all his interviews by telephone. Just me and a bloody voice modulator, and what the hell do I know about telomeres and stem cells, I had to get the *New Scientist* chatting about my love of golf and walking the coastal paths of East Anglia."

"That's quite enough," she said. "We believe that Prudence somehow broke through the layer of new memories, and reminded Capability of his first life That involved almost a hundred years of information, identity, emotion and experience dawning upon his mind in the space of a few seconds. The process triggered a psychotic episode, the results of which we all witnessed."

"And you, what... you reprogrammed him after? His research was destroyed."

"Oh, Inspector. Don't let yourself down now," she smiled. "The scrap, the scraps recovered by Prudence's plods may have been destroyed. But I worked with Capability for eight years before he became Ali, and I've been studying his progress ever since, refining the process, getting it right."

"We're a hop, skip and a jump from bringing MRT to market," Charles said. "It's going to blow everything else completely out of the water. You sign out of everything, every responsibility you've ever had, every memory, you really get another go at being young. Not just pretending, I mean the real thing. As part of the package, we'll hold your funds in trust for you. You will be looked out for throughout the whole of your life. A long lost Auntie will die, and leave you a fortune. If you ever buy a lottery ticket, you'll win.

Our team of financial advisers will continue to manage your funds for you, and our lifestyle monitors will find a way of getting all your lovely lucre into your bank account without so much as a raised eyebrow. You give us a power of attorney, and just when you hit twenty-seven years old, bang! We send in our team and you go through the whole thing again, and again, and again. Just think, you'll be young, and lucky, and rich forever!" He raised his hands above his head, and pulled them slowly apart, drawing a slogan in invisible lights. "*With Nottingham Biosciences, you can take it with you!* How's that for a strapline?"

"We haven't settled on a marketing strategy yet," Miranda said, and Charles dropped his invisible billboard.

"So after you realised what had happened," Oates said, "you had to clean up a bit to protect your science project."

"If you must put it like that."

"I hate to throw a spanner in the works, but I'm afraid you're going to have to come with me back to London."

Miranda stood up from her position by the window, and took a step towards him.

"We are going to offer you something," she said. "But I want you to understand before you hear it that you will not appreciate the true worth of this offer at this time in your life. You are a father, are you not?"

Oates nodded. He had known this moment must be coming ever since the beginning of their confession. And yet now that it was here, he felt afraid.

"I want you to picture those moments in communicating with your children when you tell them something that your experience has shown you to be true. You are aware that without the context of that experience, with indeed an immediate context of personal experience which may demonstrate the opposite, your children will not believe you. But fortunately you are the parent and so it is not essential that they believe you, because you can command them to do the thing that you know to be right, secure in the knowledge that one day they will also come to a vantage point from which they will perceive the truth upon which you acted. That is the relationship between myself and you, Inspector, with one crucial difference; I cannot command you to do anything. I must simply ask you to believe that as much as you may kick against it, what I am about to tell you will, with the lapse of time, become your truth."

As Miranda spoke, her words contrived to seal the two of them away from the rest of the room, and the rest of the world. Her will settled upon him in a focused beam, and what had been up to that point a conversation between a number of participants became a duologue.

"I understand what you are saying. And I know what you are going to say. And the answer is no."

"We can make you young again."

"I don't want to be young."

"I think that is a lie. And believe me when I tell you, if you do not yet want to be young, that means that you are not yet truly old. You may not fear the reaper, Inspector, but you should fear the Zimmer frame. Failing eyes, false teeth, weakness in your limbs, your penis flaccid, desire outpacing performance in every contest. And then finally to feel nothing, your thoughts getting slower, confusion settling over everything, to depart from the world in mind and soul whilst the body sits in some plastic covered seat in the day room."

"What's the bloody alternative? Have the Treatment and MRT, and then one day I see Lori on a street corner, and I take an axe to some bloke on the pavement?"

"Capability was the first patient. He is… imperfect. We have been working on the revised version for half a decade. If it really makes a difference to you, I will go first. As soon as we have passed on my knowledge sufficiently for the program to be running, I will be undergoing the process myself. I've had to work on this almost alone up to this point, because of the risk of industrial espionage or interference from the government. You cannot imagine how lonely I have been. How desperate I have been to bring the process to the point where I can undergo it. But none of that matters now."

"And I'll be hopping on board. And so will John," Charles said, breaking in upon their duel. "From here to eternity!"

Oates was grateful for his intervention. Miranda's voice was a mesmerising thing. The rhythms of her logic beat down on the brain. She tried to continue in the same vein, without acknowledging the interruption.

"We can discuss the best means of minimising the impact to your family. Perhaps arrange for your death in the line of duty. We would make a substantial cash contribution to their welfare. They would discover you had taken out a life insurance policy some time ago naming them as the beneficiaries. You would be giving them a start in life far in advance of anything you could hope to achieve otherwise."

"Capability. Ali. He really doesn't know he killed his brother?" Oates said, playing for time.

"He doesn't even know he has a brother. He was catatonic after the incident but we were able to subject him to an emergency MRT procedure prior to notifying the police. After that Charles offered him the Treatment to become an Eddy. We have been refining MRT for some years, and it involves periodic repetition for Capability. That is no longer the case with new subjects. We think he may be aware of the process on some subconscious level – I believe you've seen his diaries. It's as if he is trying with some part of his mind to resist the memory grafts. Editing those diaries has become a rather more painstaking process for us than the actual manipulation of his mind."

"Does he fight you? Does he... are you making him forget?"

"We act on the basis of Capability's original consent. He is no longer in a position to give informed consent, as he lacks the information to understand the process, though not, I hasten to add, the intelligence. As I am sure you will have detected in your discussions with Ali, his intelligence remains as lucid as ever. The point is we can't explain it to him without explaining to him who he was, and that really is a dangerous business. As you have seen. You should remember though that the process is necessarily voluntary, in that you have to want to believe the new life with which you are presented in order to accept it. We could no more force MRT on someone than we could make them fall in love. It only works if you are weary."

"And what do I have to do?"

"Nothing other than what you were asked to do this morning. You bring Ali down to London. We think that with the riots, the press attention will slip away from him over the next few days, and he can have his trial in relative peace. We get him a decent barrister as an act of compassion on behalf of the company, and he gets a ten year sentence. He serves five to parole, not long enough for anyone to realise he hasn't aged inside. Then he disappears again, this time for good. With our MRT program fully up and running, we can send him anywhere in the world."

"We're not asking you to put away an innocent man here, Rob," John said. "I wouldn't do that and I know you wouldn't either. The only person in the world who will think he's innocent is Ali himself, and he'll be wrong."

Oates opened his mouth to denounce them, and said nothing. His conception of right and wrong had always been founded on conscience. By that logic if conscience could be wiped clean, the rightness or wrongness of an act could be time-limited. He understood now the idea that had so horrified Lara in the tunnels. Every man was a story he told himself, and the sane and rational mind only allows for a certain amount of poetic licence – you can shift details, change the order of events quite substantially, but there comes a point where the facts of an event cannot support any further alteration without being demolished and rebuilt from scratch. At that point, you have to choose between the truth, with whatever shame and guilt such truth implies, or embrace psychosis. No rational man would choose to be mad, and so the conscience would have to bear the burden of guilt.

With MRT, that was no longer true. A rational act of evil could be separated completely from its mental consequences. With this idea of morality as a gentleman's agreement between the sane, he could not fault Miranda's logic; with MRT you could be reincarnated without sin.

As for her offer, all the outcomes would be aligned with their deserts. The guilty man would be punished, although only others would know his true guilt, and even they would lose the knowledge as they passed through MRT. Oates would have to live with the abandonment of his family only as long as he remembered it, and after that he would be free and his family would be rich. He remembered the feeling he had had in the carpark after his interview with Morrison, that to be really safe you had to cut away the people you loved. He heard Lori's voice in his mind asking him, *what good has all your remembering done? When someone's gone, they're gone, and you can't do yourself or them any good*. To be free of Anna, that was something. To be free of Anna, and all of the pain he had stored up for himself by his choices – his terror for his children, his love for his wife. All the violence he had done, all the people he had killed would wash away. He could let himself go, once and for all.

No. Oates could not fault Miranda's logic, not with the tools of his own philosophy. He simply knew it was wrong. It was an article of faith. For almost the first time in his adult life, Oates thought back to the chapel he had attended with his father as a child.

"Superintendent John Yates, Miranda, Charles Golden, I am arresting each of you on suspicion of perverting the course of justice and corruption in public office. You do not have to say anything, but it may harm your defence if you fail to mention when questioned something you later rely on in court."

John laughed at him, and sat down on the window ledge. Oates felt the absence of the gun at his thigh, the armour sitting too light on his leg. Miranda wasn't done with him.

"You haven't asked the most important question, Detective Chief Inspector."

"And what's that?"

"You haven't asked – why you?"

"You had to get someone."

"But there were a dozen men of your rank and experience available. Why you?"

Oates glanced over at John, and saw that his eyes were fixed on the floor. The fact that his superior was unwilling to meet his eye filled him with a profound unease, almost a premonition.

"Maybe you thought I was dumb enough or drunk enough that you could run rings round me."

Miranda shook her head. Charles was grinning.

"What then? Come on then. What?"

"We knew this moment might come," Miranda said. "We discussed with John the personnel files of the men in his command. We were looking for someone whose life had become unbearable to them. We needed someone in pain. Someone who would understand the true significance of forgetting."

"Dead daughter? Drink problem? Starting to crack?" Charles said. "That's our man!'"

John still couldn't look him in the eye. "I'm sorry, Rob. I really thought... I know how much it hurt, when Anna passed on. I really thought that maybe it would help you."

As they stood facing one another the sky outside the window flickered, and went out. At first, Oates thought that he had fainted, that the moment had proved too much for his damaged mind to take, and he had simply blacked out. Then Charles said, "oh!", and the faint little cry provided him with some affirmation that the experience was shared.

Oates clung to that certainty. The room was plunged into absolute darkness. There was a scream from the courtyard, and the sound became strangely twisted as if it came from the bottom of a great chasm. None of them spoke, but Oates heard the sound of movement. He tried to move towards it, but it took all his courage to inch forward. The absence of light was so complete that the atmosphere around them seemed to have a physical weight. The external world was compressed to nothing more than the millimetres of air flowing around the hairs on his skin. Oates was blinking rapidly, and with each blink the continuing fact of his blindness instilled a mounting sense of panic.

This state of affairs lasted for perhaps thirty seconds, after which he became aware of a cold ring of dawn mounting from the ground visible through the window.

Slowly, rising from the earth, up the walls and along the great dome of the roof, the concentric circles of emergency lights began to wink on one set at a time. Dimly, first, but expanding rapidly, the light swelled to alleviate the claustrophobia. The relief however lasted only as long as it took Oates's eyes to become accustomed to the new light. In place of the sunshine of a moment before, a halogen glare now bathed the room. He walked over to the window, threw the old lead casement back, and gazed out at the sky.

Without the visual baffle of the hologram on the dome's interior, the sides were suddenly much nearer than he had imagined. Not only the sky had gone, but whole chunks of buildings which he had assumed were real, along with vistas of trees and distant spires and the hazy depths with their implied freedoms. In place of that pastoral vision rose the gunmetal walls of the dome itself. What remained of Avalon was almost more changed than that which had simply vanished. The warm sandstone of the older buildings, given a flesh-like softness by the summer sun, became suddenly grey and institutional in the cold new light. As that light now came from the entire circumference of the dome and from above, shadows were banished or cast in strange and conflicting multiples, and the river which had glittered moments before became a dead mineral vein in the earth. The starlings nesting in the eaves of the buildings rose as one from their roosts, and flew frantically in an escalating spiral around the walls.

"What the hell is going on?" John said.

Oates turned back to the room, and saw to his relief that even Charles looked shocked.

"I don't know," Charles said. "It has to be some kind of attack. The power supply hasn't gone down, or we'd still be in the dark. Someone's hacked into the weather programming."

"How could that happen?" John asked.

"I don't know! The Mortal Reformers, the perimeter fence is down in fifty places. If they could get a device through the outer shell of the building–"

There was a sound of screaming deep in the earth. The room shook, the burnished bronze lamp in the ceiling began to sway gently. Just as Oates had pictured Miranda that morning as a classical goddess sitting in this room, the associations echoed down to the present moment, and the scream made him think of the titan Atlas, shifting the world on his shoulders.

In the weird, flat light of the halogen rings, the calm strip of the river began to shake and churn. A couple who had been reclining in a punt at the beginning of the disaster clung to the edges of their craft as it rocked in the new turbulence. The sound from the earth reverberated from the metal walls, bouncing up and down the curved insides of the spa walls. It was not just the visual effect which had been disturbed, but whatever technology served to regulate the acoustics of the dome had also been corrupted. Rather than sounds being carried away into the open air, they collided weirdly within the hollow space, and, finding their escape blocked, returned to the ground. That was why the first scream in that initial moment of darkness had seemed so terrible. Charles's eyes widened as he stared at the portion of the river visible from the headmaster's study.

"The turbines... they're turning the wrong way. They'll flood the whole bloody school!"

"Where's Miranda?" John said.

"She was just here..."

Oates knew who had made the noises in the darkness. Miranda had taken the opportunity to escape. She had slipped past them, and down the stairs. He strode over to the door, and looked down into the empty hall. There was no sign of her. Her disappearance made him irrationally afraid. Because she was not in his sight, he suddenly felt her everywhere. This was her world, and whilst she was invisible he was at her mercy.

The students had begun to exit their buildings, and to congregate in the middle of the grey courtyard, the late risers blinking sleep from their eyes. Oates could feel not fear, but indignance, fear's precursor amongst a rich clientele. Indignance at a service paid for and not delivered. It was also outrage at the fact that they had made themselves ridiculous – Oates remembered the seductive effect of the sunshine and the cool water on his wrist.

"Right, you two, stay here."

"I'm not in the business of taking orders from you, Inspector," Charles said.

Oates strode back across the room, and punched Charles in the stomach. His fist sunk into the soft belly bulging over the trouser top, and caused the PR man to double over as the wind escaped him in a lunch-flavoured whoosh. As he bent coughing, Oates took his arm and wrenched it backwards. He unclipped the cuffs from his belt, and fastened one around Charles's wrist. John looked at him, too shocked for the moment to react, and when Oates took his hand there was no resistance. The second after the tell-tale click, he wrenched it away, but by then it was too late. His fate and Charles's were linked at the wrist.

"You can guard the suspect, sir."

"Give me the keys, Detective Chief Inspector," John said.

Oates turned his back on them, and made for the door.

"DCI Oates... Give me the fucking keys, you little prick," John screamed, and lunged at him.

The Superintendent moved with a speed of which his physique gave no warning, and he would have taken Oates by surprise, had it not been for his tether. Charles was on his knees by the window, and the sudden yank of the metal handcuffs sent him sprawling on the floor. The torque popped something in the old policeman's arm. Oates experienced an extraordinary moment of clarity as the enraged snarl of his superior's face hurtled towards him, pulled up by a sudden pop.

It always makes a man look stupid, the second of incomprehension that precedes the recognition of pain, because the observer's understanding has outrun that of the protagonist. Oates knew the moment he heard the sound that John's shoulder was out, but it took a few seconds for John's body to admit the disaster to his mind. It was that moment of superior understanding which freed Oates from any vestigal fear he might have felt in the usurpation of John's authority. It gave him no pleasure, but here was absolute proof that he could know more about his boss than his boss knew about himself. John might be more clever, but in his moment of fear he had forgotten himself. Oates knew him more clearly. He knew him for a criminal.

When the screaming was under control, he relocated John's shoulder. By this time Charles had recovered, and he helped to hold the Superintendent down. Oates had originally intended to lock the two of them in the headmaster's lodge, but when he looked out of the window he could see that Charles's warning about the flooding had not been idle. Water was pouring into the court, not just from the doors adjacent to the river, but from every direction, as if the toilets and the drains all over the artificial school were backing up. Charles indicated he had to get to the control room to try to reverse the damage, or failing that to evacuate the guests in the induction facility. Oates refused to give them the keys, but allowed the two of them to leave cuffed together to see what good they could do fighting the chaos engulfing the spa. He set out to find Miranda.

HE SEARCHED THE rooms in the headmaster's lodge. She had left no trace. He was coming back downstairs to the hall when he noticed the water leaking in under the old oaken door. The door had a step up that was at least eight inches above the level of the courtyard. He was standing there when his earpiece began to chirp in his breast pocket. He slipped it into his ear. The voice whispered, "*Love of my life, love of my life.*" It was Lori calling. At first he was nonplussed; the dome should have blocked out the signal. Then he realised that the jamming of radio waves must have been controlled by the same mechanism as the accoustic baffle and the imagery. The shell of the egg was becoming permeable to every brand of external influence.

"Hello my love. Is everything alright?"

"Yes, I'm just calling so you won't worry."

"Have you found a place to park up? Are things alright out there? It's madness in here, I can tell you."

"Oh, no we're inside now. Some nice men came and picked us up."

"Which men?"

"Some of those men in blue overalls, the groundskeepers. They said they'd been sent."

"Where are you now?"

"Is everything alright Rob?"

"Everything's fine. I just want to come and get you now."

"Only your voice sounds funny."

"I'm a bit out of breath, that's all. Where are you?"

"We're in that big gatehouse. Isn't it strange, with the echoes? And there's water coming in everywhere. I think we were best off outside."

"Are you all together?"

"Yes. Well, Harry's upstairs. He needed the toilet."

"Is there anyone with him?"

"Your friend Miranda said she'd go with him and show him the way. They'll be back down in a sec."

"Have you still got the gun my love? Only I need to know where it is at all times. It's not supposed to be out of my holster."

"Oh Rob, I'm sorry, I didn't think. The groundskeepers took it off me when we came in. They said it wouldn't be allowed inside. It's in a locker at reception, and they said we could pick it up on the way out. Rob?"

"I'm here."

"I made sure to stay and see they locked it away. I'm sorry, I didn't think."

"Alright love."

"Is that okay?"

"It's fine, it's fine. You stay put, I'll come and get you."

"Did you sort it out then?"

"What?"

"Rob! That bloke who murdered the financier."

"Yeah, that's all sorted."

OATES STOOD FOR a moment with his gloved hand pressed to his mouth. Miranda had taken Harry, and he himself had been the agent of his family's danger. He shook his head, and tried to reassure himself. Whatever reason Miranda might have for bringing them within the spa, she could not really mean to harm Harry. She was ruthless and amoral, he knew that from her own account of Prudence Egwu's murder, but she displayed those qualities in the context and on the scale of commerce. The heads of major companies didn't hurt little boys. Wherever she had taken Harry, she would still be wearing her business suit.

But he could not quite believe the words with which he comforted himself. A memory came back to him of meeting Miranda that morning in the upstairs rooms. What had she said to him? *What about the deaths of those you love?* It echoed back to him like a prophecy that offers no guidance, but reveals its truth in the wake of the disaster. Maybe the day before she had been a businesswoman, but the sudden falling away of the comforting illusions of the spa was both symptom and cause of a change in the old rules. In London he had seen the same thing, the city unmaking itself, the skin of civilisation peeled back to reveal the passions, raw and glistening. With her artificial world coming apart at the seams, Miranda might be capable of anything. He had to find them.

He pushed open the front door of the headmaster's lodge, and a wave washed over his boots. The whole of the court was flooded. The water in the river was spilling over, flooding its banks and the school beyond. With the Victorian Gothic buildings, and the water rising above the height of the ground but not yet the stairs and doorways, St Margaret's had become a sudden Venice, with placid little canals running under the stone archways.

Although the illusion of sky and distance had dissolved, and the sunshine with it, elements of the weather system persisted within the spa – a strong wind, almost tropical in its warmth, ruffled the rising surface of the water, and rain was falling on one half of the court, so that a clear line separated the new square lake, with one half bubbling under a rainstorm, and the other rippling under the zephyr. The rising water had found odd things to play with, and a bunch of balloons floated on the surface. From an open window on the second floor a regular fall of handwritten notes came fluttering down, blown by the breeze across the clear part of the water, then borne quickly down by the weight of the rain. The record Oates had heard on his way in was still playing somewhere, only the earthquake must have knocked the stylus into a scratch, as the saccharine chorus were singing over and over in a maddening chant.

The people in this landscape were a mixture of St Margaret's original inhabitants and the crowds latterly gathered around the outside of the dome. Men and women in modern clothes were stumbling through the entrance to the courtyard, which meant Avalon's perimeter had been well and truly breached. Whether they were rioters bent on smashing the spa, refugees seeking shelter, relatives hunting loved ones, agents of the Mortal Reformers come to complete their handiwork or a volatile combination of all these constituents, the moment they came through the gatehouse into the main square they stopped. Their intentions simply washed away in the rain. Like children from a warm land seeing snow for the first time, they stood overpowered by the strangeness of the scene.

The effect on those who had been staying in St Margaret's was quite different. The management in its meticulous fostering of a youthful dependency had unmanned its guests. The initial shrill of complaint had been stifled with the rapid deterioration of circumstances. No waiter had come to cower beneath the recriminations of the customers, and with this proof of abandonment, the students were acting without any internal restraint.

Some of the guests had snapped back into command, and realising the dangers of being trapped in an overturned bowl filling with water, they were heading for the exit, where they met the press of invaders forcing their way in from outside. But a remarkable number of the guests were delighting in the chaos. They were playing in the warm rain, hanging out of the windows and hallooing in delight across the lake.

To his amazement, Oates saw a group of new-young which included a prominent actress and a footballer he recognised, but could not place, carry one of the punts from the river out through the door by the refectory, like a savage hunting party shouldering their canoe down to the banks of a jungle river. They were dressed only in their night things, boxer shorts and t-shirts. They dumped the boat in the waters of the court. Behind them came a new-young man with his arms full of wine bottles and a wheel of cheese, evidently looted from the kitchens, and the whole crew jumped into the punt and pushed off from the steps.

The scene before him in combination with his fear for Harry was almost more than Oates could bear. He felt his connection to reality, which had grown more tenuous with every moment of the last twenty-four hours, threaten to snap completely. He felt he might go mad.

He was familiar with the psychological effect of adrenaline shading into panic. Appearing first as an itch at the back of the mind, a spreading numbness would overtake the sense of self. You could do a terrible injury to your mind in that state, and not feel it until later. You could abandon a friend in trouble, run away from a battle or kill a man, and in the moment there would be no relationship between the action you took and the type of man you knew yourself to be. It was only later, when the panic receded, that you would be left to reconcile the thing you had done with the fact that you were the doer.

Oates had heard a friend describe it as feeling like you were an actor in a film, and that was half right; he would have said an extra in a film. You were not the leading man in these moments, but a bystander, rushed into the background to rhubarb whilst the real action took place somewhere else. In this respect, he almost found the state of panic to be closer to objective reality than normal life. After all, you couldn't have seven billion actors all rightly believing they had been cast as the main part in the same movie. Someone must be wrong, and at that moment Oates felt it might be him.

The scene before him created a grotesque harmony with these sensations, for it looked like nothing so much as a film set. The visible struts in the ceiling with their glaring artificial lights were like a studio hanger, the gorgeous buildings a set, the weather effects and costumes like nothing so much as themselves. There was even the actress in the punt, playing the part of herself gone mad as a teenager. Only there was no director, and no one to shout cut. No beginning or end to the scene, only the endless, merciless imperative to perform. A voice broke out above him, like the word of God in its indifferent calm, coming from everywhere and nowhere, louder than any voice he had ever heard.

"This is an emergency announcement. Would all students and personnel please make their way to the evacuation points. This is not a drill. This is an emergency announcement..."

He set out from the door of the headmaster's lodge into the court. He stumbled with his first step, having underestimated the depth of the water. Already the cobbles were invisible beneath the surface. When he first set out, he was unsure of where to go, but when he looked up he knew. There, on the roof of the buildings of the court, standing on the lead sheeting above the level of the red brick battlements, he could see two silouettes. They could have been statues, for they were motionless, looking out across the dome. One was a slender young woman, and by the hand she held a child.

Oates tried to run across the court, but with the water reaching up to his thighs he had to jump with each step to reduce its drag. He crossed the line from the dry half into the storm. As he tasted the rain, he found it faintly chlorinated. All around him the other denizens of the dissolving world pursued their own chaotic plans, but they paid no attention to Oates, and he paid no attention to them. He knew that Miranda must see him coming, and he kept his eyes away from her, fixed on the water in front of him. He knew somehow that she would not do anything whilst he looked away. Whatever was to happen on the roof, it would be for his benefit. He made for the opening into the stone staircase closest to her position, which was about twenty metres from the gatehouse.

The room into which he came on the top floor was a classroom with the ghost of a chalk equation still haunting the blackboard. He opened the little casement window, and squeezed his body out onto the roof. The run through the water and the climb up the narrow stairs had squandered his puff. He raised himself panting to his feet, standing high above the spreading riot. He had doubled back on himself in climbing the stairs, and had bisected once again the border of the storm. Where Oates stood, he was quite dry. Miranda, only perhaps ten feet away, was whipped by the wind and the tropical rain.

She was facing out over the court, looking down in the direction of the churning river and the swallows spiralling up in their giant cage. Harry stood beside her, holding her hand without the slightest sense of danger, his eyes widening in an effort to take in the meaning of the world below. She did not turn to look at Oates when he finally clambered to his feet.

Confronted with her profile, he was struck again by her extreme beauty; yet she no longer seemed young to him.

She seemed in fact to have stepped out of age altogether, to have become an avatar for some quality as old as time. The symbols and ideas in her had swollen like tumours, pushing her humanity out through the pores. The instant he saw her, he was dismayed; if she was no longer human, there was no hope of dissuading her from an inhuman act. As he stood there, Harry sensed his presence and turned. He beamed at him, but made no attempt to leave Miranda's side. Oates waved, and his son waved back with his free hand. He was about to start moving towards them across the roof when Miranda spoke. She did not shout, but raised her voice so that he would hear her through the storm.

"Do you know, I haven't left this place in four years? I haven't seen it without the sky in three. It's almost more beautiful, don't you think? You can see the genius of it, the wonder of the engineering. Really perfect technology hides itself. You never know it's there, until it goes wrong. I'd forgotten this was under everything. I'd forgotten how much I missed it."

"It's over, Miranda."

She shook her head.

"It's falling apart. We need to get you out of here."

"It doesn't matter, Inspector. This place has served its purpose. We can discard it." She gestured with her hand out over the water, her fingers taking wing and lifting at the wrist into a glorious future.

"Then let the lad go."

She shook her head again, sincerely regretful that such a thing could not be done.

"It's alright Dad. I'm not scared anymore. It's amazing."

Miranda swung fondly on the little arm.

"Then take me," Oates said, "I'll jump off this bloody roof myself."

"That's not enough, Inspector. Now, I asked for a clever policeman, and that is what I got. Can you understand why?"

"Harry, wouldn't you like to come back with your dad?"

Harry nodded, but made no move to come back to Oates. He was transfixed by the scene in the court below. The three of them stood, a frozen tableau in the cold and shadowless light of the dome. Again, the voice from the heavens intoned the evacuation.

"If you just let him come to his dad, I'll have your bloody Treatment. If that's what you want, you've got my word…"

"It doesn't work like that, Inspector. As I explained to you, the process has to be voluntary. Do you think I want to do this? I have to set you free."

Oates remembered the way that Chris Rajaram had mentioned, almost in passing, that the Tithonus Effect could amount to psychosis. Miranda must be one of the oldest women who had ever lived. She had been an early adopter of the Treatment she had herself helped to develop. Charles had said she was a student doing her doctorate at Cambridge before he was born. That could make her over a hundred. Clearly the operation of her mind was disturbed, but she was not insane. There was cold, hard rationality in her, untempered by any empathy.

He tried to think about her like any other criminal, to reconstruct her thought process from first principles. He thought back to everything he knew about her. In their very first interview in the spa, she had tried to recruit him to her vision. He had disappointed her with his failure to understand. She had chosen him because… because of his suffering. And he had disappointed her because he bore it. He had not wanted to escape his life, he had not wanted to lengthen it. He had just wanted to live it. It was not enough for Miranda, but why?

It was his stoicism that had violated her principles. It was that fragile part of him, alcohol under one shoulder, his family under the other, limping along, which endured a day like this one and still looked forward to the next. She had fallen out of love with life, and yet she could not conceive of herself as having failed. She could accept her ennui only insofar as she could convince herself that this was a basic operation of the human condition. She needed to feel that her weakness was not personal, but universal. By refusing her gift, Oates had threatened the logic by which she justified to herself the desiccation of her passions and her morality. He could bear his ageing, and his suffering. The thought of his death was not so offensive to him that he would pay the price of oblivion in exchange for immortality. But her soul's logic would bear no exceptions – having once failed to recruit him, the only recourse was to increase his suffering until it became unbearable. That was where Harry came in. Harry and the edge of the roof. The dawn of this understanding must have shown in his face, because Miranda smiled at him. It was the sad smile of a parting couple, of two people united by their shared knowledge of something both unsought and inevitable.

He looked down at Harry. Harry held on to Miranda's hand in absolute innocence, whilst his great intelligence worked its way through the apocalypse consuming the school, and his compassion encompassed the actors. Oates could imagine his thoughts, and the questions he would be formulating to confound his dad and all the philosophers. In that instant the sense of unreality was banished. He knew one certain thing. He loved his sons. All the rest of the world could warp and change. His senses and his memories might betray him, his principles collapse, the whole of England could become a TV show. But his love for his son was real. It was a thing that existed outside of him. An objective presence standing by his shoulder. It would exist after he was dead. It would exist when he was no longer there to feel it. He would die for it.

"Come on then," he said.

Miranda hesitated, and a slight hint of confusion troubled the smooth marble brows.

"We'll do it together," he said. "You said it had to be voluntary. Well, I'm volunteering. You keep hold of his hand, and I'll take the other. We'll do it together."

"You're lying."

"No. I thought I could go on. But I don't want to. I need another push, I know that now. To be free. And afterwards, I will need the Treatment, and MRT. Afterwards, I will beg you to help me."

"Let me do it. Let me save you that at least."

"If you do it alone, I won't want to forget. I'll only want to pursue you. I'll live to destroy you. But if we do it together I can be free to have the Treatment. How can I live with it, if I've done it myself?"

He edged forward on the roof. He could see Miranda wavering. She wanted to believe him. She wanted to think he was weak. His ankle still throbbed from the fall in the sewers. *Feet don't fail me now,* he begged himself, and as he moved, his begging became a prayer. He began to make promises. He would give up the job. They would leave London together. He would never go out on nights again. He would give up his dreams of his youth. He would be grateful every day. He would quit drinking. Never another drop. He would never hurt another man. He drew closer. He crossed the threshold of the storm. He felt the rain on his skin. Somewhere along the way, his thoughts became prayers. He would give his own life for Harry's, give it gladly. He prayed to the love for his sons. The only thing that existed outside of him. The rain plastered his hair to his head, and streamed down into his eyes. As he edged closer, Nottingham Biosciences had fulfilled the promise of their slogan – he no longer lived in fear of his death.

He held Miranda's eyes in his own like a hand in his. They were wild and skittish, the madness which her intelligence must have concealed for some time beginning to obtrude. She was desperate to believe in him. He sensed her need as he drew closer, her supreme loneliness drawing him in. He was whispering to her, not words exactly, but a sound like words, a comforting sound like the soft sound of the sea. He took Harry's hand. It was tiny in his own. It was the answer to his prayers. Miranda's eyes filled with gratitude as she pulled back to gather the momentum for the swing that would carry his boy out into the air.

For a fraction of a second, there was the consummation of their two beliefs, each one impossible if the other were to be true. In that single instant, Harry was both saved and sacrificed. But the impossibility could not hold. With a sudden yank, Oates tossed his son away from the ledge, on to the lead sheeting of the roof. At the same time, Miranda's expression ignited with the knowledge of his treachery. He grabbed for her, and she screamed, the sound set to an eerie echo by the steel sky above and the flooded court below. He tried to pull her away from the drop, but the force required to save Harry had unbalanced him. She was tiny beside Oates, but her fury gave her strength. She caught hold of his outstretched arm, and jumped, and the two of them pitched over the edge into the storm.

LONDON HAS HAD some bad mornings. Most cities don't know what it's like to wake up with whole streets, whole districts gone, but London does. Dawn on 6 September, 1666. Dawn on 8 September, 1940. And then the smaller outrages. The people with their riots, the prophets with their bombs, the developers with their diggers. It might be because the city is old, but there are older cities. It might be because the city is unlucky, but the streets of London haven't felt the tramp of an invader's boot in almost 1,000 years, and how many other cities in Europe can say the same?

Something in the city wants to rise and fall. Something wants to remind the inhabitants that what looks like permanence comes down in a violent minute. One day a building, and the next a patch of sky strung on the washing line between the two buildings either side. Whatever the reason, Londoners are good at tidying up and carrying on.

Most of the damage done by the rioters was cleaned up within the week. The police deployed rubber bullets and water cannons the night after the looting on Oxford Street, and the army were all ready to come in, but really the riot was spent. There had been a couple of bad fires in the East End, but architects were sharpening their pencils even as the last tendrils of smoke and steam wafted from the rubble. The only real casualty had been the Great Spa, which had been engulfed in flood and fire. The fate of the mighty dome hung in the balance, with structural engineers still poking in the foundations to see if it might be saved.

Certainly London seen through the plate glass windows of the café on the third floor of the National Theatre looked quite unchanged. The only sign of the rioting was on the front page of a copy of the *Evening Standard*, and even there the disturbances had lost their hold on the headlines, slipping to the bottom right hand column. A frenzy of opinion formers had descended on the events like carrion on the carcass of a beached whale, picking them apart with sharp little insights. Eventually there would be nothing left but the bones of history.

Eustace Morrison folded the paper and set it down on the metallic surface of the table in front of him. He stared out at the river. The tide was so low that the grey water had receded to reveal the mud banks below the stone parapet of the Embankment. White gulls circled against the white sky. A curtain of drizzle hung across the view like mild static across a television screen, as if Morrison and the world were not fully tuned in to one another.

He saw his contact running across the open space where the skateboarders practised their jumps, holding a folded newspaper up over his head. Morrison had bought him a cup of tea in anticipation, and he removed the saucer he had placed over it to keep it warm. He disappeared from view beneath the parapet, and a few moments later came to the table brushing water from the sides of his raincoat. When he sat down he had to remove his glasses, which were both steamed with the heat and flecked with raindrops.

"So?" he said taking up the tea without a word of thanks.

"I'm afraid that so far we've made very limited progress," Morrison said.

"Five days and they haven't managed to find a thing?" Putting the tea down, he scrubbed at the droplets of water with the end of his tie, but this served only to smear the lens. He squinted myopically to focus on Morrison, and it gave him a look of extreme skepticism.

"We've recovered equipment we believe may have been used. But nothing of MRT, either the results of the experiments or the scientific process itself."

"But you've accessed the Avalon mainframe?"

"Yes."

"Is it encoded? Erased, what?"

"We think it's possible the information was never actually stored on computer."

"That's ridiculous. Everything gets stored on computers. And a process that complex, there must be documentation."

"From the interviews we've conducted so far it would appear that the vast majority of the work on the project was conducted by Miranda exclusively, and performed from memory. She did use assistants, but on an extremely strict rotation, so that not one of them assisted with sufficient frequency to understand the wider context."

"We expect the Chinese to have developed a viable alternative to the Treatment within the next three to five years. When the British government loses its monopoly on the granting of Treatment licences, we will have to rethink an entire generation of foreign policy."

"May I be candid?" Morrison asked.

"No you may not."

Morrison waited politely whilst his contact sipped his tea.

"I hate candour. It's just another word for rude. Or rudeness, rather. Oh alright, fine, be candid if you must."

"Our foreign policy will soon be someone else's problem."

"Ah yes. You're taking retirement next year, is that right?"

Morrison nodded.

"What have you got planned?"

"Natasha and I are selling Oakley Street. We're going to move down to our house in St Cezaire."

"Permanently?"

"Well, not forever."

"I see. Well, they say the climate's good for old bones."

Morrison smiled faintly.

"What about that man you had, Rob something?"

"Detective Chief Inspector Oates."

"That's the one. Shot that black boy right in the middle of One New Change. They love that at the Home Office, as I'm sure you can imagine."

"He failed to retrieve any of the papers from the Mortal Reformers. But our intelligence is that he did at least try."

"Does he know anything about MRT? He must have been the last person to speak to Miranda alive."

"We haven't had the opportunity to debrief him just yet. He's only just come out of intensive care. He's in Royal London Hospital with his family."

"And your recommendation on the investigation into the shooting? Or would you prefer to wait until you've had the chance to interview him?"

Morrison nodded to himself.

"Play it straight."

"Play it straight?"

"If he murdered the boy let him go down. But don't make it so."

"Well, alright. You are an odd fish sometimes." He drummed his bitten nails on the table once. "I'd best be getting back. You're sure you won't stay with us? Compulsory retirement only applies where necessary. We could always arrange a Treatment licence…"

"But not for Natasha."

His contact said nothing.

"It's kind of you to ask me," Morrison said, "But no. I think it's time to leave."

"Oh well. Are you having some sort of leaving do?"

"No."

"No. Can't say I blame you. I can't stand that sort of thing either. Half of them are pleased to see the back of you, the other half couldn't care less. The one or two who do care, you'll see them again anyway. Keep well."

"And you."

"I just wish it wasn't such filthy weather. Filthy weather and good news I could handle. Or bad news and a lovely clear day. But filthy weather and bad news… hmph!"

His companion left him sitting alone in the theatre café. Morrison watched him once again through the streaming plate glass window as he ran for the cover of Waterloo Bridge, heading past the rough sleepers in the direction of Whitehall. He had just disappeared from view when the lamps on the South Bank flickered into life. Outside, the clouds were hastening the end of a brief day.

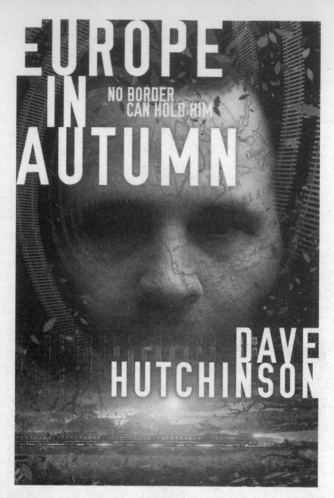

EUROPE IN AUTUMN

NO BORDER CAN HOLD HIM

DAVE HUTCHINSON

Rudi is a cook in a Kraków restaurant, but when his boss asks Rudi to help a cousin escape from the country he's trapped in, a new career – part spy, part people-smuggler – begins. Following multiple economic crises and a devastating flu pandemic, Europe has fractured into countless tiny nations, duchies, polities and republics. Recruited by the shadowy organisation *Les Coureurs des Bois*, Rudi is schooled in espionage, but when a training mission to The Line, a sovereign nation consisting of a trans-Europe railway line, goes wrong, he is arrested and beaten, and *Coureur* Central must attempt a rescue.

With so many nations to work in, and identities to assume, Rudi is kept busy travelling across Europe. But when he is sent to smuggle someone out of Berlin and finds a severed head inside a locker instead, a conspiracy begins to wind itself around him. With kidnapping, double-crosses and a map that constantly re-draws itself, *Europe in Autumn* is a science fiction thriller like no other.

'A real feat of the imagination, this is a really exceptional book, unlike anything I've ever read before.'
Chris Beckett
Arthur C. Clarke Award winner

TONY BALLANTYNE
DREAM LONDON

Captain Jim Wedderburn has looks, style and courage. He's adored by women, respected by men and feared by his enemies. He's the man to find out who has twisted London into this strange new world. But in Dream London the city changes a little every night and the people change a little every day. The towers are growing taller, the parks have hidden themselves away and the streets form themselves into strange new patterns. There are people sailing in from new lands down the river, new criminals emerging in the East End and a path spiraling down to another world.

Everyone is changing, no one is who they seem to be.

 WWW.SOLARISBOOKS.COM

Follow us on Twitter! www.twitter.com/solarisbooks

CHRISTOPHER FOWLER

PLASTIC

'A breathtaking thriller set in the dark shadow of the everyday, Plastic is a razor sharp parable of modern life.' Jake Arnott

With a foreword by JOANNE HARRIS

June Cryer is a shopaholic suburban housewife trapped in a lousy marriage. After discovering her husband's infidelity with the flight attendant next door, she loses her home, her husband and her credit rating. But there's a solution: a friend needs a caretaker for a spectacular London high-rise apartment. It's just for the weekend, and there'll be money to spend in a city with every temptation on offer.

Seizing the opportunity to escape, June moves in only to find that there's no electricity and no phone. She must flat-sit until the security system comes back on. When a terrified girl breaks into the flat and June makes the mistake of asking the neighbours for help, she finds herself embroiled in an escalating nightmare, trying to prove that a murderer exists. For the next 24 hours she must survive on the streets without friends or money and solve an impossible crime.

 WWW.SOLARISBOOKS.COM

Follow us on Twitter! www.twitter.com/solarisbooks

On the road to nowhere each step leads you closer to your destination, but who, or what, can you expect to meet along the way?

Here are stories of misfits, spectral hitch-hikers, nightmare travel tales and the rogues, freaks and monsters to be found on the road. The critically acclaimed editor of *Magic*, *The End of The Line* and *House of Fear* has brought together the contemporary masters and mistresses of the weird from around the globe in an anthology of travel tales like no other. Strap on your seatbelt, or shoulder your backpack, and wait for that next ride... into darkness.

An incredible anthology of original short stories from an exciting list of writers including the best-selling Philip Reeve, the World Fantasy Award-winning Lavie Tidhar and the incredible talents of S.L. Grey, Ian Whates, Jay Caselberg, Benjanun Sriduangkaew, Zen Cho, Sophia McDougall, Rochita Loenen-Ruiz, Anil Menon, Rio Youers, Vandana Singh, Paul Meloy, Adam Nevill and Helen Marshall.

When his elderly father suffers a stroke, Christopher Beal returns to England.
He has no home, no other family. Adrift, he answers an advert for a live-in tutor for a teenage
boy. The boy is Lawrence Lundy, who carries with him the spirit of his father, a military pilot
– missing, presumed dead. Unable to accept that his father is gone, Lawrence keeps his
presence alive, in the big old house, in the overgrown garden. His mother, Juliet, keeps the
boy at home, away from the world; and in the suffocating heat of a long summer, she too is
infected by the madness of her son.

Christopher becomes entangled in the strange household, enmeshed in the oddness of the
boy and his fragile mother. Only by forcing the boy to release the spirit of his father can he
find any escape from the haunting.

It is the biggest experiment in history...

Eidolon
LIBBY McGUGAN

...and it must be destroyed

When physicist Robert Strong — newly unemployed and single — is offered a hundred thousand pounds for a week's work, he's understandably sceptical. But Victor Amos, head of the mysterious Observation Research Board, has compelling proof that the next round of experiments at CERN's Large Hadron Collider poses a real threat to the whole world. And he needs Robert to sabotage it.

Robert's life is falling apart. His work at the Dark Matter Research Laboratory in Middlesbrough was taken away from him; his girlfriend, struggling to cope with the loss of her sister, has left. He returns home to Scotland, seeking sanctuary and rest, and instead starts to question his own sanity as the dead begin appearing to him, in dreams and in waking. Accepting Amos's offer, Robert flies to Geneva, but as he infiltrates CERN, everything he once understood about reality and science, about the boundary between life and death, changes forever.

Mixing science, philosophy and espionage, Libby McGugan's stunning debut is a thriller like no other.

 WWW.SOLARISBOOKS.COM

Follow us on Twitter! www.twitter.com/solarisbooks